8
2/09

SAY GOODBYE

ALSO BY LEWIS SHINER

NOVELS
Frontera (1984)
Deserted Cities of the Heart (1988)
Slam (1990)
Glimpses (1993)

STORY COLLECTIONS
Nine Hard Questions about the Nature of the Universe (1991)
The Edges of Things (1991)

ANTHOLOGIES
When the Music's Over (1991)

SAY GOODBYE
THE LAURIE MOSS STORY

LEWIS SHINER

ST. MARTIN'S PRESS
NEW YORK

Library of Congress Cataloging-in-Publication Data

Shiner, Lewis (1950–   )
    Say goodbye :   the Laurie Moss story   /   Lewis Shiner.
— 1st ed.
        p.   cm.
    ISBN 0-312-24110-0
    I. Title.
PS3569.H496S29   1999
813'.54—dc21   99–15934
                                                          CIP

First Edition: October 1999

10 9 8 7 6 5 4 3 2 1

FOR
MARY K.

Wife, lover,
teacher, friend:
never say goodbye.

ACKNOWLEDGMENTS

Extra special thanks to Mary
Alberts, my live-in editor and
inspiration; to Gordon Van Gelder,
editor and friend; to Richard Butner,
writer guy; and to Melody Rich,
who taught Laurie to sing. Thanks
also to John Accursi, R. P. Alberts, Sr.,
Duane Aumann, Cindy Lee
Berryhill, Danny, Jim, John, and
Viki Blaylock, Art Fein, Bill Finke,
Karen Fowler, Joan Gordon,
Steve Grant, Bobby Lloyd Hicks,
John Kessel, Cynthia Killough,
Dana Kletter, Pat LoBrutto,
Jack McDevitt, Steve Snider,
Maureen Troy, Mark Van Name,
Bob Wayne, and Paul Williams.

THE CITY

Signs and Portents

"It was my first Friday night in LA," Laurie says in her press kit for the album. "I was stuck on the Santa Monica Freeway, thinking about buffalo. A vast single herd covering the earth from one horizon to the other, the way they used to, placid, lost in their own grassy thoughts, then suddenly careering off at top speed, all of them at exactly the same time.

"So there I was, cheek to bumper with all the other cloven-tired, sunroof-humped, Klaxon-horned metal ungulates, stalled on the concrete plains, watching the hot breath steam from their tailpipes, when the sky blew up.

"I didn't know if it was terrorists or nuclear war or the Big One that was supposed to drop us all in the Pacific, but it was clearly the end. Huge concussive explosions and fat orange cinders trailing fire out of the sky. Ashes on the windshield. Cars veering off onto the shoulder and me pretty sure I could feel the freeway shake under my Little Brown Datsun. I kept driving, though, because, really, this was what I'd been waiting for all my life: Armageddon.

"Anyway, I finally rolled my window down and looked up and realized it was nothing but the fireworks show at Disneyland. They launch the rockets, apparently, a few feet from the highway and the damned things go off right there over the cars. Some freak atmospheric condition was pushing the debris back down before it completely burned up.

"So that's where 'Just Another End of the World' came from. That thought: If this is really the end, I won't have to do laundry tomorrow. My rent check will never bounce. Of course it was just one more false alarm, not even a sign from God, only a sign from Unca Walt, in his block of ice under the freeway, and it had no more cosmic message to convey than 'Hey, look at me.'

"Though I will say this. Once I was over my initial disappointment, it was a hell of a show. The human mind can't leave something like that alone. It's always going to read signs and portents wherever it can. And I remember sitting straight back in my seat, both hands on the wheel, and saying, 'Thank you. I'm glad to be here.'"

THE SILK AND STEEL

I meet "Fernando"—not his real name—in a bar called the Silk and Steel on Sunset Boulevard. It's Monday, the 11th of November, 1996, and he is my first official interview for the book.

It's chilly and overcast in LA, and even the clouds seem to be rushing off to somewhere important. I'm easing into the writing process by going to the people that are publicly available, the ones that I know will be willing to talk to me. "You'll recognize me," Fernando has promised on the phone, and he is right. He's six-foot-three, lavishly tattooed, pierced four times in the right ear, five times in the left, once in the left nostril. He's shaved his head, but not recently, and he has a soul patch beneath his lower lip.

"This is where it went down," he says, in a somewhat high-pitched, nasal voice. The walls and ceiling are painted flat black, standard decor on the Strip, and the brown shag carpet has mostly unraveled. Afternoon sunlight trickles in the open back door where a kid in shorts and a baseball cap wheels in cases of beer. It's the kind of place that needs its darkness. "I thought you should see this," Fernando says, "because it's the first place Laurie sang in LA. It was an open mike night, like they do every Monday—they'll be doing it again tonight. I put her and Summer together that same night."

Fernando works in one of the better-known Hollywood music stores. "You get jaded," he says about the job. "A lot of the big touring acts come in when they're in town. I've met Clapton, Page, both Van Halens—all three if you count Valerie. All the hot studio guys, of course. I must see a hundred kids like Laurie every year, coasting into LA in cars that barely made it over the mountains, desperate for a break. They've read about the Viper Room in *Rolling Stone* or they've noticed the LA addresses on the backs of their CDs, or they've seen palm trees in too many MTV videos."

He met Laurie in June of 1994. She'd only been in LA for a week. "How it happened was, she called the store looking for a four-track recorder. I sold her the same Tascam I sell all the wannabe singer-song-writers, on special for one-ninety-nine. I remembered her, one, because she was cute—skinny and intense, with this bright reddish purple hair that was kind of eighties retro. Also she's one of those people that are a little more, I don't know, tuned in or something. Like they're sucking everything in through their eyes. So when I ran into her a couple of days later at the Silk and Steel, it only took me a minute to place her."

Fernando might forget a face, but never a guitar. Laurie's, he recalls, was "a cream-colored mid-sixties Strat, very clean," but not suitable for the Unplugged-style format of the Silk and Steel. Fernando found her "trying to reason with the bartender, not upset or anything, just, like, 'I can't understand why playing an electric guitar in a folk club is still an issue thirty years after Dylan played Newport.' As if this kid behind the bar had any idea what she was talking about. She was very naive that way, she didn't understand that places like this aren't about music, they're about the acoustic guitar as fashion statement."

Fernando introduced her to his girlfriend, Summer Walsh, who'd been on the LA folk scene for ten years. "Next thing you know Summer's offered to loan out her Martin D-15. We all sat together, and when Summer got up and sang I could see Laurie was really blown away. Have you heard Summer sing? You know she wrote that song on Laurie's album, 'Tried and True'? She is so awesome, man. She could be where Alanis or Joan Osborne is, and she would be if—" He shakes his head and shifts around in his chair. "Don't get me started on record companies."

After Summer's set Laurie's confidence seemed to falter. "Summer really wanted to hear her, so she pulled a couple of strings and got Laurie up on stage before she could chicken out. Laurie, she was nervous at first, but she did good. And her songs, you could tell she knew what she was doing. They were structured, you know, nicely put together. And hooks that fully dug into your brain.

"She was quiet sitting around the table, but on stage she had this, like, eagerness. Like at the end of each song she couldn't wait to get to the next one. It was some very contagious shit."

Afterward the three of them went down the street to the Rock and

Roll Denny's, a musician's hangout for decades. "You could really see the
energy happening between Summer and Laurie. It's like . . . it was
enough for me to have done that, to have introduced them. I'm happy
just being *around* the buzz, I don't have to *be* the buzz, if you know what
I mean.

"Not Laurie, though. She had that bone-deep hunger. I liked her
from the first, but that hunger made me scared for her too."

MIRACLE ON SAN VICENTE

Bobbi D'Angelo is in her forties, her blonde hair a little brittle, her voice
rough from chain smoking. She—"and the Bank of America, honey"—
owns the Bistro d'Bobbi on San Vicente. It's upstairs in a small, exclusive
strip mall: burgundy window treatments, tasteful neon signage, tiled bal-
cony with umbrella tables. Inside, behind the garlic and oregano, you can
smell the yeast in the dough that waits on steel trays near the oven. A
hostess in black pants and a tux shirt shows me to a small, cluttered office
next to the kitchen.

The restaurant, Bobbi explains, grew out of her divorce settlement
from "a very rich asshole." She lights a Virginia Slims menthol and says,
"Sooner or later I'm sure I'll get in trouble for it, but until somebody
puts a gun to my head, I'm not hiring any men here. No offense, doll.
We're a self-sufficient little matriarchy, and Laurie fit right in. All the girls
have their *noms du pizza*—builds morale, keeps a little extra distance between them and the customers, like this joke we're all in on. We knew
her here as Gladys."

Bobbi seems to remember every detail about each of her girls, as if
they were her daughters. "She was pretty desperate when she first came
in. She'd been looking for work for a couple of weeks, and it was all either fast food or topless or prep work. I hired her on the spot and put her
to work that night. She used to say it was her Miracle on San Vicente.

"She was good with people, got along with the other girls, hell, I
didn't even know she was starstruck until the week before she quit. She'd
been with us four months, and then one night she started writing the
words to a song on the back of one of her tickets and that's how I found
out."

Bobbi knows firsthand about being starstruck. "I arrived here in 1966, with a few hundred thousand others. I was just eighteen and I knew in my heart of hearts that Destiny had her hand on the telephone, about to dial my number. I was something then, you wouldn't believe it to look at me now. Smart, good-looking, ambitious. I stuck it out for two years. All I ever got were walk-ons, which I took, and propositions, which I didn't. Finally I ran out of money and hope and I went back to North Carolina and married Steven, who was in love with me in high school and incidentally heir to a textile business. I hated myself for being a failure and a quitter, and I drank for a while and slept around a little bit and I spent more than one afternoon with a bottle of pills in front of me, wondering if I might just take them all.

"Everybody in the world—my various agents, my roommates, producers, casting directors, strangers on the bus—all of them had reasons why I wasn't famous. Maybe I had no talent. Maybe I had too much. Maybe I needed bigger breasts. Smaller breasts. A different agent. To stop changing agents. The one thing nobody could accept—least of all me—was that it might not be anybody's fault at all."

She seems eager to distance herself from the eighteen-year-old beauty that I can still clearly see behind the makeup and the cigarette smoke and the sardonic tone. "If it's nobody's fault," she says, "then everything is random. It's out of control. It means being a star doesn't really prove you're a good actor, or beautiful, or, God help us all, lovable.

"I told all this to Gladys—to Laurie, I mean. Not because I thought it would change her mind, but so that when it happened to her she would maybe feel a little less alone. She said something about how I hadn't turned out so badly. But the truth is I set myself up to get hurt when I was just a kid, and by the time I got over being hurt it was too late to do anything else. Like get an honest job, say waiting tables. Like go to college in my spare time, write some film criticism, get my jollies at some local theater if I absolutely had to be on stage.

"I could have saved my breath, of course. She was convinced it was all going to be different for her, even if she had the decency not to say so. We all want to think that, don't we?" Bobbi grinds out her cigarette. "Then, a year or so later, there she is on VH-1. You could have knocked me over with a feather."

OVER THE HILLS AND FAR AWAY

On Tuesday afternoon I take 101 north, over the Hollywood Hills to
Ventura Boulevard, then make my way back uphill to Sunshine Terrace. I
park across the street from 11163, a wood-sided bungalow nestled in
front of a row of apartments. The air is vastly sweeter here than on Ventura, and magnolias and fruit trees and cedars arch over the street. I get
out and stretch my legs, hearing the ticking of the rent car's engine, the
low murmur of a TV, and distant childish laughter.

I take a few pictures of the front of the house. Someone is obviously
living there; they've put out a blue patio umbrella, a single lawn chair,
pink mums in a bed along the front wall. I walk down the driveway a few
feet, hoping for a glimpse of something beyond the louvered wooden
shutters that line the windows. The high-pitched, snorting laugh comes
again, and then a woman's voice says, "If you're looking for Laurie, she
doesn't live here anymore."

I turn to see a woman in her late twenties, bending over to pick up a
puckered beach ball. She has long red hair, gray jeans, and a pink sweater.
From behind the house a girl of about four, dressed in brand-new over-
alls, runs out saying, "Who you talking to, Mommy?" Seeing me, she is
instantly paralyzed by self-consciousness.

I wiggle my fingers at the girl, explaining to her mother that I know
Laurie is gone, that I am writing about her. I go back to the car for a paperback of my latest book to provide credentials.

"I'm sorry," the woman says, turning it over in her hands. "I'm afraid
I never heard of you." A light breeze animates her fine red-gold hair,
trailing a wisp of it across her face.

"Don't worry. Millions haven't." I convince her to keep the book,
which I autograph, and that earns me a proper introduction. Her name is
Catherine Conner, originally and intermittently of Salem, Oregon.
Shannon, age four, is by this point hiding behind her mother and unwilling to shake hands, even when asked in a very nice Donald Duck voice.

Eventually Catherine invites me in. Over a glass of herbal iced tea,
with Shannon watching *The Rescuers Down Under* in the next room,
Catherine talks about meeting Laurie. "I used to see her come home
from work in like her uniform thing, with her hair up and the black

pants and the white shirt, and then a few minutes later there would be this electric guitar playing. Not loud or anything, but I always knew it was there. I thought it was so cool, and so one morning when I heard her I went over and I was just like, 'Hi, I'm your neighbor.'

"I mean, my own life is such a mess. I spent four years at Oregon State without ever fully getting a handle, you know? Came to LA to see the bright lights, got pregnant by this underemployed actor, and now I'm living from day to day on temp work and child support. And here's Laurie, so full of ambition and working so hard for it, day and night, you know?"

As I listen I can tell that Laurie's life has became more real to Catherine than her own. It's a feeling I can relate to.

"I would go see her sometimes when she played," Catherine says, "and sometimes we would stay up late afterwards, just talking all night long." The memories light up her face, and she's happy to go into Laurie's background. Some of it I've read or heard about elsewhere, but many of the details are new.

"Her family is basically her mom, who's divorced, and her younger brother Corky, who is this kind of slacker screw-up. That's me talking—Laurie always went the long way around not to criticize anybody. She was also real close to her mom's father, who she always called Grandpa Bill. They used to go listen to jazz and stuff when she was growing up.

"It was some friend of her brother's who used to live in that apartment. He ran out of money and was looking for somebody to take over the lease. And Laurie was living in San Antonio with this creepy guy, and her brother was like, 'You have to do this. It's a sign or something.' "

Laurie had been going over the bank statements and mentally loading up her Datsun for a couple of weeks. She was living in a rented apartment with rented furniture, and at that moment her relationship didn't seem very substantial either. "Jack is like this insurance adjuster," Catherine says, "good-looking from the picture I saw, but not Mr. Sensitive. The kind of guy who takes you to a sports bar on a first date, if you know what I mean?"

Catherine said that Jack was stressed out at work, drinking too much, and staying out late at clubs, "with Laurie or without her." When Laurie mentioned the merest idea of a trip to LA, "Jack totally lost it. He took her guitar out on the back patio and smashed it. She was laughing about it when she told me, this kind of nervous laugh, but you could see that it scared her to even remember it."

Laurie ordered Jack out of the apartment, packed up, and hit the road for Dallas, where her father lived. "She talked about her father a lot. He was the reason she started playing guitar in the first place." Laurie's father, Michael Moss, played with a band called the Chevelles at Richardson High School in the mid-sixties. He gave up the guitar when he married Laurie's mother and moved to San Antonio. One Saturday when Laurie was in sixth grade her father came in from raking leaves, got the guitar out of the closet, and started to play. Until that afternoon she had never known what was in that odd-shaped tweed suitcase; when the guitar came out, Catherine said, "it was like the sun coming up in the middle of the night."

The guitar transformed her father into a creature of glamour and mystery and Laurie wanted that change for herself. She begged and pleaded until her father showed her a couple of chords. Years of piano lessons had never spoken to her as persuasively as her first five minutes of guitar, and "she would have kept playing all day except her mother came in and gave her father a look. She said it was the kind of look you would give your car as it was slowly rolling over a cliff."

It was apparently a defining moment for her father as well. He moved to Dallas and filed for divorce shortly thereafter.

"You know that's her father's guitar she plays on the record?" Catherine asks. "She talked him out of it on her way to LA. He didn't want to give it up, even though he never played it. But he had to have seen how determined she was, how bad she needed it."

She sighs and looks into her tea. "She really loved that guitar."

FOLKIES

The Sly Duck Pub has been a fixture in Santa Monica since the forties, though it didn't come into its own until 1962, when it began to feature live music on its Tuesday hootenanny nights. By 1963 it was serving espresso and music seven nights a week, with big names like the Limelighters or Jim Kweskin on the weekends.

These days it's reverted to its English roots, serving draft ale in ta-pered glasses and sporting a menu of some one hundred and fifty im-ports. The manager is a young, earnest man named Brad Mueck (pronounced "Mick") who wears wire rims and blue oxford cloth shirts and whose light brown hair is at least a third gone.

"If I'd had my way," he says, "Laurie and Summer would still be headlining here as a duo every Saturday." From his second-floor office above the bar, Brad can look out on 4th Street, which runs parallel to the ocean four blocks away. "This is not the way that history shall remember them. But together they were far more than the sum of the parts—like Joan Baez and Mimi Fariña, or the Weavers. Summer has a fabulous voice and sincerity and an instinct for harmony. Combined with Laurie's wit and energy and guitar playing, it was magic. Magic, pure and simple."

Brad had heard about Laurie from Summer long before he ever saw her. "Then one night Summer called to tell me she's going to get Laurie up to sing with her. Laurie had apparently just written a song on the back of a ticket at some pizza place where she was working and Summer was enthralled with it. Laurie was calling it 'Teen Angel' at the time, though eventually she changed the title to . . ."

"'Angel Dust,'" I say.

"Naturally. So at the end of her first set Summer handed over the guitar and Laurie played 'Angel Dust.' If she was nervous I saw no sign of it. She connected with the audience the way a candle connects with oxy-gen, and you could see the light she gave off on all their faces. Summer kept her on stage and they did her song 'Tried and True,' and dedicated it to Fernando, the married man that Summer was seeing."

I can't stop myself. "Fernando is married?" I ask.

"He was then. Still is, as far as I know."

"I'm a little stunned," I admit. "Summer seems smarter than that."

Brad leans back in his oak swivel chair and takes a deep breath. "It's not a matter of intelligence. You know that. You've interviewed other musicians. How many of them act in their own best interests even a frac-tion of the time?"

"That's true of most of us," I say carefully.

"But entertainers are the worst. And the more damaged they are, the more we love them. Kurt Cobain, Judy Garland, James Dean."

"Laurie Moss?"

"Oh yes. I can't tell you the details of her particular history, but she was absolutely the type. To flog my favorite hobbyhorse again, if all she truly cared about was a great setting for her material, she had that in abundance with Summer. But the maximum seating capacity here is one hundred and eighty. She needed more love than this place can hold."

Laurie's guest shot impressed Brad enough for him to offer her work. "I would say I used her every week or ten days. She would do the opening sets at nine-thirty and eleven-thirty." Summer at that point headlined every Tuesday, but it turned out to be almost three months before the two of them wound up sharing a bill.

"I'm embarrassed to say they came up with it on their own, with no prompting from me. Summer would only tell me she had a surprise for me. The surprise was that they'd gotten together over the weekend and rehearsed, and that Tuesday—I'm going to guess this was about late January of '95—they played all four sets together. Summer was on acoustic, Laurie played electric through a little practice amp under her stool."

For all his criticism of entertainers, Brad's own emotions run very near the surface. He seems close to tears as he describes their debut as a duo: "It was not polished. There were songs of Summer's where Laurie just played guitar, and songs of Laurie's where Summer just improvised a harmony part. Mistakes were made. But my God. What I wouldn't give for a tape of that night."

After a moment he pulls himself together. "Well. I may be slow, but I'm not stupid. I offered them the headline spot on the next Saturday I had open. The irony, of course, is that by that time Laurie had already met Gabriel Wong."

THE SESSION

"I'm a session player," Gabriel Wong says on Thursday afternoon. "My heroes were always session players, even as a kid. Sly Dunbar. Tony Levin. Session players sleep in their own beds, they make top money, they don't get in a rut of the same set every night."

Gabe's apartment is small, clean as an operating theater, and organized for maximum efficiency. He is sprawled at one end of a tasteful oak-and-taupe-cotton couch that is not much larger than an armchair. He's wearing black jeans and running shoes, and a black collarless linen shirt. He has a rangy build, cocoa skin, three-inch dreadlocks, and lively eyes.

The night he met Laurie he was backing a local favorite named Dick O'Brien, an irregular gig always advertised as "Dick at the Duck." "Let me paint you a quick portrait," Gabe says. "Short, thin-skinned, hairy. Knows a minute or so of every song ever written. Buys a drink for any woman who'll come up to the stage and show him her bare chest. Thinks it's the height of humor to put a condom on a beer bottle.

"O'Brien doesn't like me, but he needs me. His bass players have a tendency to quit on him. And since part of his thing is doing instant requests from the audience, and since it so happens that I myself also know a minute or so of every song ever written, every now and again he finds himself paying me more money than he wants to."

Laurie was O'Brien's opening act. "O'Brien's reputation had preceded him, and Laurie was headed for the door before we even started, so that she wouldn't have to listen to us. Somehow she got hung up talking to friends and heard the first song. It turned out she really liked my playing."

In fact she liked it so much that she made a poor first impression. "She came up after the set and she was totally nervous," Gabe remembers. "She kept saying one wrong thing after another. Like, she couldn't seem to process my name. I'm adopted, see, and my dad was Chinese and my mother was Korean, so I've gotten a lot of shit about my name all my life. And Laurie, you could see that she just couldn't understand how a black man could be named Wong, but she was raised too nice to come out and say it.

"My girlfriend L'Shondra was there and she thought Laurie was some groupie or something and kept trying to pull me away. But I had a feeling, and I waited her out until she could get it together to say what she wanted."

What she wanted was Gabe's signature style, which is heavily influenced by reggae and ska. "The timekeeping is solid, but you leave out notes and move the accents around. It makes the audience hear the music instead of the singer, which gives Dick O'Brien apoplexy. I do it to him whenever I can."

In an interview with the British magazine Q, Laurie describes Gabe's playing as "a taste behind my tongue, a pressure in my solar plexus, a color behind my eyes. It wasn't discovery, it was recognition. Yearning backbeat. Precise, articulate silences. I'd been waiting for it all my life and probably several other people's."

"I hadn't seen any of her set," Gabe admits, "so I was copping this real cool, superior attitude. She said something like, 'I've never heard anybody play bass like you before,' and I was like, 'Funny, that's what Dick kept saying all through the first set. At least that was the gist of what he said.' And she was so sincere, it was scary. She looked like she was about to cry and she said, 'As far as I can tell Dick is a real asshole, and you're the greatest bass player I've ever heard.' How are you supposed to respond to that? I just kind of said, 'Well, you're at least half right.' So I introduced her to L'Shondra and said, 'This is Laurie Moss. I'm the greatest bass player she ever heard.' It's really kind of amazing that Laurie didn't turn around and walk away, I was being such a smartass.

"We all sat down at her table and I asked her, since she liked me so much, if she happened to have a record contract or anything. That was when she told me she was doing a four-track demo in her living room and wanted me to play on it. She was real embarrassed about it, but at the same time she had this absolute determination, like, 'I have to ask this guy, so I'm going to do it, no matter what.'"

"What did you say?"

"I told her I'd listen to her second set and see what I thought."

"And . . . ?"

"She had something. She's one of those people that seems too weird or intense until you see them on stage. Then it all clicks. Good songs, you know, where everything dovetails. Good with the audience. She got them to where they really liked her and were pulling for her. And that was Dick O'Brien's crowd, total animals, not the kind of house you'd want to show fear in front of."

After her set Gabe told Laurie he'd do four songs for a hundred dollars. "Chicken feed, compared to what I usually get paid. But she'd made *me* like her too."

Gabe kneels by his stereo, which is almost at floor level. The much narrower shelves above it are full of alphabetized CDs and neatly hand-labeled cassettes. He puts a tape in the deck and listens intently to the faint hiss before the music. A crisp electric guitar starts in the left speaker, then pans to the center as the bass and the simple but effective lead guitar come in.

It's "Angel Dust." Laurie's voice, a little tentative, with no reverb or sweetening, starts to sing about stepfather's hands that make you burn with shame, the hot breath of boys in crowded halls, the bright flash of gunfire on TV, the red-orange coals of forbidden cigarettes on a window ledge in the sleepless night. Burning, burning, turning these angel's wings to ashes.

It's not the bravura performance on the album, but it makes up in intimacy what it lacks in raw power. "It's all there, isn't it?" says Gabe, enjoying my surprise. "That's her playing both guitars. From the start she knew exactly what she wanted. Not that she acted like it when I first got there for the session."

She had the four-track set up on the dining room table, along with headphones and lyric sheets with the chords penciled in. "She said she wanted me to play the way Dick O'Brien hated. I remember I made some feeble joke about her not having my parts written out for me, and I swear she went so pale I thought she was going to pass out. Nothing I said seemed to calm her down, so I went ahead and did a take.

"You have to understand, I was wearing the only headphones, and I was plugged straight into the recorder, so she had practically no idea what was happening. I had to turn my back to her because she was starting to make *me* nervous. That's my first take you're listening to right now.

"When it was done I handed her the headphones and she listened to the song, just staring down at that cheap veneer table—apartment furniture, you know—and this time it's me who can't hear what's happening. All I know is she looks like her dog just died. Then she turns off the machine and jumps up and goes into the kitchen. So there I am, standing in the kitchen doorway going, 'Listen, if it's that bad, I won't take your money.' She's actually crying into a dish towel. I start to apologize again and she looks up and says, 'No, it's perfect. I love it.'

"I said, 'Has anybody ever told you you're a little weird?'

"'Actually, no,' she says. 'I've done a pretty good job of hiding it until now.' Maybe she was pulling my chain, but I believed her. I believed I had walked in on the first stage of her metamorphosis from something kind of ordinary and simple into, like, the refined essence of Laurie

Moss. It was like this other person was coming right out through her skin, and it was intensely, physically painful for her.

"She said another thing that really touched me. She said, 'Listening to that tape just now was the first time, ever, that I believed something might happen with my songs. That somebody might actually want to buy an album to listen to them.' And she said it was me that made that happen, which is ridiculous, but it was still a really nice thing for her to say."

They wrapped up the other three songs in less than two hours. "One or two takes was all it took. I mean, I still remembered them from hearing her play them, once, at the Duck. She wrote me a check while I packed up, and I started out the door, but I couldn't do it. I couldn't just walk away."

Suddenly Gabe switches off the tape player, puts the tape back in the case, and hands it to me. "Here. I've got another one. I can see that you really need to have this."

I protest unconvincingly and then let him give me the tape. The insert, obviously produced at Kinko's, features a fuzzy photo of Laurie, her name, and the title *Red Dress of Grievances*. "Thank you," I say. "I can't tell you . . ."

"You don't have to," he says. "I basically feel the same as you do about her. I was already feeling it when I played on that tape. Which I guess is why I turned around in her doorway and asked her what she was doing the next night. She stood there and stared at me—I mean, she obviously thought I was coming on to her. So I said, 'It's not like that. It's just that there's some people I think you ought to meet.'"

THE BAND

WHITTIER

One truth about LA is that it's a city made up of small towns. Each has its own personality—from the cool, piney elegance of Pasadena to the carnival excess of Venice, from the high-walled pretensions of Bel Air to the border-town hustle of Santa Ana—and at the same time they're united by a top-down, palm-trees-and-stucco, drive-in kind of feeling that is the essence of LA. The only part of the city that doesn't belong is the concrete and mirror-glass heart of downtown Los Angeles itself.

What better place for the entertainment industries that service the world than a city with a hundred different faces, all wearing the same distracted smile?

It's the evening after my first interview with Gabe, a clear Thursday night in November, and I'm in Whittier, ten miles southeast of LA's central business district. This was once a Quaker city, named for their poet laureate, as is Greenleaf Avenue, which runs through the middle of their one-story 1950s downtown. Richard Nixon grew up here, working at the family grocery store, back when Whittier was covered by orange groves. The orange groves are gone now, of course, throughout LA County and neighboring Orange County too. The land is worth too much to waste it on trees.

Jim Pearson, Laurie's keyboard player and coproducer, lives five minutes from downtown Whittier in a neighborhood of fading three-bedroom, forty-year-old California ranch-style houses. As I park at the curb I can hear music straining through the foil-covered windows of his garage. It's a presence more than a sound, bass guitar and the faint crack and swish of drums.

I try to imagine how Laurie felt walking up this sidewalk for the first time. Gabe had told her only that it was a garage band, that they played a couple of times a week, that there were three others besides himself: a guitarist, a drummer, a keyboard player. She knew how good Gabe was,

and how reluctant he was to talk about the group. She must have sus-
pected something—slumming superstars, illegal Haitian Kreyol musicians,
Buddy Holly back from the dead. If she was nervous about playing a tape
for Gabe in her own apartment, she must have been petrified at the
thought of jamming here with strangers.

Or did she feel, as Bobbi D'Angelo put it, Destiny's hand on the
phone, about to dial her number?

The concrete slab that forms the porch is sinking, and oleanders have
overrun the wooden trellises on either side. At the front door I'm afraid
to ring the bell because I know Jim is recording. I knock quietly and the
door opens on a light-skinned black woman in her thirties, close to my
height, very thin. Behind her is a seven-year-old boy in shorts and a navy
blue sweatshirt, holding one shoe in each hand. He is fair-skinned with
dark brown peppercorn hair. "These are the *new* shoes," he is patiently
explaining. "I want the *old* ones."

I introduce myself.

"I'm Molly," she says, offering her hand. "This is Sam." Without
looking away from me she slightly hardens the pitch of her voice. "We
can't find the old shoes. Put those shoes on and let's go." She smiles.
"Jim's in the garage. Take a left at the kitchen to the end of the hall.
Don't knock, just go in."

It was barely a two-car garage to start with, and Jim has turned the
back third, the third I've just entered, into a sound booth. Jim sits on a
barstool in front of a plywood countertop, his fingers lightly touching
various knobs and faders. He has curly orange hair over his ears and an
orange beard and mustache. He's wearing black jeans and a worn, tan,
seventies-looking sport shirt that stretches tight over his stomach. Next to
him, inch-wide brown recording tape runs through an Ampex deck with
reels the size of dinner plates.

He nods to a second stool and I sit down. In the rest of the garage is
a four-piece band, three women and a man. The music is dissonant in a
practiced, deliberate way that appeals to me. The singer makes sudden
leaps with her two-octave range while the drummer keeps up a steady
throb with her toms and kick drum.

Moth-eaten blankets hang from the rafters and there are egg cartons
glued to the ceiling. A battered sofa leans against one wall next to a half-
sized refrigerator. What light there is comes from various mismatched

table lamps on the floor, some of them with bandannas over them, casting odd shadows on faces and making the corners seem to writhe.

The take breaks down and Jim says, "Not bad, that was really close," into an intercom. "Why don't we start fresh tomorrow night?"

I introduce myself, and Jim says that he's glad to finally meet me in person. We shake hands and he tells me the band is called Estrogen. "Actually, they knew Laurie. We did some shows together, and Laurie used to borrow Danny's amp in the early days."

We move into the kitchen, where Jim gathers up Little Caesar's pizza detritus from the green Formica table and takes orders for coffee and Cokes. Danny, the dark and massive lead guitarist, leans on his forearms and says, "She had to remind me of it later, but I actually talked to her on her second night in LA. We were doing a no-cover Monday at the Whiskey and she came up after and told me she really liked us. She said if there was any justice we'd be famous. I told her I'd settle for luck. This was around the time of the O.J. murders and all. I told her justice was tricky and you never knew what it was going to cost."

Jim finally sits and pours himself a Coke from the three-liter plastic bottle in the middle of the table. He talks to the band about the evening's work for a while, then they excuse themselves to pack up for a gig. When they're out of earshot, Jim says, "They're pretty talented. Also very professional and patient. They've all got day jobs and they're funding this out of their own pockets, so I'm undercharging them rather seriously. They'll press about a thousand CDs, which they'll sell at their shows. With any luck they'll eventually get their money back and maybe some college stations will play a cut or two when they hit town on a tour."

I get out my recorder and set it in the middle of the table. "Is this okay?"

Jim nods, and tells me how he'd wanted his own studio since he was in a bar band in the late seventies. "Some people build model railroads. I wanted to put together overblown rock symphonies—you know, the whole pretentious classic-rock keyboard trip. It started out as pure self-indulgence, but eventually I fell into recording other people to help pay for my habit. Now I bring in enough from recording and producing that I only have to work twenty hours a week at my straight job." The straight job is printed circuit design, which gives him a flexible schedule and lets him do a lot of work from his house.

The jam sessions evolved over a period of two years "or thereabouts. There were three of us that were the core, with different drummers. It was what we did instead of poker, I guess, an excuse to get together and drink a few beers and not have to talk about anything too serious. Dennis had been drumming with us for three months. He was younger than the rest of us, but reasonably unobnoxious for a drummer, and we were pretty sanguine about the whole setup."

Jim pauses, then says, "Obviously Gabe was not that sanguine, or he never would have brought Laurie in. I remember when he told me he'd invited somebody, I nearly had a seizure. It was a bit like telling your wife you'd invited a movie starlet to sleep over. We didn't do things like that."

"So you didn't like the idea."

"No, actually, I thought it was great. So maybe I wasn't that sanguine either. But there were those among us who were definitely not going to like the idea. One of us. There was one of us. Gabe said, 'I don't care. We need this.' And I said, 'Fine, but you're telling him, not me.'"

"'Him' being the legendary Skip Shaw."

Jim nods and refills his glass.

JAMMING

Jim remembers answering the door to find Laurie on the porch, flanked by her father's guitar case and a practice amp the size of a large purse. She shook his hand and said, "Laurie Moss."

"Well," Jim said, "I guess you won't be dating Mick Jagger."

"Pardon?" She was nervous and confused and Jim saw this had sailed right past her.

"Rolling Stones?" Jim said, embarrassed now himself. "Gathering no Moss? Sorry. I can't seem to learn not to make fun of people's names. It only pisses everyone off and makes me look like an idiot. This way."

Gabe was already in the garage. Jim introduced Dennis, no more than a mane of yellow hair behind the drums, and Laurie nodded. She seemed to be trying to take in all the details without looking naive. There was Jim's Yamaha DX-7 keyboard, state of the art in the eighties and something of a relic in 1995. In the corner was a beautiful black vintage Fender Twin Reverb amplifier that was unaccounted for.

Jim pointed to her practice amp. "You want me to plug this in, or do you want to use Skip's amp until he gets here?"

"I don't think Skip would like that, man," Gabe said.

"My amp is fine," Laurie said. "Who's Skip?"

Jim made covert eye contact with Gabe. "Our guitar player," Gabe said, at the same moment that Jim said, "Skip Shaw."

"You mean, *the* Skip Shaw? As in 'Tender Hours' Skip Shaw? He's still—"

"Alive?" Jim said. "Ambulatory? Able to play? Yes to all the above, amazingly, despite certain ongoing efforts on his part. I'm surprised you know who he is, actually."

"My dad absolutely loved him. He's really coming? My dad will simply die."

From behind her a hoarse baritone said, "He's here. Feeble, wizened bastard that he is."

She turned and Jim saw their eyes lock. Skip was well over six feet tall, thin in the chest, somewhat thicker around the middle. He wore faded jeans, cowboy boots, a mostly yellow Hawaiian shirt unbuttoned halfway to his waist. His face was weathered to a walnut color and crinkled at the corners of the eyes and mouth; his long, graying brown hair was combed straight back from his high forehead. He had a battered guitar case hanging from one hand and a Lucky Strike burning in the other.

"Laurie," Jim said, "this is Skip."

"Hi," Laurie said. Jim thought she looked twelve years old at that moment. "I always loved 'Tender Hours.' It's a beautiful song."

"Ah yes," he said, walking to his amp. "'Tender Hours.' Those were the days. Folk rock. Model As. Flocks of passenger pigeons that blotted out the sun."

She looked to Gabe for a clue as to how she should react. Gabe shrugged and turned away. Skip opened his guitar case and took out a weathered red Gibson hollow-body and strapped it on. "Don't pay me any mind, sweetie," he said. "Deep inside I'm touched that you've heard of me at all."

The "sweetie" must have seemed especially patronizing, but then Skip was, in fact, old enough to be her father. Jim watched her opt for professionalism, crouching on the floor with her electronic tuner and getting ready to play.

"Jim," Skip said. "Gimme an E." He was still watching Laurie. Jim played a note on the keyboard and Skip tuned up at full volume, giving each peg a sharp, strong twist. Laurie plugged in her father's guitar and, when Skip stopped to light another cigarette, tried a chord.

Jim put a microphone in front of her amp. "Don't want you to get drowned out."

Skip took a Budweiser out of the refrigerator. "Anybody else?"

"Me," said Dennis from behind the drums. Skip took one over to him, walking closer to Laurie than strictly necessary, clearly and deliberately moving through her personal space. Jim noted the way she held completely still as he passed, not even breathing.

"So," Skip said. "You guys want to try and play something?"

"We could," Laurie said shyly, "do something of yours."

Skip waved the idea away. "I'm sick of all that shit. Why don't we do one of these songs of yours that Gabe was so hot and bothered about?" She glanced up too late to find sarcasm, if it was ever there.

"What about that minor 7th blues thing?" Gabe asked.

"Um, you mean 'Neither Are We'?"

Gabe nodded. Skip said, "Go for it."

Laurie ran through the chords for Skip and Jim with self-conscious bravado. Gabe fell in as soon as she began to play in rhythm, and it visibly buoyed her. "What do you want from me?" Jim asked. "Kind of a three A.M. tinkly piano?"

"Organ," she said. "That B-3/Leslie sound, real throaty and spare." She eased in beside him as he changed his settings, saying, "The melody goes dah da-da-dah da-da-dah dah, and you do a response, dat daaaah dat, like a horn part." She played it on the DX-7. "Then through the progression." She showed him the rest of the chords.

"So you play keyboards too?"

"Not really," she said, stepping back, trying not to look too proud, Jim thought, at having successfully shown off. "Some piano lessons as a kid."

He played the part through a couple of times while Laurie went back to guitar. "I get it," he said.

Dennis built quietly on his toms, then went to the ride cymbal and snare.

Her face relaxed into quiet pleasure. After half a minute Jim saw her glance at Skip, but he was no longer watching her. His eyes were closed and his head leaned forward as if he'd fallen asleep on his feet, except that his left hand moved silently up and down the neck of his guitar, feeling its way toward something. Suddenly it slid high up to squeeze out a single prolonged, piercing note.

Laurie walked over to a vocal mike in the middle of the room, stopped playing long enough to switch it on, opened her mouth, and sang.

It came together that fast, and everyone in the room knew it. Jim looked at Gabe and got a nod and slow smile in return. The air was sweet with the smells of hot electronics, camphor from the drums, the creme rinse in Laurie's sweat-damp hair, the ancient musky odor of the garage. The pressure of the sound waves caressed their skins and vibrated all the way through them.

At some point Skip stopped them long enough to say, "How about we roll a little tape on this?" And much, much later, after Laurie did a final vocal take, standing alone in the center of the garage in headphones while Gabe and Skip sat on the couch and Dennis lay on his back on the floor, she looked at her watch and said, "Oh my God. I have to be at work in five hours."

Everyone left at the same time. Nobody said anything about doing it again. "But really," Jim says, "I think everything after that first look that passed between Skip and Laurie was inevitable. Every one of us knew the two of them were going to end up in bed together, and every one of us, for our own individual reasons, tried to talk ourselves into believing we were wrong."

Jim plays me the version of "Neither Are We" they recorded that night. It is nearly the same arrangement as on the album—the recording quality not as pristine, the fit of the parts somewhat looser, Skip's guitar more drawn out and showy, Laurie's voice slightly hoarse from the long night's work. Getting to hear it is a privilege, payback for these long days and nights away from home.

"So," Jim says, walking me out to my rent car. "Have you been in touch with Laurie at all about this?"

"I wrote her. And left a couple of messages on her machine. But she hasn't answered. I don't think she wants to be involved with this. Which I can understand."

"Have you tried e-mail?"

"E-mail?"

"She hates phones, and she thinks letters are too much work. But I still get e-mail from her a couple of times a week. If you've got an address, I'll pass it along to her. No promises, but it's worth a try."

I give him the address. This seems too good to be true, especially after the unexpected bonus of hearing the tape. I head for my kitchenette in Anaheim, feeling hopeful for the first time in days.

S U M M E R

On Friday night I drive back to Santa Monica to catch Summer at the Duck. She is headlining and the bar is two-thirds full as she takes the stage for her first set. I've gotten a definite sense of scene-in-progress for the last half hour, with people moving from table to table exchanging glancing kisses and handshakes, but now everyone quickly finds a seat.

Summer herself is wearing jeans, a Faulkner-caricature T-shirt, a thrift-shop plaid sport coat, and running shoes. She is medium height, full-figured, with black hair cut straight at the bangs and shoulders. She is relaxed and comfortable on stage, and I sense her taking satisfaction in this long, respectful silence.

With the first chords come whistles and applause. She smiles and nods and starts the first verse. There is nothing in the words or the music or the singing to tell you what year it is outside. It could be 1962. Brad the manager's comparisons to Joan Baez are appropriate: Summer has a strong, clear voice, crisp diction, a big range, perfect pitch, vibrato, all the tools. If this were in fact 1962 she might have a great career ahead of her. But from my outsider's viewpoint it seems obvious why she hasn't been signed now, in 1996. Her passion is implied and not obsessively delineated. She has no edge.

Toward the end of the set she introduces "Tried and True" by saying, "I guess this is my 'hit.' Some of you may have heard it by another singer. . . ." She pauses for effect and the crowd responds with some laughter and also, to my surprise, some hisses.

"Hey, now," she says. "It was nice to make some royalties." She makes an ironic grimace and launches into the song.

Afterward, in the office that Brad has loaned us for the occasion, we talk about her past. "Born in Iowa—like most people in LA, I'm from someplace else. My mom teaches math at the university in Iowa City. My dad split when I was six, so I never really knew him. He claimed to be a poet, but he never had anything published that I've ever seen. The last anyone heard he was in Mexico somewhere. That was ten years ago.

"I went through a phase in high school where I tried to find out about him. The truth is I didn't find a lot to like. I still blame him for deserting us and I think there's something to be said for holding a good grudge."

She went to UCLA on scholarship and hung on as an English undergraduate as long as she could, reluctantly and eventually moving on to grad school and teaching assistantships. She'd been writing songs since her teens and she started playing professionally when she moved to the city. She met Fernando in a coffeehouse in Westwood and he convinced her to drop out, take a low-paying job at a bookstore in Long Beach, and pursue her destiny.

"I'm not kidding myself," she said. "I know I'll never be Madonna, or even Joni Mitchell. I don't have the looks, I don't have a gimmick. Live performance is not that big a deal to me anyhow, it's just a way to get the songs out there. I keep thinking I ought to be in Nashville, where there's a real community of people who make their living writing music."

"Are you serious about that?"

"Why not? It's something I think about a lot these days. Tennessee is beautiful, with real seasons and big pine trees. And they don't bulldoze everything every ten years whether it needs it or not."

"You say you're good at holding grudges. Does that apply to Laurie?"

"Most of the time I'm fine about Laurie. I mean, she never meant to hurt me, and she put my song on her record and all. It's just that every once in a while I look out at the audience and wonder if I'm going to be playing at the Sly Duck to the same hundred, hundred and fifty people until I die.

"It's not something you can reasonably blame somebody for. Why did some guy sleep with you and not fall in love with you, even though you fell for him? Laurie wanted a rock and roll band, she wanted *that* band, and I knew from the start that I was her second choice."

"So she'd already played with Skip and the others before you two did that first night as a duet?"

Summer nods. "Twice." She is sprawled back in the wooden desk chair, playing with a letter opener from the desk. Brad is nearly invisible, standing in a dark corner with his arms folded over his chest, as if ready to swoop down and defend Summer if necessary. "The first time was apparently pretty spectacular. She called me the next day and was all atwitter over it. She'd played with Skip Shaw, they'd worked on one of her songs, it was like they were reading her mind, they all played these perfect parts, and every blind person within a five-mile radius could see again after they were done. I remember trying to talk her down a little about Skip Shaw."

"Talk her down?"

"Don't get me wrong, I'm as big a fan of his songs as anybody alive. But he's been in LA forever, and you hear a lot of stories. Like, that song 'Tender Hours.' You've probably heard this. Supposedly he wrote it in fifteen minutes to win a twenty-dollar bet with his producer. Then he turned around and spent the twenty bucks to get high. I didn't want her to think Skip Shaw was God or anything, is all. Which she found out herself a couple of days later when she went back for another practice.

"I don't know exactly what happened, but Skip was apparently in a territorial mood, going around pissing in all the corners in that charming, testosterone-driven way guys have—no offense."

I incline my head for her to go on.

"She'd taken in a new song and all Skip wanted to do was play old blues crap. Just froze her out, until there was nothing left for her to do but pack up and go home."

"Did she ever figure out what happened?"

"Just Skip's little way of having cold feet. Being a jerk to run her off. Needless to say, Laurie was pretty low. I was not in a very good place myself. You've met Fernando, I hear."

"Word gets around."

"It's a small town. Several of them. Anyway, Fernando was going through one of his periodic this-is-going-to-hurt-me-worse-than-it-does-you phases where he went back to his wife for a while, and my opening act had just stood me up, so I suggested the duet thing. I thought it would cheer both of us up. Purely as a one-off, not with the idea of a recording contract or Letterman or" —she raises an eyebrow at me—"tell-all biographies somewhere down the road."

She bends her head, folds both hands behind her neck, and holds that posture for a beat or two. "Okay," she says as she straightens. "Part of me wanted us to be a duo from the first time we sang together, really from the first time I heard her sing at the Silk and Steel. Not that she was that earthshaking, I just had a feeling. I knew we'd be good together."

I nod. "How long did it last?"

"Sixteen weeks, fifteen of them headlining on Saturday night. By the end we were playing to standing-room crowds. It was starting to break. But by then her band was ready to come out, and—well, there really wasn't a choice as far as she was concerned. Her heart wasn't in what we were doing. I knew it. I could feel it. But I still wanted to hang on, you know?"

"So she was rehearsing with the band at the same time that you two were playing together."

"Oh yeah. In fact, Skip started courting her back that very first night we did the duo. We were on stage and I looked up and saw Gabe in the audience and I thought, Uh-oh. He was nervous, and Laurie started to squirm and make mistakes. During the break Gabe came up to her and they talked, and then she went out by herself. I gave her a couple of minutes and . . . this is going to sound petty, but I followed her.

"She walked down toward Ocean Boulevard, and there was a dark blue sixties Mustang parked at the curb, and I knew it had to be Skip's car. I never saw his face, just his arm hanging out the window with a cigarette burning in the fingers. She went up to the car and stood there, and then after a while she got in. That's when I went back to the club."

"Did she tell you she was back with the band?"

"Eventually. I mean, I know it was hard for her. She said there was no point in telling me about it until she'd tried it a couple of times to see if it was going to work. What does that remind you of? But she did tell me, and she said she wanted to keep working with me while they were rehearsing, and she meant it, at least at the time. But I knew I was losing her.

"I can tell you when I realized it was over. I went to their first gig, at Club Lingerie, which I had to read about in the *Weekly,* by the way. The veil, as they say, was lifted from mine eyes. I couldn't kid myself after that about us having a future together. The crowd was eating her up, and vice versa. She was even *singing* better than she did with me.

"How could I begrudge her that?"

K I T C H E N E T T E

My kitchenette is small and antiseptically clean. I can smell the fresh paint on the walls, and the beige industrial carpet is as firm and new as the mattress. There is a single living room/bedroom, a bathroom with a shower stall, and a black-and-white-vinyl-tiled nod to a kitchen. I am within walking distance of both Disneyland and the Anaheim Convention Center. I have a twin bed, a sofa, and a coffee table. The TV gets fifty-two cable channels.

My laptop computer is set up on the breakfast bar that separates the kitchen from the rest of the room. I check my e-mail over orange juice and a blueberry muffin. Nothing from Laurie, of course, but there is a message from my four-year-old son (with obvious help from his mother) wondering how much longer I'm going to be here. In fact I have only today and Sunday left of the week I allotted myself for on-site research, all I can spare for a book that I not only haven't sold, but may not be able to sell. I am to fly back to San Jose at noon Monday.

I create a new category folder labeled "Guilt" and file the message. I don't need anyone else to ask me what the hell I'm doing here when I ask it of myself every day. Sometimes it feels like pure self-indulgence: scoring a copy of Laurie's demo, getting to hear Jim's garage tape, and later today my biggest coup yet, an interview with Skip Shaw.

I have almost everything I came for, and it isn't nearly enough.

E Y E   C O N T A C T

"This would all be easier if I'd died when I was supposed to," Skip says with an easy smile. He's wearing a Wild Bill Hickcok shirt in red satin, with a flap that buttons up one side. He stands with his left cowboy boot planted against the wall, brushing a hank of long brown hair back with one hand while the other holds a burning Lucky Strike up close to the knuckles.

The most recent picture I've seen of him is twenty years out of date. He's always been good-looking, in a dissipated sort of way, and age has given him the weather-beaten authority to back it up. His voice goes with the rest of the package, lazy in a way that is not quite Southern, part rural Californian and part world-weary, seasoned with two-pack-a-day huskiness.

We're in a cinderblock jingle factory in Van Nuys, far and away the least glamorous part of LA I've yet seen, on a side street crowded with repair shops, warehouses, and sheet metal plants. Eighteen-wheelers parked along the curbs force traffic into the middle of the crumbling pavement, and the air is purplish with exhaust fumes.

Inside there are window air conditioners mounted in the brown veneer paneling, mismatched furniture, and bulletin boards layered with fourth-generation xeroxed notices from unions, tax authorities, and pest-control companies.

"If you'd died?" I ask. "What do you mean?"

"It's hard to keep up that mythic pace year after year. What if James Dean had lived to be in *The Towering Inferno?*" He shakes his head. "I was in a car wreck in 1971. That was right after I made *One More Lie* for Columbia, which was the best work I ever did, and they dropped my contract and didn't even want to release it. I came to in the hospital and I looked around and I thought, Man, this was not in the script."

"That was when your daughter was killed."

He looks startled, but doesn't lose the smile. "You do your research, don't you?"

"I like research. Good research is like armor."

He nods, slowly. "Armor's okay. Makes it tough to change directions sometimes."

"Let's try anyway. If you were dead you would never have played on Laurie Moss's album. Or was that your *Towering Inferno?*"

"No. No. That was a good record. Jim Pearson produced that record, him and Laurie. No, this is my *Towering Inferno,* right here. Cheese puff commercials. The love theme from the eleven o'clock news."

"Don't you get royalty checks?"

"If you're talking about my illustrious solo career, my royalties wouldn't feed a cat. Hell, nobody had lawyers in those days. None of us expected to see forty, let alone have to make a living when we got here." When he says "us" I think of the LA scene he was part of at the end of the sixties and the beginning of the seventies: Neil Young, Tim Hardin, Gram Parsons, some of whom did not, in fact, see forty. He shrugs. "Studio work is easy. There when I want it, easy to walk away from."

"You almost walked away from Laurie, the week you met her."

"I ran her off, is what happened, out of sheer contrariness."

"Why?"

"I listen to the radio, you know, still, and she sounded to me like that was where she was headed. The big time. I had to ask myself if I wanted to go through that again. Fame is the crazy guy on the subway in New York. You don't want to make eye contact with it, because then it's all over you, breathing in your face, haranguing you, wanting things from you."

"But you changed your mind."

"It wasn't about me. Gabe and Jim wanted her back."

"But you were the one that went out to Santa Monica to talk her into it."

He's shaking his head. "That's not why I went out there. I went out there to tell her that if she wanted to keep playing with Gabe and Jim and Dennis she shouldn't let me get in her way. I told her that night that she should count me out. I'd already been to the mountaintop, I'd swallowed all the tablets, I'd fucked the fatted calf, I didn't have it in me to do it all again."

"And she said?"

Skip shrugs. "She said she didn't want to do the band unless I was in it."

There is a knock at the door and a guy with sideburns and a threadbare green button-down shirt sticks his head in the office. "Skip, we're ready for you."

He nods and reaches for the guitar case at his feet. "Sorry," he says. "I warned you this might happen."

"Can I watch?"

The question seems to surprise him, as if I'd asked to look on while he washed the dinner dishes. "I guess so," he says.

The studio is more thoroughly run-down than the offices: a small, cluttered room with a bare forty-watt bulb in the ceiling, carpet patched with duct tape, ripped Naugahyde chairs, cigarette burns in wood-grain Formica tables. There's a small drum kit in one corner and a keyboard in the middle of the floor. Skip plugs his guitar into a distortion box which is connected to an old blackfaced Fender amp. The guy in the green shirt, whose name is Jeff, hands Skip a pair of headphones. Skip adjusts them while he lights another Lucky, then puts on a pair of reading glasses to look at the handwritten charts on the music stand in front of him.

Through a pane of glass I can see the control room and Steve Weitz, who is producing the session. He's unshaven, dressed in a leather jacket and T-shirt, and seems preoccupied as he speaks into the microphone in front of him. "This first one is your basic 'Brown Sugar' ripoff, just give me that Keith sound. . . ."

Skip nods and tunes down to open G. His smile is cocky now, and once he starts to play he hams it up, imitating Keith Richards' splay-legged squat and outthrust right arm.

The second piece calls for surf guitar. He retunes and cranks his reverb to get the signature wet-sounding echo. For the third he plays syncopated funk, swaying to a rhythm section I can't hear, eyes closed, cigarette smoldering in the corner of his mouth. Something is different about him, and it takes me a few seconds to realize that he's finally stopped smiling.

"One more," Weitz says. "We can use a couple three minutes of lead here, go ahead and cut loose a little." Skip closes his eyes and plays jazz chords, 7ths and 9ths, interspersed with single-note runs. Then he slides up to a solo and moves outside the progression, playing long, convoluted lines that are both melodic and fiercely intense. At one point, sustaining a long trill, he reaches up with his right hand to snag his cigarette and grind it into the carpet with his boot heel.

It's at least eight minutes from the time—well into the take—that I think to look at my watch until Skip finally stops. In that time Weitz shuts down the tape deck and comes into the studio to stand next to Jeff and me. Weitz begins to get impatient, looking at his own watch. I can see other faces inside the control room. Skip seems oblivious to us all, despite my growing self-consciousness.

The solo finally crashes and burns in a flurry of muted strings. In almost the same motion as his final downstroke, Skip wrenches the cord out of guitar's socket with an explosive crack. The amp is still emitting sixty-cycle hum at high volume as Skip leans his guitar against it and abruptly turns and walks out of the room.

I can see the people in the control room laugh and shake their heads as they walk away. A few of them applaud. Jeff smiles at me awkwardly and shifts his feet. I can see my own discomfort in his face. "Does this happen a lot?" I ask him.

"I've known him twelve years. He doesn't go off like that every time, but, yeah. I'd say more often than not."

"Skip calls it his 'dirty little secret,'" Weitz says. "He gets off on the whole *verkakte* scene. Playing some tune he's never heard before, under pressure, for money. You know what limiters are, supposed to keep you from blowing out your recorder with too strong a signal? Skip hasn't got those. He starts playing, he's wide open."

"How can you stand to watch him do that?" I ask them. "It's like watching a car wreck."

Weitz shrugs. "He likes it. Who am I to judge?"

I assume the interview is over. I stop to get my tape recorder and find Skip in the office, sitting now, glasses gone, hair freshly combed straight back from his face, leaning forward with his chin in his hands.

"That wasn't exactly what happened," he says as soon as I walk into the room. "That business about Laurie not wanting to be in the band if I wasn't in it." I realize he has resumed the conversation from exactly where we'd left off and I turn on the recorder. "I guess what I went out there for was to take another look at her. Kind of like walking in a liquor store just to look around when you've been sober for years and years.

"We sat in my car and smoked a J, and I asked her what it was she wanted. She said she didn't care if she got rich, she just wanted to make a decent living. I didn't entirely believe her. I was pretty sure even then that she wanted it all, the limos and the dark glasses and the sunken marble tubs, but it didn't matter. Either way, I still wasn't the ride she wanted to catch, and I told her so. That I wasn't one for going the distance. She got out of the car like she was going to walk off, then she stuck her head back in and asked me why the hell I'd dragged her out of her gig to tell her that.

"I told her everybody'd gotten together at Jim's place the night before and this thing—that had never had to have a reason before—was now somehow sad because it wasn't going anywhere. And she nodded and said, 'I told you what I want. Maybe you need to think about what *you* want.'"

"And did you?"

"Mister, it's twenty years too late for me to think about what I want. I think about what I need, to get from one day to the next. And the smart thing for me to do would have been to walk away."

"Why didn't you?"

"I could sit here all day and give you reasons. It would have meant not seeing Jim and Gabe anymore—I didn't know then it was going to mean that anyway. Maybe I thought I could deal with it. The truth is people don't do things for reasons, they do things because they ate too many powdered sugar donuts for breakfast or because they caught a whiff of perfume standing in line at the bank.

"So I ended up at Jim's house two nights later, on the phone to Laurie, telling her I'd do whatever she wanted. She could call the album Laurie Moss and the Lichen, and I'd be a Lichen."

Even at this distance in time there is something else behind his attempt at humor; bitterness, maybe, or resignation. "This would have been January of '95, I guess, almost two years ago. She came over and we played and then somewhere around one or two in the morning we had a council of war. Her blood was up. She'd just got fired from some horrible coffee shop waitressing job and so the band was all she had. Jim and Gabe and Dennis had caught the fever from her and I could see right then I'd made a mistake.

"I'd put her in the position of having to make trade-offs. For every label exec in this town who has fond memories of 'guitarist and singer/songwriter Skip Shaw' there's two that I screwed out of a big advance. I told her I'd play on the record and maybe do some gigs, but anything beyond that—up to and including putting my name on the record—had to be in my own way and my own time."

"Was 'Don't Make Promises' your idea?"

"Talk about guilt? Yeah, that was me. We were sitting around putting together a set list, talking about cover tunes, and she showed us 'Say Goodbye' by what's his name . . ."

"Tonio K."

"Right. And somehow we got to talking about Tim Hardin, who she'd heard of but never actually heard. And I told her about hanging out with Tim at the Chateau Marmont before he died, and I played her 'Don't Make Promises.' I was against putting it on the record, and so was she, but Jim talked us into it."

I check my notebook. "In the press kit for the album she described your singing on that song as 'a working man's voice trying to make it to the next verse without being torpedoed by emotion or giving up from the sheer weight of the experience it had to carry around.'"

Skip leans back and for a second his eyes lose focus. Then he smiles, finally, with something like real pleasure. "She was really something, wasn't she?"

A N G E L S

From a pay phone in the waiting room I call Melinda Lee, Laurie's former manager, who's been trying to get me an interview with Mark Ardrey. Ardrey was Laurie's A&R man, her principal advocate inside General Records.

He has politely declined, she tells me. "Sorry. He's just not talking to anyone associated with Laurie."

I call Jim Pearson in Whittier. He's been trying to locate Mitch Gaines, who toured with Laurie. It seems Mitch is on the road again and won't be back for at least a month. He and Dennis, Laurie's drummer, were the last names on my list; I've talked briefly to Dennis in San Diego, where he's living now, and he's agreed to a longer phone interview once I get home to San Jose.

"Well," I say. "I guess that's it."

"I guess," Jim says. "Unless you happen to like football?"

And so, after a perfunctory Saturday night tour of the clubs on Sunset Strip, I spend my last Sunday in LA with Jim Pearson and his son Sam, watching the Miami Dolphins on television.

"Laurie and Dennis and I used to go to Angels games," Jim says. Jim seems aware of the game at all times without having to focus on it. Sam is playing with Star Wars action figures on the carpet in front of the electronic fireplace of the TV. He is older than my son Tom, but still makes me miss him profoundly.

"I'm a bit of a sports freak, and so is Dennis," Jim goes on. "Laurie was not deeply into sport, but I think she found the formalities of baseball soothing. The sense of rules and order and knowing what's expected of you. Dennis bought her an Angels cap at one of the games and she used to wear it every night on tour—you know, what with 'Angel Dust' and everything."

I point out how often people talk about Laurie in past tense.

"You're right, of course. And it's not that I think of her as deceased or anything. It's just . . . the distance."

"When you think about her, are there pictures in your mind? Particular defining moments you remember?"

He closes his eyes to think. "When we were on stage, I was always behind her. I can see her standing in front of the microphone, the neck of the guitar sticking out to her left, arms close to her body, bouncing up on her tiptoes and leaning forward because she's fully into it, blinding white lights in front of her, silhouetting her. That's a moment.

"Sitting around the kitchen table at my house, late at night, her hair matted with sweat, collapsed in her chair with this exhausted smile. For her to do what she did—driving halfway across the country to get to LA, waiting tables eight or nine hours a day, and then going home to work on her demo or coming out here to rehearse, all the auditions and open mike nights and free gigs—we're talking about a very intense, focused, driven human being here. Every once in a while she did remember to enjoy it. You could see it sometimes, at two in the morning when we were working on the record and we'd nailed a take, it was like the momentum of the band physically pushed her back in the chair and spread this smile across her face and for a little while the tension that was holding her together went away."

He must see something in my face because he reaches over to squeeze my shoulder and says, "Sorry."

"What for?"

"I'm not sure." He shrugs. "I guess that I got to be there and you didn't." He picks up a cassette from the coffee table and hands it to me. "I dubbed off some of the rehearsal stuff for you. Maybe it'll help. And I did e-mail her about you."

I thank him for the tape and then hesitate, afraid to ask the next question.

He shrugs, anticipating me. "She remembers you, that *Pulse* story you did. If she'll talk to anybody I think it'll be you. It's just asking a lot for her to talk at all right now."

RED DRESS

A week later I am back in San Jose, transcribing interviews. It's the day
before Thanksgiving. I find I have e-mail from someone named red_dress
and I know it is Laurie. I hesitate before I open it because this is a pivotal
moment: If she brushes me off like Mark Ardrey did, I won't have
enough material to do the book. I try to imagine how that would feel
and discover, to my surprise, the possibility that I might be relieved. I will
have failed, but it won't be my fault.

I open the message. "I liked the story you wrote in Pulse," it says.
"Jim assures me you are very sweet, and Gabe, apparently, thinks so too.
They want me to tell you everything. Should I?"

There is only one reasonable answer. "Yes, please," I reply.

Over the next week, at the rate of two and sometimes three messages
a day, we set the ground rules. E-mail only, no phones. Phones make her
feel like she's being stalked. I can use anything she tells me for publication, provided I make reasonable attempts to verify her chronology and
cross-check her facts with Jim and Gabe. If she starts feeling wonky she
can end it—no arguments, no recriminations.

I try to find a starting place that feels safe yet gives her room to talk.
"Most bands play for months or even years before they record," I write
her. "You had a finished master tape before you ever played in public.
How did things get so turned around?"

"Panic," she writes back. "Sheer, visceral panic. . . ."

THE TAPE

BRAVE NEW WORLD

When she first left San Antonio for LA, in June of 1994, she had money enough for three months' rent and food. Even so, she'd made the trip in her Little Brown Datsun and not on the back of a turnip truck. She knew full well that three months was not long. Music careers were apt to take years, if not decades; were more prone to fail grimly and quietly than spectacularly; were fraught with dangers both unimagined and painfully obvious.

She counted not on her voice or her songs, whose worth she could never really know from the inside, but rather on her own ability to make a decision and live with the consequences—a skill she'd managed to develop in the complete absence of family role models.

In three months she thought she would have time to look for a day job, and perhaps find one. Time enough to put smells and colors and feelings with names she'd heard all her life: Malibu, Pasadena, Hawthorne, Long Beach, Anaheim, Burbank, Hollywood, Venice. Time enough to stretch herself against the city and see if she fit. Time enough to make herself available to good luck, if good luck should be so inclined. In short, she decided the time had come to invest her emotional life savings in a three-month lottery ticket.

Her reasoned, low-pressure attitude vaporized on contact with the city. In the first two weeks she found herself fighting panic on multiple fronts: Even as she was awed by the fabulous houses, the travel-brochure beaches, the palm-lined boulevards and oleander-covered hillsides, she was stunned by the amount of time she spent in bumper-to-bumper traffic, surrounded by concrete embankments and ice plant turned gray by congealed exhaust fumes. Every dollar she spent seemed to take a little of her substance with it. She begrudged herself every hour not spent in hot pursuit of her future at the same time that she found there was only so much rejection she could tolerate in a single day. Most mornings she woke up with relief to find that Jack was not in the bed next to her, and every night she listened to the noises of barking dogs, passing cars, and rattling garbage cans, all of them seeming hostile for no other reason than that she did not yet have her own connection to them.

Finding work at the Bistro d'Bobbi meant money coming in that nearly equaled the money going out. It lowered the incline of the daily uphill struggle at the same time that it consumed the majority of her waking hours. It got her through July's barrage of phone calls from Jack that began with incredulity and quickly moved through pleading and threats to acceptance and self-pity, as if he were going through the text-book stages of death and not merely the end of a relationship—though by that time he was only talking to her answering machine.

Having a job got her through August's humiliation of asking her father to buy a new transmission for the LBD, which meant she could no longer even say she was managing on her own. When her birthday, always the low point of the year, rolled around in September, at least there were people at work to make her a baked apple pizza with all twenty-six candles on it. And by the time she had to quit the Bistro in October for a once-a-week opening slot at the Sly Duck Pub—supplemented eventually with a coffeeshop day shift to make ends meet—LA had at least become familiar. She had worn paths in the freeways that knew the shape of her tires, and there was comfort in the long, slow curve of Sunshine Terrace that led to her apartment. Her three months came and went and she saw that her stay was no longer limited by money but by the strength of her own resolve.

The resolve was the hardest part.

Once, during her two years at San Antonio College, she'd gone floating down the San Marcos River with a boy from her English class. At the shop where they rented the inner tubes she'd watched the boy talk to the owner, whose name was Ron Tuggle, about a place called Jacob's Well.

Jacob's Well was a vertical limestone shaft filled with clear water from the Edwards Aquifer, and scuba divers liked to work loose the grating that closed it off and explore the tunnels that fed into it. From time to time Ron had to go into the well after the bodies of divers who'd drowned there. The day Laurie met him, Ron had a shaved stripe across the top of his head and stitches in it that belonged on Frankenstein's monster. He was explaining how a cave had collapsed on him the last time he'd tried to bring a body out. He talked in a low voice, his eyes dazed and haunted-looking, stopping periodically as if he couldn't quite remember what he'd just said. His partner had been ten or twenty feet behind him when the roof fell in. And of course his dive light went out. He was in total blackness, pinned by boulders, deep underwater, and running out of air. He knew he was going to die, he said, only he had this obsessive thought that he couldn't get rid of. He was absolutely convinced that if he panicked, the doctors would be able to see it when they autopsied him, and he would have set a bad example to all the people he'd taught to dive. So he lay there in the darkness and took the smallest sips of air that he could manage. In the end, he said, he sucked so much air out of the tank that it collapsed under the pressure of the water around it. He'd just lost consciousness when his partner finally got to him and dragged him back to the surface.

The idea of someone she had met and shaken hands with lying in the cold and dark waiting for death was not one that rested quietly in her head. Humor was the only defense. Whenever anything went wrong for the rest of that weekend—a long wait at a restaurant, or a rude and meddlesome clerk at the motel, they would look at each other and say, "What would Ron Tuggle do?"

She was still thinking of Ron Tuggle on Thanksgiving in Los Angeles as she carried a small, hemispherical mound of turkey and dressing to a table in a deserted downtown cafeteria. She was fifteen hundred miles from her family and the house she'd grown up in but only hours away from a job she hated, so tired at night she could barely open her guitar case, thinking that good luck was perhaps not inclined her way after all. "What," she asked herself, "would Ron Tuggle do?" less as self-exhortation than as an admission of hopelessness. She took tiny bites, imagining that each one was a sip of air, possibly her last, and in that way made it through the meal. But the next morning, peeing in the coffee shop's dank and airless restroom, one feeling of release unleashed another and she was overwhelmed by a flood of homesick tears. When she got back to her apartment that afternoon she called her mother, who offered up a round-trip ticket to San Antonio for Christmas. Laurie said yes, not knowing the change that waited just around the corner of the new year, when she would meet Gabe at the Duck in January and ask him to play on her demo.

TEXAS

Grandpa Bill was standing next to her mother when Laurie got off the plane. He was dressed like a college professor in herringbone, pressed cotton, and corduroy, though he was in fact a retired postal clerk. He seemed terribly thin and pale to her, and there was more gray in her mother's long, dark brown hair than Laurie remembered, as if her own subjective sense of enormous time lapse had somehow aged them. But she was groggy from airplane sleep, which, like airplane food, had left a bad taste in her mouth without satisfying her.

When she and Grandpa Bill finally let go of each other, her mother hugged her quickly then held her at arm's length. "What in heaven's name did you do to your hair?"

"Henna, Mom," she said, "just henna," hating the defensive tone that came so automatically from her mouth.

She woke up at ten o'clock the next morning—only eight California time—in the same worn-out double bed she'd slept in all through high school. She remembered countless vertiginous mornings-after with pale pink stucco looming above her, and endless broiling summer afternoons with a guitar lying across her sweat-damp stomach as she imagined herself on the big concrete open-air stage of the Sunken Gardens Theater in Brackenridge Park. She'd conceived and made endless mental revisions to her first album cover in that bed, and worked on her Grammy acceptance speech. She'd sought the appropriate attitude to take when Mick Jagger called to say he loved the album and would like to see her naked.

She'd dreamed of being transformed, not just different hair or more perfectly matched breasts, but a different walk, a new expression behind her eyes, like she'd glimpsed once in her father and seen again in other men with guitars, Paul Westerberg in the early days of the Replacements, or local hero Charlie Sexton, or countless others on the MTV of her adolescence, and so rarely seen in women, except of course for the iconic Chrissie Hynde, with her defiant stance and trademark eyeliner, tough and vulnerable and rebellious, the snarl that launched a thousand careers.

Her fantasies were simpler now, though still the fuel that kept her engines turning during hard times. That fewer than one in a thousand had ever materialized was irrelevant, or should have been if she'd been able, in the gray December morning, to see past the other nine hundred and ninety-nine.

She dragged a box of old cassettes out of her closet and played them on her mother's stereo: Bowie, Replacements, Scandal, INXS. Her head felt swollen with memories of dancing at the pavilions at McAllister Park, drinking tequila at Freddy Sandoval's house with his parents out of town, cruising back from Austin on I-35 all alone at three o'clock on a Sunday morning. Colors and smells and overpowering emotions, family and lovers and friends.

At six-thirty Grandpa Bill showed up to take her to dinner and Laurie hustled him out the door before he broke down and invited her mother along. Then, when he stopped to hold the door of his pickup for her, she wrapped her arms around him. She'd thought about this every Friday she'd been away: catfish, yams, and roasted corn at the Clubhouse, Fifth Army Band veterans from Fort Sam Houston playing jazz in the corner by the ice machine, Grandpa Bill with a plate of ribs, beans, and greens, eyes closed, smiling.

Unlike LA, San Antonio was not built around its freeways; the shortest route to the Clubhouse was on surface roads, through upscale Terrell Hills and Alamo Heights, then south into aging neighborhoods on the edge of downtown. Suburbs were the same across Texas and across the country, but urban San Antonio was the very essence of Tex-Mex: palm trees and red tile roofs looking out on acres of parkland, low-riders blasting conjunto and country-western, plywood shacks selling cabrito in the shadow of plastic golden arches.

She'd thought, on the days when LA had seemed ugly, cumbersome, and painful, that she would slip back into San Antonio as if it were the perfect pair of shoes. And it was in fact comfortable, and full of still more memories: milkshakes from the Broadway Fifty-Fifty; pizza in her best friend Miriam's car as they sat in Volare's tiny parking lot; her first kiss, at her father's company picnic; her first concert, Dallas's Bugs Henderson, playing the Sunken Gardens when she was fourteen.

They'd passed Incarnate Word University with its millions of Christmas lights and were only a few blocks from the Clubhouse when a street lamp highlighted the shaved place on the back of Grandpa Bill's head.

"What's that?" she asked.

"What's what?"

"On your head."

He sighed. "I had a couple of little growths taken off."

"What kind of growths?"

"A couple of melanomas. No big deal."

"Grandpa, that's cancer."

"Just a couple of little skin cancers. The doctor did it there in the office with a local anesthetic. I drove myself home afterwards. The worst part of it is I have to have a lot of annoying tests for six months to make sure they got it all."

"Mom doesn't know. Does she?"

"I told her it was a wart. You're not going to say any different, are you?"

"*If* you let me talk to your doctor, and *if* he backs up your story, then I'll consider it."

"I don't want you getting yourself exercised over this. You can't imagine the good it does me to know you're where you are and doing what you do. If I got in the way of that, if only because you were worrying about me when you should have been concentrating on your music, I couldn't forgive myself."

"Not the guilt, Grandpa," she pleaded. "Anything but that."

The parking lot was full, as always, and they parked on North Alamo. Claudis, the owner, stood by the open back door, surrounded by fragrant white smoke from the fifty-five-gallon pit. He was well over six feet tall and massively built, with hair and beard starting to turn white. He raised his eyebrows and jabbed one finger toward Laurie as she got out of the car. "Lord, girl, where you been?"

She walked up to shake his hand, feeling a smile stretch her face. "California."

"No shit. You playing guitar out there?"

"A little."

"You get famous, don't you be forgetting your old friends, now."

"Not a chance. You'll be catering my Grammy award party."

Inside, the band was tuning up. Laurie moved automatically toward an empty booth on the north wall, Alice's station, then saw that Alice wasn't there. She looked at Grandpa Bill, who said, "She's been gone since July."

"What happened?"

"Apparently one of her customers complained about something and she quit."

Laurie understood that she had no claim on Alice. They had no relationship outside the Clubhouse; Laurie herself had left for California with no warning, had abandoned her customers at the Bistro d'Bobbi just as abruptly. Still she felt the loss of one more silken strand tying her to the world.

The band sat down to business and Cecil, the keyboard player, caught her eye, winked, and without her having to ask for it, played the crisp, delicate runs that led the band into "Take the 'A' Train." In the middle he took a Basie-style solo, one perfect, ringing note at a time. Take this train, the music said. Roll with this train and don't look back.

FELIZ NAVIDAD

She didn't get up until noon on Christmas Eve, and when she did she found Corky sprawled in their mother's recliner, watching junk sports on ESPN. "Hey, sis," he said, not looking at her. He'd dressed up for the occasion in a Rage Against the Machine T-shirt and a small, tasteful, dangling cross earring. His hair looked like he'd cut it himself with a pocketknife.

She brought in her breakfast and ate at the coffee table, watching him watch the screen, curious to see if he'd actually start a conversation. The five years' difference in their ages had seemed like an entire generation, a lifetime, when she was negotiating the social land mines of high school and he was still learning long division, and she'd been pressed into involuntary baby-sitting at least once a week. It had left her feeling more like a mother than a sister. In the months she'd been gone he seemed to have leapfrogged past her to some premature world-weariness. One arm dangled over the side of the chair, the wrist intermittently twitching as he worked the remote control.

"So how's that apartment working out?" he finally asked.

"Good," she said. "I mean, it's expensive, but it's . . . safe. I'm glad you talked me into it."

"You needed to get away from that asshole."

"What about you? Mom said you lost your job."

"Yeah, like it fell through a hole in my pocket or something. I got fired, is what happened, 'cause I kept coming in late and calling in sick and all. 'Cause I couldn't manage to give a fuck about photocopies. Excuse me, *reprographics*."

"So what *do* you want to do?"

"Fuck if I know. You are so lucky to have something you really care about."

"I guess. I'm still working shit jobs, just like you."

"Not for long. You're too talented. Me, I'll be doing it the rest of my life. I'll be that pathetic old guy you see at the Stop N Go at midnight, one hand on the sawed-off under the counter all night long, trying to work up the nerve to empty the till and head for Mexico."

She didn't know how to reassure him. He'd tapped into some deep reservoir of despair she'd never seen in him before.

"Have you still got your place over by SAC?"

"Nah. My shit's all up in the attic, next to yours. I'm crashing on my buddy Ray's sofa right now."

"What about, um, Angela?" She'd had to concentrate to come up with the name of his most recent girlfriend, whom Laurie remembered as bleached hair and a pretty face with eyes always turned to the ground in front of her.

"I may be worthless, but I ain't stupid. Even if she was up for taking me in, which I doubt, she'd end up throwing me out again in a few days. Whatever we got left is pretty goddamn shaky."

He was motionless while he talked, still in the way that a drawn bow is still, or a baited rat trap. The sympathy she wanted to feel for him seemed to evaporate in his presence.

In the afternoon her mother began her Christmas Eve tamales, a matrilineal tradition that stretched back for unnumbered generations, lately (and reluctantly) modified to use vegetable oil instead of lard and black beans instead of pork in a separate-but-equal batch. Grandpa Bill took up his accustomed place at the kitchen table while Laurie assisted, the house gradually filling with warm seasonal smells.

Corky played his father's part, numbing himself in front of the TV with Miller High Life. By the time dinner was over and Laurie had seen Grandpa Bill to his truck, the recliner was horizontal and Corky was snoring quietly. Laurie's mother threw a coverlet over him and turned off the lights and the TV.

"Thanks for dinner, Mom," Laurie said quietly. "Great tamales."

"I'm glad you liked them."

Laurie lingered another moment in the hallway. "Are you okay?"

"Just tired," her mother said. "I'll see you in the morning."

It wasn't that she and her mother didn't talk. It was that the substance of the conversations hadn't changed in years, only the details. "You look so thin," her mother might say, or, "This California business isn't really working out." If Laurie mentioned Mazola Mike, the balding, oily, forty-year-old manager of her coffee shop, her mother might say, "Is that what you drove all that way out there for? To work in a coffee shop and play once a week in some bar?"

In ninth grade, sneaking home late through the back yard, Laurie had recognized the smell wafting from her mother's open bedroom window. Once past that momentous discovery it had been easy to deduce the rest: a single joint every night at bedtime, supplemented with medicinal use at certain high stress periods—such as Christmas, when she would put off shopping until the last minute, then wander through the mall in a cannabis fog, buying shiny things at the Imaginarium and the Nature Company.

For her part, Laurie was happy with what she'd done on a micro-scopic budget, and she put the results under the tree the next morning. She'd found her mother a set of matching Art Deco ring, earrings, and necklace at an antique store in Pasadena. For Corky she'd gotten CDs by up-and-coming LA death-metal bands that had yet to score national record deals. For Grandpa Bill there was a history of LA jazz, lavishly il-lustrated, which he didn't look up from for the rest of the day.

Throughout Christmas afternoon people dropped by for a plate of tamales—neighbors, Laurie's fifth cousin from Helotes, lawyers from the office where her mother worked as a legal secretary. Around seven o'clock Laurie answered the phone and heard her father say, "Merry Christmas. Did you get your present?"

"No . . ."

"I mailed it last week. Better ask your mother."

She covered the mouthpiece and asked, and her mother did in fact come up with an envelope which looked suspiciously like it held a check,

moving Laurie to equal parts hope and guilt. Inside, instead, she found
words and music to a song called "Last to Know."

She picked up the phone again. "I found it."

"It's . . ."

"Shhh. I'm reading."

It was a story song, her favorite sort, with a natural voice and un-
forced rhymes, about a boy whose girlfriend was going to leave him
rather than let him find out she was pregnant. When he does find out,
though he's the last to know, he makes her stay and marry him because
he loves her and wants the baby. At the same time he has figured out
what she knew all along, that it's going to change everything, that it already has, and once again he's the last to know.

Though it was a story she'd never heard before she was not so naive
as to believe he'd made it up. She was touched by the lyrics at the same
time that she felt disoriented and a little hurt that the singer—she made
herself think of him as the singer—had entered into the marriage with so
many reservations.

"Sing it to me," she said.

"I wrote the music out . . ."

"I want to hear you sing it."

"Besides which, I don't even have a guitar, thanks to you."

"Please."

Eventually, hesitantly, he began to sing. It was good enough, she
thought, that if he'd ever recorded it he would at the very least have
made it to where-are-they-now status.

"Daddy, it's wonderful."

"It's the only song I ever kept, out of all the ones I wrote. I thought
it was pretty good, except by the time I wrote it I didn't have a band anymore and I didn't know what to do with it."

"I do. That's what this is, isn't it? For me to sing?"

"If you want it."

"I want it."

When she got off the phone she read the song through twice more
to fix it in her memory. Then, since no one was looking, she held it
tightly against her chest.

CLASS REUNION

She was scheduled to fly back on Tuesday. On Monday, when she got up, she found a note from her mother saying Rudy had called, with a local number under the name. Rudy had been a minor guitar hero in high school, possessed of more swagger than real skill, and had moved to Austin afterward to pursue a career in death-metal. The last time Laurie had seen him, more than a year before, he'd had dark brown hair to his waist and a shaved chest. She and Rudy had been friends and intermittent lovers until she'd gotten involved with Jack, at which point she'd lost track of everyone. Including, she thought, herself.

She called and got his mother. Rudy was out, but he'd left directions for a party that night at Christian Walker's house, one of the socialite kids from high school who'd always tried to hang with musicians. No, Rudy's mother said, Jack wouldn't be there, Rudy had made sure of it.

A party, Laurie thought. Just the thing.

She roamed the empty house, missing her guitar, knowing that if she had it she might never leave. It was so safe here. By working fifteen or twenty hours a week she could pay her own way and have enough left to help her mother with the mortgage. There would be barbecue at the Clubhouse every Friday, coffeehouse gigs in Austin an hour and a half away, and all the sleep she'd been yearning for.

After dressing carefully in new jeans, antique silk blouse, and black blazer, she took her mother out to an early dinner at Aldino's and then borrowed the car to drive to old-money Olmos Park, where Christian's parents lived on Contour Drive, as narrow and twisting as it was exclusive. The Walker house was fieldstone and high hedges on a block of scrub oaks and palms, lush December lawns, Spanish-style castles and drab brick blockhouses.

The front door swung open to her touch, decanting shouts and high-decibel music and the fumes of beer and popcorn. She walked over hardwood floors and under vaulted ceilings to the sunken living room, with its walk-in fireplace and Victorian curved, padded, and skirted furniture. Two dozen people drifted in a great circle from the den to the living room to the kitchen. Laurie nodded to familiar faces with unremembered names, who nodded back. In the kitchen she found a stash of Snapple in one of five identical plastic tubs, drowned in half-melted ice. Through sliding glass doors she could see the vortex of the party spin around the edges of the L-shaped swimming pool, where the obligatory *Queen's Greatest Hits* played and dancers camped it up in their best Travolta style. She could hardly wait for the seventies to be over again.

"Laurie?"

It was Shawn Moore, heartthrob of MacArthur High in his day: six-foot-one, rumpled blond hair, track, tennis, family money, a nice enough guy who'd been lockstepped onto his career path since day care. Everyone knew Shawn; he only knew Laurie because of the way institutions turned alphabetical proximity into physical.

"Hey, Shawn." He stuck out an awkward hand and she took it, noticing at the moment of contact how his hair had thinned and his middle thickened, taking a sudden and irrational dislike to his expensive leather deck shoes and the white strip of T-shirt that showed under his polo shirt. "How's law school? You must be almost through with it."

"Oh," he said, turning still more awkward. "I guess you didn't hear. I'm, uh, taking a break from that."

"What happened?"

"My grades took a pretty bad slump last year. I just kind of, I don't know, burned out, I guess. I'm going back. Next year, probably. I've been working for my old man at the dealership in the meantime."

"How do you like it?"

"Are you kidding?" He said it with a bitterness that made Laurie want to run away. "So what's up with you? Still in San Antonio?"

"LA."

"No kidding? Hey, that's right, you used to sing, didn't you?"

She had inadvertently ignited Shawn's interest eight or nine years too late, now that he could no longer change her social status or perk up her self-esteem. It took her five minutes to extricate herself to the sweet cool air of the patio.

She found Rudy on the far side of the pool near the beer keg, with Christian hovering nearby. Rudy had trimmed his hair to his shoulders and was wearing baggy olive shorts below his knees and a black Nine Inch Nails T-shirt. "Hey, Rude," she said. "Hey, Christian."

Christian, in jeans and a brown sport coat, smiled vaguely and let Rudy thrust him aside.

"Laurie!" Rudy threw slightly drunken arms around her, then

stepped away for another look. "What you been doing in LA, starring on *Babewatch* or what? You are fully foxed out."

"Waiting some tables, playing some solo gigs. How about you?"

"Doing good, really good. That whole Black Sabbath thing is happening again, we've been playing a lot, same lineup for four years now. This guy wants us to come to Houston and cut a record for him, I don't know, maybe next month."

"Maybe next month" was Rudy's "mañana," and Laurie knew he didn't have a record deal. It was, however, all he could talk about, and whatever interest he might have had in Laurie's West Coast adventures evaporated next to the heat of it.

She hadn't meant to do it, hadn't known it was happening, but apparently a low-grade fantasy had been simmering in her mind all day. She'd come to the party prepared to be seduced, if sufficient care and effort were taken. Sex with Rudy was only part of the distance she realized she'd been willing to go. Once, years ago, Rudy had wanted to abandon metal godhood and start a pop band with her, and she saw she'd been waiting for him to ask again tonight, and that such an offer could have become a reason to stay.

She felt like a fool, like she'd fallen for a retouched photo in a catalog, and now the merchandise would have to go back. "Listen, Rudy," she said, driving a wedge into the first crack in the conversation, "I have to circulate a little, but you hang tight, okay?"

Toward the back fence she saw Connie Sigurdson, part of Shawn Moore's high-school A-list, leading lady of drama club and senior musical, in a knot of admirers. She was dressed in a black silk sweater and black slacks, her blond hair cut sharply to chin length. It didn't hurt her popularity that she was sharing a couple of tightly rolled joints she'd brought with her from New York, where she'd landed an understudy role on Broadway. "I do some Tuesday nights," she shrugged, "and all the Sunday matinees." Her acting had improved; Laurie nearly believed her nonchalance.

"So," Connie said as Laurie moved into the circle and accepted a hit. "I hear you're in LA now."

"Waitressing, mostly."

"But you *are* playing, aren't you?"

"Yeah, I've got a regular club gig." Laurie was embarrassed to find herself resorting to false modesty in the face of Connie's palpable hunger for an audience. In high school Connie had promised suicide if she wasn't a star by twenty-five; but that was high school, and understudy on Broadway was the real world, and closer to stardom than 99.9 percent of anybody ever got, closer in fact than Laurie had ever been.

"See?" Connie said, looking around. "She knows. I love San Antonio, and I'll always think of it as home, but pro basketball and a Hard Rock Café do not a cultural Mecca make. If you're headed anywhere, the very first thing you have to do is leave town. Laurie? Am I right, here, or what?"

Laurie shrugged, feeling her heart sink. "You're right."

"So," Connie said, the argument, if there'd been one, clearly over, "how long are you in town for?"

"Tomorrow," Laurie said. "Just till tomorrow."

AULD ACQUAINTANCE

She regained the two hours she'd lost and was safely back in her apartment, showered, and tucked into bed by ten Tuesday night. She apologized to Los Angeles for being tempted to return to her mother's. "I didn't mean it," she said. "I'm glad to be home."

If it hadn't been true before, it was true once she said it, both the "glad" and the "home."

On New Year's Eve she and Summer did the Strip until eleven, then opted for a bottle of cheap champagne and a slumber party at Laurie's. They watched the countdown on TV, where the commentators had already seen the clock roll over in three time zones and there was not much left for California but empty bottles and confetti all over the stage. But then, Laurie thought, being in her twenties at the end of this particular century, she was used to the party being already over.

They made Summer a bed on the couch and talked by the flicker of a candle on the coffee table, Laurie sitting on the floor so their heads were only inches apart. Summer told her that Fernando was married, and that was why they weren't together for New Year's. Laurie played her the song her father had sent her for Christmas.

There was a quiet tap at the front door and Laurie opened it to find a slightly inebriated Catherine from next door, her hair up, wearing a low-cut black dress that no longer fit as well as it once had. "Join us," Summer said from the couch. "There's a little warm champagne left."

"No more champagne," Catherine said.

"Where's Shannon?" Laurie asked, sitting back where she'd been.

"With her grandmother in Santa Barbara for the weekend. Allowing Mom to go out on a real date and get a little schnockered."

"How'd it go?"

Catherine sighed and sat on the floor next to Laurie. "Maybe I will have just a taste of that champagne." She topped off Laurie's glass and drank half.

"A jerk?" Summer prompted.

"No, he's actually very sweet. Known him since college, brought me flowers, good-looking, not gay, not married."

"Maybe you should introduce me," Laurie said. "What's the matter with this guy?"

"It's not him. It's me. I'm bored. I can't help it. I think I'm genetically programmed to fail. The only men I'm attracted to are jerks like Shannon's father. Cocky, arrogant jerks who never grew up and who will inevitably dump me for somebody closer to their own mental age."

"Maybe it's all part of Nature's plan," Summer said. "If we hooked up with somebody stable, instead of these philandering Neanderthals who knock us up and move on, they'd always be around to screw up the kid."

Laurie got another glass and split the rest of the champagne three ways. "A toast," she said. "To 1995. May this be the year for all of us. May we find fame, fortune, and true love."

They touched glasses and Summer said, "Or any two out of the three."

FIRST CONTACT

A week later she met Gabriel Wong at the Duck. She kept her foot inextricably in her mouth for the entirety of their first conversation, rescued only when Brad announced her second set. The warm tide of resultant applause carried her back toward the stage. I'm for real, she reminded herself. People clap for me.

She set about her conquest of the audience as a stepping stone to winning Gabe for her demo. It started with one stranger and then another setting down a drink, looking up at a break in the conversation, allowing her voice to slip from background to foreground. At some pivotal moment the very nature of the experience changed; then none of them were strangers, and a silence opened up under the music where the murmured voices and scraping chairs and clinking glasses had been only a moment before, and she owned them.

It never lasted long, but it came that night when she needed it and it came with the reckless energy of falling in love. When she walked off stage, soaking wet, giddy and exhausted, Gabe was there to hand her a business card and say, "Call me. It'll be good."

And it was good, despite her terror, despite her fleeting regrets at the hundred dollars she could ill afford to pay him for the work, despite the fact that as soon as it was time to actually start she was seized with profound loathing for her songs, for her voice, for her pitiable lack of talent.

And it was good on that Sunday in the garage in Whittier, where, of all the emotions that surged through her, the strongest was wonder: that her familiar song could be transformed into this rich new entity with life of its own; that she could be drawn so deeply, so suddenly, so comfortably into a sense of community with these men that she barely knew, one of them a certified legend; that they could simply sound so good.

The next night she called Gabe and he confirmed that yes, it had really gone well.

"I knew that."

"Sure you did. That's why you called, right? Well, it went so well, in fact, that I think some of us got scared."

"Like maybe one of you in particular? Maybe with the initials Skip Shaw?"

"Maybe."

"So you guys all, what, sat around and talked about me after I left?"

"Some. We all think you're too good to be playing in a garage in Whittier. Not merely too good. Too commercial. We think you're going to be very, very big."

Her heart was in her throat. "If that's true, then you could all be very big with me."

"Maybe, but some of us seem to like garages."

"One of you? Skip again?"

"Two. It *is* Jim's garage."

"It's very safe there."

"Right the first time."

"So," she said. "What happens next?"

"We thought maybe we should try it again. Wednesday night, day after tomorrow? Maybe it'll be terrible."

"I can see how that might make things a lot simpler for some of us."

"It might indeed."

ONE TO GO

On the lunch shift Tuesday she'd served too much coffee to a girl with matted hair and last night's mascara bruising her eyes. The boy with her, shirtless under his black leather jacket, seemed disappointed with whatever he kept seeing on his watch. At the end the girl said, "Two more cups of coffee," and he said, "Make one of them to go."

The words had lodged in her head and anchored a refrain that played there all afternoon. Once at home with a guitar the right chords all seemed to recognize each other and settle in comfortably together. Verses followed, winding up with an extended meditation on an empty styrene cup clattering down a deserted gray-guttered street.

If it was a bit bleak, at least the pieces all snugged together perfectly, and what's more she'd written it top to bottom in forty minutes, a time not, perhaps, in league with some of Skip Shaw's, but a new personal best.

Wednesday, faced with two girls sick and unable to persuade Laurie to work a double, Mazola Mike said, "You find this all rather puerile, don't you?"

She had seen him on break studying a battered red paperback called *Vocabulary Is Power!* "Of course not," she said, showing him the truth in her eyes while her mouth went through the motions. "It's just too late to change my plans, that's all."

Five minutes later he'd cornered Mildred, late thirties, three kids, no husband, in debt twenty or thirty dollars to every woman in the place, and he had her nodding tiredly to the rhythm of his supermarket erudition.

That will never be me, Laurie thought, holding the new song in her head like a plane ticket and a passport, like a numbered Swiss account.

She and Jim and Gabe and Dennis had been working on "One to Go" for an hour when Skip arrived, wearing jeans and a stained white T-shirt, unshaven, his hair apparently unwashed since the last time she'd seen him. She attempted to keep playing despite his looming in her peripheral vision as he set his guitar case by his amp and stood with folded arms, staring, Laurie thought, right at her.

He waited until she had struggled through to the end of the song to walk slowly to the refrigerator for a beer. Once he had everyone's undivided attention he said, "Don't mind me. You just go on ahead."

Jim said, "We've been here since seven." It sounded to Laurie more like apology than accusation.

"I got held up." Skip took a leisurely drink, then opened his guitar case as if unsure what he might find.

"Did you hear the new song?" Jim asked.

Skip paused in the act of strapping on the guitar. "'The new song,'" he repeated, as if these were words he could not be expected to interpret.

"Laurie's new song," Gabe said.

"Yeah, I heard it."

Jim and Gabe both looked away, avoiding confrontation without, she thought, being consciously aware of it. The song was barely a day old, fragile, with no strength of its own yet. It could be so easily crushed. "What is it, exactly," she said, "that you don't like about it?"

He finished plugging in his guitar and turned to face her. His eyes, if they indeed opened on his soul, had steel shutters over the windows. "Nothing, darlin'," he said at last. "There's nothing I don't like about it."

He hit his low E string and waited for Jim to sound his pitch. It was the alpha male's call for submission, and the sight and smell of it made her queasy and desperate for fresh air. To her disappointment, Jim played the low E.

Skip tuned up quickly, at high volume, and went immediately into a shuffling blues. He played by himself for a long time, long enough to have sensed the reluctance all around him, if he cared to, while Laurie stared at him. His own expression was vacant, as if she'd ceased to exist, or at least to matter. Behind her Laurie heard Dennis take up the rhythm on his cymbal. Jim hit a tentative chord and Laurie unplugged her guitar.

Gabe crouched next to her as she packed up. "Listen, I'm sorry about Skip." He was not playing, but neither was he unplugged. "Stick around, will you? He'll calm down in a minute."

"I don't need this," she said, hating the way her voice came too close to a scream in order to top the noise. Jim's hands dropped away from the keyboard as she passed him, and by the time she'd slammed the door to the studio Dennis had dropped out as well. That left only Skip, and she heard him all the way out to the street, where the car keys fell out of her trembling fingers twice before she could open the LBD's trunk to stash her equipment, and a third time opening her door. He was still playing as she drove away.

PARTNERS

She was home and showered by ten, making sleep an unexpected option—though in fact she was so tense that the mattress felt like steel plate. She called Summer and let her wring the entire sordid story into the open. At the end of their commiseration Summer proposed the duo, and the timing, it seemed to Laurie, couldn't have been better. Skip had flattened her ego with the indifference of an interstate trucker running over a soft drink can, and if a duo with Summer wasn't the future she'd been imagining since the previous Sunday and her first very different trip to Whittier, at least it was a future where somebody wanted her, and not a future of lying on a sheet-metal bed listening to her bones creak as her muscles wound ever tighter. "Come over Saturday," she told Summer, "and we'll work a few things up."

Saturday, cloudy and cool, was a dozen glazed and two Styrofoam vats of decaf, five hours of guitar and gossip, a song list and tentative arrangements. Sunday night was a long black knit dress fresh from the thrift shop, two songs on her own, then the crowd's eager pleasure as Summer joined her, a performance that felt like an event, that felt, Laurie tried to convince herself, like history in the making. All in all it would have been perfect had she not looked into the audience during the third set and seen Gabe.

When, during the next break, he came to her table and told her Skip was outside, she saw disappointment flicker over Summer's face, and tried to ignore the sudden jump in her own pulse. "And?" she said coolly.

"He didn't tell me what he wanted. I would guess he wants to apologize."

"Go," Summer said. "If you don't you'll be pissed off at yourself, and probably me besides."

When she got out to the car, in the clouds and moonlight, with the Pacific crashing into the rocks below, she found herself leaning with her back to the car, talking to a disembodied hand with a cigarette in it. "So," Skip said. "What exactly is it you want?"

"Excuse me? I didn't call this meeting."

"If you were to come back to Jim's studio, if we were to play again, what would you want out of it? What would your intentions be?"

"You sound like I'm trying to date your daughter."

"I had a daughter, as a matter of fact, and she would have been about your age if she'd lived, though that doesn't have jack shit to do with the topic at hand. Just spitball a little for me. If you could have your way, what would you want from us?"

It wasn't the death of his daughter as much as the offhand way he exploited it that upset her balance, and of course that was exactly what he'd meant to do. Still she let herself be lured inside and even smoked a little weed with him, and she told him exactly what she wanted. "I want to be part of a real band, not just have some backup musicians. I want to make a record, with my name on it, and hear it on the radio in my car. I want to play out a couple of hundred nights a year, some of it on the road. I want to make enough not to be in debt and not to have to waitress anymore."

Skip barely seemed to have heard her. "I stood outside," he told her, "and listened to your new song for a while before I went in the garage last Wednesday. I stood out there and thought, Man, you better run this little girl off right now. Because if you don't you're going to fuck up and let her down and break her heart."

The rest of what he had to say was a variation on the same theme: a species of arrogant masochism, with no gesture of contrition or of commitment. When she got back to the club Summer was already on stage, singing "One More Lie" by Skip Shaw, and when she saw Laurie she winked and smiled.

"How'd it go?" Gabe asked her.

"I think you were wrong," she said. "He didn't seem to want to apologize after all."

Laurie waited out the end of the song, then took the stage to no inconsiderable applause. She knew Gabe heard it; she allowed herself the small fantasy that Skip might have pulled up to the curb outside long enough to hear it too.

They played until two, counting the four encores, and afterward Brad called them into his office to offer them a standing Saturday night gig as a duo, two hundred apiece, two sets instead of four, approval of opening act. "Give us a minute," Summer said.

With Brad out of the room she said, "I don't know about you, but I loved tonight. I think we make a hell of a combination."

Laurie, buzzing with Skip's dope and the crowd's approval, said, "Me too."

"Should we do this?"

"We should absolutely do this," Laurie said.

"Your thing in Whittier, that's not going to happen?"

"It doesn't look that way." She stuffed her second thoughts where she didn't have to listen to them and stuck out her hand. "Partners?"

Summer took it and drew her into a hug. "Partners," she said, and after they told Brad, the three of them repaired to the Rock and Roll Denny's to celebrate. At three-thirty, however, consensual time took hold again with the suddenness of an enchanted carriage reverting to a pumpkin. She saw that, with the exception of the clientele, this was a Denny's like any other, with ugly plastic booths and brown Formica tabletops, too much like the booths and tabletops where she was due in three and a half hours.

She woke up in her own bed at a quarter of seven from a dream of a room filled with telephones, where as soon as she answered one of them another began to ring. She saw then that she'd slept through forty-five minutes of alarm with her head under a pillow.

She was an hour and a quarter late to work, and as Mazola Mike wrote out her termination check he said, "Here's a week's pay in lieu of notice." A banner day for him, she thought. He not only got to fire her, he got to say "in lieu of."

At home with blinds drawn, having laboriously gone through all her uncollected mental trash without coming upon sleep hidden behind any of it, she found herself returning to two items over and over:

With all the jobs she'd walked out on, she'd never been fired before. What had the world come to when she couldn't even hold on to a crummy waitress job?

And . . .

Why had she committed herself to a semi-acoustic duo when what she really wanted was a band with bass and drums and high amperage?

By afternoon she'd developed all the symptoms of a full-blown cold, contracted, she was sure, while standing drenched with sweat in the chill night air talking to His Highness, Skip Shaw. No recrimination too petty for me, she thought, no forgiveness in view.

Gabe's phone call caught her on Wednesday afternoon when her immune system, having triumphed over the forces of disease through the application of Nyquil, sitcoms, and vitamin C, was back in the driver's seat. She had, after all, her severance pay and two hundred a week coming from the gig with Summer. She could find another job. She was freshly showered and dressed in clean black jeans that fit her for the first time in months. It was enough, in the words of a song she'd written in college, to make her carry on.

If Gabe had not caught her in such an up mood, if Skip had not been cute and funny with his Lichen act, history might have sauntered onto another path. As it was she grabbed her guitar and amp, got in the LBD, and drove to Whittier, putting on mascara and Carmex on the 101 South.

GAME PLANS

Back in San Antonio, in another life, Jack had once explained male sexuality to her. Put a balloon over the end of a faucet, he said, and turn the water on. If it doesn't get relief on a regular basis, something's going to explode. Her first reaction had been horror, then eventually a grudging pity as she saw how well the explanation fit her own observations.

For Laurie sex was more like eating dessert. It was a pleasant habit she could fall into, but the longer she went without, the less she missed it. Except, of course, for the occasional craving.

Jack had been very concerned about his balloon exploding, which meant there had been a number of times that Laurie had ended up with dessert without a meal first, dessert when she wasn't hungry, dessert first thing in the morning when she hadn't yet brushed her teeth.

And yet there had been times when what she'd begun in resignation had become so much more than that, when their bodies had locked into a call and response so effortless and universal that it seemed as if she'd just that moment fallen in love. As if love and contentment were imprecise synonyms for the simple, mechanical state of existing in synchrony with an external rhythm.

It was the only explanation she could find for the way she felt when she walked into the garage where the band was already playing "One to Go," when she tuned up, plugged in, and fell into the rhythm. Skip was exactly the same person who had driven her out of the garage a week before, the same person who'd sat next to her in his Mustang on Ocean Boulevard, staring straight ahead into the red and green neon reflecting off the damp streets, and yet now they were both wheels on the same locomotive, roaring down a steep grade in total darkness.

They did three takes, and after the last one Laurie said, "Harmony. Anybody here besides Skip sing?" Gabe and Jim both raised their hands and they spent another two hours working out parts for "Neither Are We" and "One to Go" and doing overdubs. It was after one o'clock when they settled around the kitchen table to watch coffee trickle into a pot.

"Is it too soon," Jim said, "to start talking game plan?"

Skip looked uncomfortable and Gabe cleared his throat. "Jim always wants a game plan." He seemed to be apologizing to Skip even as he looked directly at her.

"Thinking out loud," Jim said. "Four or five songs is a good number for a demo. We've already got two. I could get us listened to. If we do a few live dates, get any kind of press at all, I can probably swing us a showcase at the Whiskey."

Images stampeded through Laurie's mind. Before she could recover, Skip said, "To what end?"

Jim shrugged. "Get Laurie a record contract. Go on tour. Become obscenely rich. Buy a huge farm and raise rabbits and live off the fat of the land."

Which was when Skip finally shook his head and made his speech about how he was on some mysterious "never work in this town again" list, and how he would play on the demo and maybe do some gigs, and if there was an album, maybe that too, but in his own way and his own time.

And so what they'd had in the studio began to slip away, and eventually she did too—after promises to meet them again on Friday—back to Studio City and unemployment, back to an answering machine with Summer's voice on it wondering where she'd been, back to guilt pangs and the worry of where her next month's rent would come from, back to an uneasy sleep from which she awoke more than once with "One to Go" still playing in her head and visions of record contracts shimmering just out of reach.

DON'T MAKE PROMISES

Summer caught her flat-footed after they practiced on Thursday, suggesting they do it again the next night. As Laurie stammered out transparent excuses, Summer looked straight into her eyes, as if daring her to tell the truth. But she couldn't, not yet, not when all the band had was a game plan and one scheduled rehearsal. She still didn't know for sure who would be there Friday night, whether it would still be the Good Skip or whether the Evil Skip might be taking alternate practices.

In fact it was yet a third Skip who showed up. This one sat on a folding chair to play and drank one beer after another all night long. He was pliant and subdued, and at one point Jim actually had to ask him to turn up his guitar. They spent most of the night on "Angel Dust," Laurie playing thick, distorted power chords while Skip strung slow, single-note phrases between them.

Inevitably they found themselves sitting at Jim's kitchen table afterward. Ley lines must have crossed there, or some Indian mound lay directly under the linoleum; the spot's emanations of comfort had little to do with the tubular steel and blue-and-green-patterned plastic of the chairs. While Laurie warmed her always-cold hands on her coffee cup, Dennis paged through the sports section of the *Times* and Gabe read an essay that Sam had brought home from kindergarten. Skip put his boots on the table and tilted his chair back as he drained his sixth or seventh beer, then crushed the can and hooked it into the green recycling bin by the back door. "So," he said, suddenly focusing on Laurie, "where'd you learn to play guitar?"

Other than lending a reddish tint to his eyes, the beer didn't seem to have affected him. His attention rendered her excruciatingly self-conscious. "When I was twelve my dad showed me, like, a G and a D, and told me that now I could play every Velvet Underground song ever written. That was the beginning of it. I'd had enough piano lessons to know some theory, so after that every time I saw guitar players on TV I would watch their hands. It went from being, like, the Eleusinian myster-ies, to something possible, like using a sewing machine."

Skip nodded encouragement.

"Then, in ninth grade, there was this boy." She tried to ignore the rush of blood to her face and neck. "He kept asking me to come watch his band practice, and one time I did. And it was the same as when I saw my father play, only more so. This scrawny little kid put on a guitar and he was still bratty and he still had bad skin but he was completely trans-formed. He was instantly sexy."

"So did you sleep with him?" Skip asked.

She looked at her hands, folded on the table, and did not look any-where in Skip's direction, but she could nonetheless see the gently mock-ing smile on his face. "Yeah, eventually. But it wasn't what you're making it out to be. It wasn't sex for guitar lessons. It was because of the way he made me feel when he played. And part of me was amazed and appalled that anything could affect me that way. So I asked my mother for a cheap guitar for Christmas, and I made Eric teach me so I could break that hold he had over me."

Finally she looked at Skip, expecting condescension at the very least, and what she saw instead was another scrawny kid who used to get beat up on the playground, who knew exactly what it meant to find redemp-tion in the electric guitar. She couldn't seem to look away.

"So," Jim said finally, splintering the moment, "are we going to do cover tunes?"

After a sip of coffee Laurie's parched mouth worked again. "Sure," she said, and went to the garage for her guitar. She was weaker about the knees than she would have preferred to be, so she perched for a second on the edge of Skip's folding chair to catch her breath. She could smell the ashtray on top of his amp, and she could see the stains and scratches that he'd worn into his guitar over the years. For God's sake, she thought. He's halfway civil to you for once and you go all to pieces.

She brought her guitar into the house and showed them "Say Goodbye," from Tonio K.'s *Amerika* album, a raggedly pretty song about the death of everything and how to let it go. Everybody liked it and Jim wrote the title on the right-hand side of a legal pad page he'd labeled "Originals" and "Covers."

Then Skip took the guitar and started talking about Tim Hardin, about knowing him in the strange twilit interval in the seventies between the time Hardin stopped writing and the time he OD'd. All the while Skip was sounding chords very quietly, and at some point he started singing "Don't Make Promises," a bouncy little countryish song full of the blackest hurt and despair. It was the first time Laurie had heard him sing an entire song, live and in person, and his singing revealed things that most professional singers learn early on to hide.

She slept badly that night. She kept seeing Skip's face, and it seemed to her that the face wanted something from her, or, more precisely, it wanted something and was asking her if she was the one who could give it to him. Every time she found herself going down that road she would hurl herself into a new position and pound her pillows into a different shape and start with a fresh thought, like, How many other women has he given that look to this week? Or, This is why men complain about having women in the band, because they want to go to bed with us, and God help us if they get what they want. Or, Why don't you just act like a professional and go to sleep?

Summer knocking on her door at noon woke her up. As Laurie wandered through the apartment in a fog, making coffee, putting on odds and ends of clothing, it seemed an easy thing to simply tell her everything. Then, when she saw the hurt and disappointment on Summer's face, she wished she could suck the words back into her mouth.

"A week ago," Summer said, "you said the band wasn't happening." She had her arms folded over her chest and her eyes were glacial.

"A week ago it wasn't. I'm sorry, okay? Look, this doesn't change anything between you and me." The sentence trailed off unconvincingly.

"Of course it does. Don't play the naïf. It's insulting."

"What I'm saying is, I want us to keep playing together. I already told them I have to have Saturdays off."

"And what happens when you get a record deal and a tour?"

"*If* that happens, then I'd have to make a decision."

"Sounds to me like you already have. I can feel your footprints on my back as you climb right over me."

"Come on, Summer, everybody in town is in more than one band."

"Not me. I'm over thirty, which makes me an old woman by the standards of this industry, and I don't look like I'm on sabbatical from *Melrose Place.* Which means this is about as far as I'm ever going to go on my own. I haven't learned to live with that—I mean, who could really learn to live with a thing like that?—but I'd kind of gotten used to the idea. Then you come along and start throwing hope at me, and then inside a week you're gone again."

"I'm not gone," Laurie said. "I'm right here. Playing with you at the Duck is the only *real* thing in my life right now."

"The only thing that pays real money, you mean. But that's okay, don't panic. I need the money as much as you do. So I'll see you tonight, and we'll do our job and collect our pay." She picked up her guitar and was gone so fast that Laurie was left staring at the open door.

GET READY

At the Duck that night Summer apologized and Laurie apologized and they got up and played two great sets, better sets, ironically, than they'd played the week before, even as Laurie knew that the crack that had opened between them would only get wider and deeper.

Over the next two weeks the band learned her father's song, "Last to Know," and one of Laurie's oldies, "Carry On." She brought in "Just Another End of the World," her song about the fireworks over Disneyland, and they did Tonio K.'s "Say Goodbye." Not to mention a half dozen other attempts that didn't stick. The process seemed virtually effortless.

Late on a Sunday in February, while everyone else repaired to the kitchen, Laurie stayed with Jim in the garage and watched him mix her five originals onto a cassette. "*Voilà,*" he said. "*Une demo,* as the French say."

Laurie took the cassette into the kitchen and they listened to it on Molly's jam box that sat over the sink. Dennis's feet tapped out the drum parts on the linoleum. "This is good," he said, smiling.

"I could get a cleaner sound," Jim said. "One instrument per track, get more control over the levels . . ."

"Would you guys be quiet?" Laurie said.

When it was over Dennis said, "I'd hire us."

"Wouldn't that be nepotism?" Jim asked.

"Gross!" Dennis said. "No way I'd do it with a dead person."

"It sounds great," Gabe said. "Really great." Even Skip was nodding. For her part Laurie was fairly sure it was either brilliant or it was the Emperor's New Demo and club owners would laugh her out of town. She desperately wanted to listen to it another eight or ten times but was embarrassed to ask.

"So," Jim said, "whose name goes on the label? Do we cobble up some hokey band name, or are we Laurie Moss?"

"How about Muhammad Dali," Gabe said, "after the famous surrealist boxer?"

"That would be good," Jim said. "Or the Pro-Crust Dough Boys, from the makers of Procrustean Bread."

"I think we're Laurie Moss," Skip said quietly. Jim and Gabe turned to look at him. "I think she wants to hear a record with her name on it on the radio."

So, Laurie thought. He'd been listening after all, sitting in his car that night. For him to repeat her words was a gesture of such intimacy that she could feel a bright spot of heat in the exact center of her body.

On the drive home she pushed Skip out of her mind and focused on the tape. She played it over and over, objectivity eluding her. She'd have gone deeply in debt to buy herself temporary amnesia, to let herself hear her own music with innocent ears, but instead she was left hanging on every note, searching for clues.

Tuesday was Valentine's Day. She took Summer to the LA Natural History Museum for the day rather than sit around the house. "You're a genius," Summer said, looking at the life-sized woolly mammoth replicas in the La Brea tar pits. "On this day of days, to have found the perfect metaphor for love."

On a Wednesday in early March Laurie took a couple of old, unfinished songs to Whittier. Skip was late again. She'd run through what she had of "Brighter Day" for the others, remembering the last time Skip was late and promising herself that nothing, absolutely nothing, would bring her back if it happened again, when Skip's voice behind her said, "That was nice. Why'd you keep going to the F? The B7th is a lot prettier."

"I don't know," she said, giddy with relief. "I was young at the time. Do you always sneak up on people?"

Skip picked up the scrap of paper with the verse and a half and the chords. "Is this all there is?"

"I never finished it. I thought maybe we could . . ."

Skip nodded and turned toward the kitchen with the paper and his guitar case.

"What are you doing?" she asked.

"I was going to take a shot at it." She could see him start to retreat into himself. "That is, if you wanted me to, of course."

"Uh, yeah. Sure. I guess."

Skip nodded again and closed the door behind him. Laurie looked at Gabe, who shrugged. "Who is he supposed to be?" she asked. "Lord Byron? Heathcliff?"

Gabe and Jim looked at each other and then Gabe said, "He hasn't written a new song, all by himself, in fifteen years. But he's still Skip Shaw. He's got that voice, and he plays the shit out of the guitar, and he knows more about songwriting than anybody else I've ever known. And he's got history. You can hear it in everything he does or says. I guess that buys him a lot. From me, anyway."

Jim nodded and gave Gabe an E.

"So anyway," Gabe said when he was tuned. "How do you feel about Motown?" By the time they'd worked their way twice through "Get Ready," with Laurie faking the words and Gabe and Jim stepping up for the "ah ah ah ah" harmonies, Skip had returned. He was smiling. He laid the sheet of paper on Jim's Yamaha and Laurie turned it to face her. He'd added two verses and a bridge, crossed things out and written between the lines, drawn circles and arrows and sketched a couple of chord diagrams.

"This is weird," Laurie said. "I never wrote a song with anybody else before."

"I didn't write it with you," Skip said. "I just doctored it a little, that's all. Hell, I used to do it for Elvis."

Laurie looked to Gabe for confirmation and Gabe shrugged.

Skip said, "Those last few albums, in '75, '76? *Promised Land, From Elvis Presley Boulevard*? I'd come in, do a polish in an afternoon, pick up some change. Some of them turned out okay. You ever hear 'Moody Blue'? It got pretty big after he died."

"You worked on 'Moody Blue'?" she asked in amazement.

Now it was Skip who shrugged, as if it didn't matter. He seemed to want her flustered and confused, and she preferred to disappoint him, if possible. "Okay," she said, "fine, whatever you say." She pointed to "Brighter Day." "What does it sound like, now that it's been doctored?"

The answer was that it sounded good. Still jazzy, yet anchored by a rhythm guitar on 2 on 4. Still her song, only now a complete thought, with an edge to the words. And he'd used the B7th instead of the F on all but the last line of each verse.

"Works, doesn't it?" he said.

"I can't believe you're really this good," she said, hung up between her renewed pleasure in the song and her annoyance that she hadn't found it on her own. "I think you're just lucky. I think sooner or later your luck is going to run out."

"Sweetie," Skip said, "if I was lucky I wouldn't be in a garage in Whittier."

"Untrue," Laurie said. "If you *weren't* lucky you'd be in a garage in Whittier with somebody besides *us*." Gabe and Jim whistled and applauded quietly.

She strummed idly through the chords again. They not only sounded better, she liked the way they made her hands feel. "This is so amazing," she said. "I can't believe you did this in fifteen minutes."

Skip uncoiled a slow, cocky smile. "I'm a fast worker."

For an instant it seemed to slip her mind that she and Skip were not alone in the garage. Since the night they'd first met, Skip had been pulling rugs out from under her—flirtatious, then hostile, then indifferent, running hot, cold, and lukewarm—and she'd begun to suspect it was deliberate. She had no choice but to call his bluff, or at least that was what she tried to tell herself afterward, after she had looked straight at him and said, "You couldn't prove it by me."

He flinched first, glancing down at his guitar and saying, "Maybe we could roll a little tape on this one?" in a cramped voice.

Jim attended to the tape deck and Laurie faced the wall, feeling the flush burn across her face. What in God's name had she been thinking, swapping high school double entendres with a man the same age as her father? At least, she thought, the tape hadn't been running, but when she was finally able to look around again she saw that Gabe was not laughing at her but in fact looked sad and scared and she saw that this, in the words of her sixth-grade teacher, was going to go on her permanent record.

They practiced again Friday. Laurie taught the band her favorite of Summer's songs, "Tried and True," and one of her own stalwarts, "September 19th," a song she'd written in the gloom of her eighteenth birthday. Skip was dressed in new jeans and a tattersall shirt with the sleeves rolled to the elbows, pacing while he played, conducting with the neck of his guitar, drinking a lot of beer but actually seeming to enjoy it for once. It was drizzling outside and the garage was warm and dry and no one seemed to want to leave it.

"We could play through what we know," Jim said.

Laurie nodded. "Or . . ."

"Or what?" Skip said. She'd been feeling his glances all night.

"Or we could do that Tim Hardin song."

He smiled privately, as if he'd seen this coming. "Okay. I'll write the words out for you."

"Okay. Or . . ."

"Or what?"

"Or we could try singing it together? Like a duet?"

"Shit. For a minute I thought you were going to let me sing the whole thing."

"Do you want to?"

Laurie saw that she had successfully called his bluff again. "Nah," he said at last. "You're Laurie Moss. I'm just a Mossquito."

They worked out the arrangement as he showed her the words. It seemed to fall naturally into place: They began alternating verses, then lines, then sang the chorus together. After a couple of false starts they pushed on through, watching each other intently, finding themselves at the end trading the title line back and forth, slightly overlapping each

other, each time changing the feel: accusation, admission, promise, acceptance.

When they were finished Laurie could not manage to get her breath.
"Once more?" Jim said.

Skip was looking at Laurie. "No," he said. "I think we got it."

In unspoken agreement they began to wipe down guitar necks and
unplug patch cords. Laurie had the Duck the next night and Gabe had a
gig in San Diego. They all agreed to the following Monday and Laurie
walked out the door with Skip close behind her. She couldn't remember
the two of them ever leaving at the same time before. The rain had
stopped and the air was cool and sweet with the scent of something flowering. She was acutely conscious of the movement of her hips and thighs
as she walked, feeling gangly as a heron.

She set her guitar and amp by the trunk and turned toward Skip as he
passed. "'Night," she said.

He seemed to slow just long enough to smile at her. Not unaffection-
ate, she thought, but a trifle condescending. And then he passed her and
got into his Mustang and drove away with a guttural roar.

S U N D A Y   M O R N I N G

Though things had gone well enough at the Duck, Laurie still woke with
a sense of foreboding. She had promised herself she would get the Sunday *Times* early and call the likeliest ten jobs, and instead she lay for another two hours with the covers over her head.

Her life in San Antonio had not prepared her for the intensity of the
Southern California spring, a continuous ambush of brilliant color and
delicate perfume. It was a day to stay in bed, preferably not alone. It was
not a day for financial responsibility, even if her rent was now two weeks
overdue and she'd given up hope of ever being able to pay it. Still, a deal
was a deal, and the price for breaking a promise to herself was guilt, de-
pression, recrimination, then a little more guilt for good measure.

She put on her ugliest clothes to teach somebody—she was not quite
sure who—a lesson: oversized sweatshirt, jeans that had suffered a Clorox
accident, Docs. She tied her hair into a loose ponytail and drove down to

the market at the bottom of the hill for a paper, a cup of bad coffee to go, and a blueberry muffin.

She spread the paper out across the dining room table and started on the classifieds while she ate. She wanted three things: part-time work, because she was making some money already with Summer; an afternoon shift, so she could sleep in after a late night in Whittier; a decent place, so the tips would actually signify. These did not seem like impossible conditions to her, but then she had not had her compassion surgically removed so that she could become the manager of a restaurant and treat all staff, past, present, and potential, like an ancient, tedious aunt that she hoped would die soon.

She started her own pot of coffee and made her ten phone calls, from which she gleaned one unlikely interview the next day in Pasadena. Then she pushed the phone away and pillowed her head on her folded arms. How had she gotten to the point of complete financial disaster? What would be the end point of this metamorphosis? She'd developed weird habits from living alone too long, like snacking on cold leftover Kraft macaroni and cheese at all hours, and leaving her underwear to dry in the dish drainer next to the sink. She'd come to structure her days around the back-to-back *Brady Bunch* episodes every weekday at noon.

Worst of all, she'd begun to ponder the metaphorical dessert cart, and more and more it was Skip she saw bringing it around.

When the knock came, however, her first irrational thought was that it was the landlady, possibly with the police. It wasn't until she looked through the peephole and felt her knees weaken at the sight of Skip leaning against the doorjamb that reality collided with fantasy and completely uncoupled her train of thought.

It was entirely too late to repair her wardrobe. She could only open the door and stare at the bright yellow Tower records bag in his right hand.

"I found a CD with all the really good Tim Hardin stuff on it," he said with a nervous smile. "Only I don't have a CD player."

"Come in," she said, slipping into autonomic hostess mode as she tried to remember if there was anything he shouldn't see in the dish drainer. She backed into the living room, reflexively grabbing clothes off the furniture as she went. "Sit down."

"I should probably go," he said unconvincingly. "Maybe this is a bad idea."

"No," she said. "No, it's great. Want some coffee?"

"Please. Three sugars."

As she snatched a pair of errant panties and stuck them in a cupboard above the kitchen sink, she could hear Skip pace the living room. His boots seemed to stake a claim to everything they touched. Her heart pounded and the smallest tasks—finding a spoon, say—confounded her. "I like this place," she heard him say. "Kind of early Swiss Family Robinson. You probably never heard of them."

"The Disney version's on video," she said. She brought him a cup with a Boynton kitten on it.

"Thanks," he said. "How bad would it piss you off if I smoked?"

"I'll risk it," she said, and gave him the brown clay ashtray that had come with the place, made in summer camp by some stranger's child before she was born. Her hand didn't touch Skip's, not then and not when he handed her the CD, but she knew within a millimeter exactly how close she'd come.

The first song was "Don't Make Promises," faster than Skip played it, deadpan except for the cracks in Hardin's voice. She stood at the mantel in front of the boom box and looked at the pictures of Hardin in the booklet: receding hair, rumpled shirt, halfway between a wino and a class clown.

"You could turn it up a little," Skip said. "If you don't mind." He'd slumped on the couch, eyes closed, and he hadn't actually lit a cigarette, though he'd set the pack and a book of matches next to the ashtray. He'd made himself so thoroughly at home, and made her feel so taken for granted, that she hovered on the verge of annoyance.

"What's that?" she asked. "Marimbas or something?"

"Vibes," Skip said without opening his eyes. "Tim wanted to be a jazzman, so he had vibes on a lot of his stuff. Gary Burton, mostly." He opened one eye to check her lack of reaction. "He was hot shit later in the sixties. Why don't you sit down and listen?"

She perched on the farthest edge of the couch from him, tired of the emotional hoops he had her jumping through, more tired still of the calm amusement with which he did it. She waited through a couple of songs and then said, "Tell me what happened to your daughter."

He sighed and took out a cigarette and turned it over and over in his fingers. "I wasn't driving, thank God. But it amounts to the same thing. It was twenty-five years ago, fall of 1971. I was living in San Francisco, married to a woman named Carol. Everybody called her CC, like in 'CC Rider.' I was drunk and lying in the back seat and I started to throw up. It had been a long, long day and we were coming back from a party, and CC wigged. I mean, she lost it. She turned around and started hitting me when she should have been driving. Our little girl, SueAnn, was lying on the front seat in a blanket, two years old—they didn't have all those laws about car seats for kids back then. And CC rear-ended an eighteen-wheeler."

He finally lit the cigarette. "You got anything stronger than coffee?"

She brought him a glass of wine and watched his Adam's apple move as he drank half of it. Then he wiped his mouth on his sleeve and said, "SueAnn went through the windshield. The driver door came off and CC got thrown. I was sealed up in the wreck for four hours, they tell me. They had to use acetylene torches to cut me out. I never heard a thing. I wasn't bad hurt—that was the booze, it really shows you how to roll with the punches—but there was this noise like a waterfall in my head, so loud I couldn't hear anything else. It started to fade after a few days, and it took six months to go away completely. It was a mercy, really. Otherwise I would have had to listen to my own thoughts."

"I'm sorry."

"Hell, it surely wasn't your fault."

"I mean I'm sorry I brought it up. Made you talk about it."

"I can talk about it or not. After a couple of years it got to where I could go on living with it, but it's never going to go away. It's not like I ever forget it happened."

He emptied his glass, and as she reached to refill it a new song came on, sad major 7th chords on a piano, and she saw it hit Skip between the eyes. It was called "It'll Never Happen Again," and like most of the others it was only a couple of minutes long. She waited it out, and poured more wine, and then said, "What do you think of when you hear that song?" From where she was sitting, with one arm along the back of the couch, her left hand was very close to the warmth of his neck.

"It's not like that," he said slowly. "There's not one specific memory. It's more the sound of his voice, the mood of the words. He's got a song he wrote to Hank Williams where he says, 'I never knew you, but I've been to places you've been.' And I did know Tim, a little, but it's the same thing. I've been to places he's been."

He looked over at her with a look that seemed destined to end in a kiss. She was self-conscious, curious, scared, and terribly impatient all at once, and she knew that she'd crossed the line into inevitability minutes, if not days, before.

The phone rang.

Skip was the first to look away. "Don't you need to get that?"

"It's probably my mother," she said. "We always talk on Sunday. I can call her later."

The ringing seemed to put Skip on edge. He knocked back the last of the wine, took a final drag off his cigarette before crushing it out. The answering machine clicked on and a voice said, "Laurie, it's Gabe. If you're there, pick up, will you?"

Something in Skip's look made her pick up the phone. "Is Skip there?" Gabe said.

"What?"

"Don't play coy with me, Laurie, is he there or not?"

"Yeah, he's here."

"Put him on, will you?"

"What's going on?"

"Just put him on. Please?"

She held the receiver out toward Skip, who looked as guilty as a dog caught with its head in the kitchen trash. He got up and took the phone and said "Yeah," listened for a while, then said "Yeah, okay," and hung up.

"I got to go," he said to Laurie.

"What's going on? How did he know you were here?"

"I didn't know where you lived. I had to ask somebody."

"Well, what did he want?"

"He . . . reminded me of something I have to do."

"This is all way too mysterious for my taste."

"It's no mystery, Laurie." She couldn't remember him ever actually using her name before. She loved the sound of it in his mouth. It was like a caress. "I got to go," he said again.

She followed him to the door, befuddled, unable to think of what to say, either to make him stay or to make him explain himself, or both. "Your CD," she suddenly remembered.

"You might as well hang on to it," he said. "I got nothing to play it on."

"But—"

He touched one finger to her lips. It sent a wave of heat all the way down to her ankles. She reached up and took his right hand in her left and kissed it, just behind the thumb.

"You got to stop that, now," he said. He didn't take the hand away. She took one more step toward him and he backed quickly out the door. "I'll see you," he said. "Tomorrow night."

She had to hold on to the doorframe to keep her balance. Skip hesitated as he opened the door of his Mustang, looked at her but didn't speak or wave, then got in and drove away.

She slammed the door and dialed Gabe's number. "What the hell was all that about?" she said.

"Down, girl. I just reminded him of something he had to do."

"That's what he said. So what was it he had to do?"

When Gabe didn't answer, she felt her muddled emotions snap into focus. "You're treating me like a little kid, and that really sucks, Gabe."

"Yeah, okay, you're right. I'll be there in fifteen minutes."

She was listening to a dial tone. She slammed the phone down and furiously cleaned the apartment until Gabe arrived.

"So what was it you had to remind him about?" she said to him at the door.

"Hi, Laurie, it's nice to see you too. Come in? Why yes, I'd love to."

He sat on the couch where Skip had been and put a brown clasp envelope on the coffee table. "Something to drink? Why yes, that'd be lovely. What do you have?"

She stood in front of him with her arms folded across her chest. "What did you remind him about?"

Gabe sighed. "I reminded him not to break up the band by screwing the lead singer."

"Whoa," she said. "Back up. Start at the beginning. Remind me when I appointed you my nursemaid. Convince me this is any of your business."

"I never wanted to be in somebody's band before. Part of what makes this different is your songs and part of it is this thing between you and Skip, that tension. If you two get in bed together you're going to end up not talking to each other and it's going to screw everything up. If you're lonely, need a boyfriend, I can sympathize. But not Skip. For God's sake, not Skip."

"Because he's in the band?" She looked at the manila envelope. "Or is there something else you're not telling me?"

Gabe seemed to lose his momentum. He picked up the newly cleaned clay ashtray and turned it over in his hands. "Did you make this yourself?"

Laurie grabbed it away from him. "Talk to me, Gabe."

"Did Skip tell you any stories while he was here? About his deal with Capitol, maybe?"

"No, what about it?"

"Another time. Did he mention his daughter?"

"He said she died in a car wreck in San Francisco. His wife was driving and he was throwing up in the back seat."

"Interesting," Gabe said.

"Is that all you can say? 'Interesting'?"

"It's just, it's a story he likes to tell a lot. When he told it to me it was set in New York City. His wife had just left him and taken Janey with her."

"Janey?"

"His daughter's name, supposedly. He hailed a cab and was following them when his wife went through a red light and a truck hit them broadside."

She couldn't seem to find solid ground, and it was making her panicky. "You're not making sense, Gabe. Are you jealous of Skip? Did I miss something?"

Gabe opened the envelope and took out a stack of xeroxes. He paged through them and handed one to her. It was part of a page from the *Los Angeles Times* dated October 10, 1972, copied from microfiche: "Singer Faces Manslaughter Charge." Skip Shaw, who'd had a hit a few years earlier with "Tender Hours," had been involved in a fatal accident the previous evening. His daughter Jenine, age three, was pronounced dead at the scene. Arresting officers claimed that Shaw, twenty-three, was "highly intoxicated and belligerent, possibly under the influence of narcotics, certainly in no condition to have been driving." After treatment for minor injuries, Shaw was charged with manslaughter as well as driving under the influence and criminal negligence. Shaw's wife, Carol, in New York at the time, could not be reached for comment.

"What are the rest?" she asked.

One was a xerox from a 1979 issue of *Billboard* with the headline, "Former Folk-rock Frontman Fails to Fork Over Five Figures." Sources at Capitol records were quoted as saying they had no plans to take Skip Shaw to court to recover the thirty-thousand-dollar advance he'd been given to record an album for them. The money was gone, Shaw was destitute, they only hoped that one day he'd make good on his contract. "We'd still love to have a Skip Shaw album," the source said. "We just don't know if such a thing is possible anymore."

"I take it this isn't how he tells it?"

"In one version he told me a vice president at Capitol tracked him down to a motel in Mexico and set fire to his room. In another he actually delivered an album—a brilliant album, of course—and Capitol was 'afraid' of it and destroyed the master. Look, Laurie, don't get the idea I like doing this. I hate this more than you can imagine."

"Do you? I find it disturbing, to say the least, that you're keeping this little secret file of evidence on somebody you claim is your friend. You're a regular one-man CIA, aren't you?"

"You don't know what it's like yet. Being around Skip can make you doubt everything you ever knew. It's dizzying. It's hard to remember which way is up."

"Does Jim know about this?"

"Jim helped me put it together."

"Dennis?"

Gabe nodded.

"Have you ever shown this to Skip, given him a chance to explain?"

"I tried. Either the papers got the stories wrong, or he was trying to protect somebody else, or I wasn't remembering what he'd really said, or somebody was lying to get even with him."

Suddenly it was all simply too hard to think about. She didn't want to do it any longer. "I think you should go."

He got up. "I'm sorry, Laurie."

"Just go."

He stopped again at the door. "I know how you're feeling. I really do. And if you want—"

"Get the fuck out, okay?"

She locked and chained the door after him and curled up on the couch with a blanket, hugging herself until she stopped shivering, watching TV until she drifted into an uneasy sleep where she was trying to solve a sort of three-dimensional crossword puzzle, fitting letters into words and words into meaningless phrases like "the ashtray was full of dimes."

It was dark when the phone woke her. A tentative voice said, "It's Skip."

"Hi," she said fuzzily.

"I just . . . I wondered—"

"Don't wonder," she told him. "Don't explain. Just come over. Come over now."

A U B A D E

She woke late, smelling coffee and cigarette smoke, at first startled at the slap of bare footsteps in the living room, then relieved, amazed, flattered, to realize they were Skip's, that he hadn't pulled his boots on and escaped in the night. Only then did terror flood her heart.

She pulled the covers over her head and curled fetally around a pillow, her eyes squeezed shut. They had not even, for God's sake, used a condom, though at the moment she was less afraid of disease than she was of facing Skip in the light of day.

When she tried to see herself through Skip's eyes she found only her high school self-image: awkward, naive, poorly formed, tongue-tied, childish. Why hadn't he run away?

By far the worst was her sure and certain knowledge that she had destroyed the band. It could not possibly survive the contempt for her that Skip was surely feeling now. She pictured each step on the path ahead: the awkward silences at practice, the knowing looks passing from face to face, then Skip finally disappearing somewhere into the bowels of LA.

As he surely would. The man was a liar, a drunk, a bitter has-been, as Gabe had tried so hard to tell her.

She found her sweatshirt tangled up in the bedclothes and put it on. Even that small gesture of independence gave her strength. She got out of bed, pulled the sweatshirt down to her knees, walked into the living room, and screamed.

He looked up from the spiral notebook he'd been reading. His jeans and belt were on and fastened, but his shirt was unbuttoned to the waist. He exhaled cigarette smoke through a bemused smile, and said, "Good morning to you too."

"What are you doing? That's *mine!*"

"Some of this stuff is pretty good. The one with the foolscap and the dunce—"

She lunged for the notebook and tore it out of his unresisting hands. He was still smiling. "This is not funny, you asshole!" she yelled, wrapping the book against her stomach with both arms. "This is private. You've got no right—"

"Hey," he said, hands halfway up in tentative surrender. "I'm sorry, okay? I just wanted to see the rest of your songs—"

"If you want something that's not yours, you ask for it. Understand?" She took the notebook to her bedroom, pitched it into a drawer, and slammed the drawer shut again. If there'd been a lock on the drawer she would have turned it and swallowed the key. No, she thought, lock and key were not enough. Obviously she would have to burn it, so that when he mocked her there would be no evidence to support him and she could deny everything.

She jumped when she felt his hand on her arm. "Don't touch me," she said.

"It was just laying there," he said. "I promise I won't ever look again unless you tell me."

"You're goddamned right you won't."

"I said I was sorry, and I am."

She turned around and looked at his bare feet. He hadn't put his socks on, let alone his boots. "Okay?" he said.

"I guess. I woke up feeling awkward, and then I saw you going through my stuff . . ."

"Me too."

She looked up at him, which was probably a mistake. His eyes were soft and dark and full of hurt. "What?" she said.

"Awkward. Me too. I was laying there in bed next to you and I felt this chill of pure remorse, like I'd screwed something up."

"You're sorry we made love?"

"Darlin', that would be like a comet being sorry it fell into the sun. It wasn't like I could keep away from you. If this hurts the band, if it hurts your chances, I don't know how I could live with myself."

"It's your chances too."

"I used up my chances a long time ago. Besides, you're Laurie Moss, and I'm—"

"I know. You're just a tree." Without quite meaning to she found her cheek pressed against his tanned, hairless chest. His skin smelled like a lawn on a late summer afternoon. And then somehow they were in bed again.

Later he brought her coffee and said, "Can we at least talk about the song?"

"What song?"

"The foolscap song."

"That. That was my Elvis Costello period. Too clever for my own good."

"Is there a tune?"

When she got up for the notebook she knew she'd somehow lost a contest she'd never meant to enter. Paging through the half-baked ideas, clichés, and shopworn revelations made her cringe. "This song," she said, "is exactly the kind of thing I didn't want you reading." The lyrics were full of forced puns and odd rhyme schemes:

> Leaves of empty foolscap
> Left me feeling like a dunce
> I've gone so wrong
> Every time I try to write
> The phone has wrung me uptight
> With a long
> Wrong number
> More than once

"Yeah," Skip said, "but is there a tune?"

She brought her father's guitar back to bed with her and sat naked, one leg crossed over the other, working through the chords, the melody returning to her in fits and starts.

"Have you considered playing the Duck like this?" Skip said. He was propped up on a mound of pillows, his hands behind his head, long strands of brown hair fallen across his weathered face. "You'd really pack 'em in."

She sang through one verse, ignoring him. Skip had her do it again, then said, "Go up a step to the C for two bars, then to the E flat." She played and he sang, "'The phone rings around the roses/You sent to deliver me/Everything stems from this . . .' or something like that."

"It needs to go to A minor instead of E flat," she said, and for the next hour she didn't think about the consequences of what they'd done, only about watching the song open like a flower in time-lapse photography. Before Skip touched it the song had been words and nothing more. After, it meant something; it glistened with subliminal sadness.

"How do you do that?" she said. Beneath her sense of wonder lay the conviction that she was doomed to a life of waitressing, that greatness was simply not in her.

"Practice, my dear." Skip got out of bed, his back to her, and pulled on his pants.

"You're leaving me," she said. "I'll never see you again." She'd meant it to be a joke, had let it escape before thinking how it would sound, how nakedly the words would hang in the air.

Skip put on his watch and said, "You'll see me in six hours." He put on his shirt and his boots while she sat on the bed, hunched over her guitar, and then, as he stood looking for an exit line, she climbed over the bed to him and wrapped him up in a kiss. When she let him go, he smiled and said, "You got to stop that, now."

PANIC

The apartment was a hundred times emptier when Skip left than it had been before he came, as if he were a particularly insidious thief. Overnight she'd lost all comfort in silence. Dressed again in sweatshirt

and jeans, she huddled on the couch, knotting her fingers until the
knuckles crunched. She didn't even have Skip's phone number. Probably
for the best. She'd missed her interview in Pasadena entirely. Gabe would
know what had happened the minute she showed up at practice, and that
thought made her cringe. Looking ahead, she could always start planning
for her eviction, which couldn't be far off.

More than anything, she hated the idea of sinking without a trace
when she had been so close. If she could just finish the master tape, she
thought, she could endure the humiliation. She could hold the CD in
her fingerless gloves as she lay starving in her cardboard box on Venice
Beach. Worse come to worst, she could make do with a cassette that Jim
dubbed off for her.

Then that's it, she thought.

We'll finish the tape.

Of the Same Name (1)

That night they learned "Fool's Cap" and two more originals: "Linda,"
which went back to college and a friend of Laurie's who'd cut off all her
hair and tried to kill her boyfriend, and "Midnight Train," which wasn't
about much of anything beyond its own "na na na na" chorus. Laurie
had spent the entire afternoon frantically reworking them both, going
through the notebook that Skip had violated and folding down the corner of every page that held a scrap of poetry capable of being hammered
into a bridge or an extra verse.

After practice, sitting at the kitchen table, Jim added them to the song
list and said, "You know . . ." He stopped and counted the songs again
and then scratched his orange beard with the butt of the pen. "You
know, there's enough songs here for an album."

"Really?" Laurie said. "No kidding." She should have been grateful
that Jim had raised the subject first, but instead she was full of the sudden
and rare terror of getting what she'd asked for. What if I get what I want
and it still doesn't make me happy? she thought. There were so many
ways to be wrong, so few ways to get things right. How was it ever possible to know?

"I make it ten originals," he said, "your pal Summer's song, your dad's song, and 'Don't Make Promises.'"

She and Skip were both shaking their heads. She said, "Skip already told you—" at the same time that Skip said, "I can't sing lead on—"

They stopped and looked at each other across the table. "We'll discuss it," Jim said. "But I'm telling you right now, that arrangement is killer. It's a great piece of material, it was born to be a duet, and I can't believe nobody ever thought of it before."

She looked at Gabe, but Gabe was still neither talking nor meeting her eyes. She and Skip hadn't deceived anyone—when she presented "Fool's Cap" and Skip kept suggesting lines they'd thrown away that morning, she could barely maintain a straight face—but they'd all pretended nothing was happening. Everyone except Gabe.

"I think we should go ahead and start it," she said.

"What," Dennis said, "you mean tonight?"

"We could start tomorrow. Work on the set for a couple of hours every night, then spend a couple of hours recording."

"It's your band," Skip said. "Only what's your hurry?"

She held on to her coffee cup with both hands, needing heat. "I'm broke," she said. "I can't find a job. I'm scared. I want to feel like something in my life is for keeps." Her gaze caught on Gabe as she said that and she wished she could close her eyes, but he stared right into her until she finally turned her head away.

"We can talk about it," Jim said.

"Let's," she said. "I want to talk about what it would sound like. Here's what I think. I think you should be able to hear the space between all the instruments. I think it should sound like everybody's playing really hard, but you can hear everybody, all the time. Everything should have texture and rough edges that catch in your brain. Weird instruments—toy pianos and plastic trash cans and tonettes, tucked away for people to discover."

Jim's eyes lit up. He had a glockenspiel, he said, that would fit on "Brighter Day" and a cheesy twelve-tone electronic doodad that had exactly the right sound for "Fool's Cap."

He went to Sam's room to find it and in the silence Dennis said, "So, what are you going to call the record?"

"Laurie Moss," Skip said. "What else?"

Dennis leaned forward, hands clasped on the green Formica tabletop, blond hair falling in his eyes, an intent expression on his face. "You know what I always thought would be a good title for a record? *Of the Same Name.*"

Jim, on his way back with the doodad, stopped in the kitchen doorway to listen.

"That way," Dennis said, "when they announce it on the radio? They could say, 'That was Laurie Moss, from her album *Of the Same Name.*'"

Jim, standing behind him, looked stricken. "My God," he said. "Dennis made a joke."

"You guys think I'm stupid—"

"Yes," Jim said, "we do."

"—but I'm just keeping my lice under a bushel basket."

For a second Jim didn't seem to believe what he'd heard, then he sank to his knees and started to roll around on the floor. Gabe bent over in his chair and Skip shook his head in silent laughter.

"What?" Dennis said. "What'd I say?"

"Nothing," Laurie told him. "I think it's perfect. It's exactly right. We'll call it *Of the Same Name.*"

When the silence wore off Gabe said, "And then what? Do we shop it to the majors or what?"

"Of course," Laurie said. "Columbia and Warner's first."

"Well," Jim said.

He'd left a black hole in the conversation. He sat down again and put the doodad in front of him. It was a six-inch miniature keyboard with an octave and a half of little round buttons instead of keys. He played a three-note version of the "Neither Are We" riff.

"You could get really hurt in the majors," he said, "even if we did get a deal. They pretty much want a gold record first time out anymore. And if you don't hit with the first single, they won't even take your phone calls."

Laurie's hopes began to melt and run. Her father had done this to her in grade school, and her mother stepped into the role when he left. If she wanted a new dress, he told her she'd just grow out of it. A puppy would be endless work. The lines were too long at Disney World.

"Let's not do this now," she said. "No pissing on the album until it's done, okay?"

"Fair enough," Jim said. "Let's see what we end up with. Anything could happen."

"You got that right," Gabe said, a bit ominously, she thought.

She stood up. "Tomorrow?" Everybody agreed, and Skip got up too. She felt her heart pick up speed.

She leaned down for her guitar case and Gabe said, "Hang on," in her father's voice.

It had gone so well. Skip fully present and playful, rehearsal productive, the album now consensual. She might have convinced herself she was going to get away with it if not for Gabe's relentless guilt-inducing stare. "It's late," she said, the way she would have said it to her father in sixth grade. "Can't we—"

"No," Gabe said.

She looked at Skip, who crinkled his eyes in a way she believed no one else could see. She realized she would have to settle for that. "See ya," she said. He nodded and walked out.

She looked at Gabe. "What did you want to talk about?"

"Let's take a walk."

They got outside as Skip was pulling away. Laurie wanted so badly to be sitting next to him, smelling stale smoke and leather, night wind in her eyes, that it felt like some essential part of her had in fact stowed away in the Mustang's passenger seat and left the rest of her behind to cope alone.

"So," Gabe said. "I hope it was worth it."

"Were we really that obvious?"

He sat on the trunk of the LBD. "Give me a break."

"Okay." She sat down next to him. "It was pretty fantastic."

Gabe sighed. "Maybe I should have pushed you two at each other from the start. Gotten it over with." He folded his arms across his chest. The effect was somewhere between stern and pouty. "The band will either survive this or it won't."

"I'll hold it together with my bare hands if I have to. At least until we finish the record."

"If making a record is so important to you, why did you have to— oh, never mind."

"Where do you get off being such a Puritan? What did you do with that black-leather fantasy at Duck the night I met you? Play mah-jongg?"

"I've known L'Shondra since grade school, actually. We've only been lovers for five years. She's an orphan too. Neither one of us has got much in the way of family history, you know? But we've got each other. She's got a master's in social work, by the way, and helps run United Way for LA County. She dresses differently for work than for clubbing, if that's any of your business, but then I'm not sure there's a huge difference between judging people by the way they dress and judging them by their skin color."

"Are you ever going to slow down long enough for me to apologize?"

"I don't know. Should I bother? I'm still pretty pissed off at you."

"I'm trying to tell you I'm sorry."

"Yeah, okay. I guess you are."

They sat and looked at the night sky, muffled in haze and reflected light. "Your real parents," Laurie said. "Did you ever find out who they were?"

"My birth parents, you mean?"

She'd never seen Gabe this way before: quibbling, sarcastic, contentious. This is my fault, she thought.

"Yeah," he went on. "My father was a black soldier in Viet Nam. He died over there. My mother was what you call Eurasian—half French, half Vietnamese. She died over here, when I was five months old. Heroin OD. My dad got her hooked on it when they were shacked up together. That's one of the reasons I'm so rabid on the subject."

"I don't remember that being the subject."

"We were talking about Skip, remember?"

"Oh my God. Are you saying Skip . . ."

"You mean you didn't know? You honestly didn't know?" She shook her head and Gabe sighed. "As far as I know he's clean right now, been clean as long as I've been playing with him. And I think I could tell. In his day, though, he was one of the king junkies of all LA."

At the same moment that she was thinking, My God, I had unprotected sex with an IV drug user—at that exact moment she was also thinking, You poor son of a bitch, there truly is a world of pain in those eyes.

"So you can see," Gabe was saying, "why he has a lot of mixed feelings where success is concerned. That 'five-figure' advance from Capitol you read about went straight into his veins. If he ever really hit the big time he'd probably do himself in."

"My God," Laurie whispered. "What else is there I don't know about?"

"Well, there's Dennis. He's into teenage prostitutes."

Laurie stared at him and he waved one tired hand. "Kidding. Just kidding, for Christ's sake."

"We're doomed," Laurie said.

"That," Gabe said, "would be the most obvious conclusion."

She thought of Ron Tuggle and took a modest sip of air. "What are we going to do?"

"We'll do what you said. We'll rush right into making the album instead of waiting until the songs are road-tested and refined and totally solid, because the more successful we get, the faster the clock is ticking down."

"You must hate me."

Finally Gabe unfolded his arms and scratched his forehead. "Nah. I'm a little pissed off, but I'm not going to hang on to it. If it wasn't for you, we'd still be pissing our lives away, going nowhere, twice a week." He stood up. "I guess I'm done, if you are."

"Gabe? Thanks."

"For yelling at you?"

"For giving a damn."

"The Buddha says the more you care, the more you get hurt." He shrugged. "Let's go see if there's any coffee left."

TRACKS

Nothing on the answering machine from Skip when she got home, and by the next afternoon he still hadn't called. Three washouts from the want ads left her nostalgic for Mazola Mike. She cleaned the entire apartment for the third time in a week to distract herself from the twin specters of guilt and anxiety.

When the phone rang around three o'clock she snatched it on the first ring. It was Jim, who had just finished using Dennis on some other singer's demo. "You want to come over and work on a couple of drum tracks?"

She'd been so sure it would be Skip that she had trouble orienting herself. Working on drum tracks was exactly what she should have wanted, but she had to struggle not to let disappointment creep into her voice. "I'm there," she said. "That's me, knocking on your front door."

She made it to Whittier in forty minutes flat, under a cold, gray sky. Intellectually she knew Skip wouldn't be there. Reality tap-danced on her emotions just the same.

For the first half hour Dennis battered away while she and Jim moved microphones and fiddled with echo and EQ to get the drum sound she wanted: crisp, contained, not the Led Zeppelin recorded-in-a-stairwell boom she was tired of hearing every day on the radio. Periodically she glanced over her shoulder, convinced someone had that moment walked in behind her.

Finally they went to work. Isolated behind padded plywood partitions, Laurie did a guide vocal and guitar track so Dennis could keep his place in the song. Playing helped. She was able to lose herself in the music for entire seconds at a time.

They ended up with finished drum tracks for "Neither Are We" and "Angel Dust," and Jim took them to Taco Bell to celebrate.

They ordered and took their drinks to a table by the window. Jim stripped half the wrapper off his straw and shot the other half at Dennis. "Cheer up," he told her. "We got two tracks today."

"Two *drum* tracks," she said. "With four more instruments, plus vocals, plus overdubs, plus eleven more complete songs, to go."

Their number came up and Dennis went after the food.

"You don't realize how good that guy is," Jim said, once he was out of earshot. "Two tracks in an hour and a half is major league. And even without the rest of the band, or a click track, he still moved around the beat, swung in behind it to push on the choruses, and never lost the tempo."

"Despite my screwing up."

"It's a different discipline, that's all," Jim said. "You'll get used to it."

"If Dennis is so good, why do you give him so much grief?"

"He's a drummer. It goes with the territory."

Being on the road, she thought, would be like this. Junk food, casual put-downs, all the music talk she could ever want. And Skip would be there, with nothing to distract him from her.

Dennis returned with two heaping trays. "What did he say about me?" he asked Laurie.

Jim didn't give her a chance to answer. "I was telling her our motto. 'Those who can, play. Those who can't, drum.'"

"Can't what?"

"Never mind, Dennis. I'll explain it to you later."

Laurie poured hot sauce onto a chicken taco. "Your wife," she asked Jim. "Molly? Does she work?"

"She's a secretary for Parks and Recreation. High stress, low pay. With me working only half-time at my real job, and never knowing what money's going to come in from the studio, we've always depended pretty heavily on her paycheck. But it's getting better now, and we're almost to the point where she can quit. Unless Sam wants to, like, go to college or something ridiculous like that."

"I went to college once," Dennis said. "It sucked. If I'm going to get up at eight in the morning, I expect to get paid or laid, one." He looked at Laurie. "Speaking of which, is it true that Skip has this really enormous dick?"

She felt her face go hot and then cold. "Excuse me," she said, with a reflexive smile. She went to the bathroom and stood over the sink, scrubbing at her face, thinking, This is exactly what you were so convinced you could handle. How do you like it? Still want to shut yourself up in a van with these people?

She gave Dennis long enough to think about what he'd done—a favorite concept of her mother's—and then went back to the table. Jim said, "He's sorry. He's an asshole and doesn't know how to behave."

Dennis said, "Sorry."

She'd had time to think it out. Pretending she hadn't slept with Skip had no mileage in it, and she wasn't about to apologize for it. "So," she asked Dennis. "Who told you he has a big dick?"

"I don't know," Dennis said, squirming like an adolescent. "I read it somewhere. What d'you call it, *Vanity Fair* or something."

"*Vanity Fair?*" Jim said. "*Vanity Fair?* You've never read *Vanity Fair* in your life. They have a minimum IQ requirement for *Vanity Fair.*"

"You're making that up," Dennis said in a mildly offended tone.

"You ever read *Harper's*? *Atlantic Monthly*?"

"Hell, no. Why should I?"

"Well, see? There you are."

Dennis ate a taco in two bites, wiped his mouth, and said, "Neither of them ever had Demi Moore naked on the cover."

It was over that quickly, the crisis more or less averted and the subject changed, albeit self-consciously. Dennis hadn't meant anything, Laurie saw, had simply said the first thing that popped into his head. Still, the knowledge of what she and Skip had done was loose in the general population, free to multiply. The first cracks had appeared in the band's foundation, and it was nobody's fault but her own.

THE SET

Skip was plugged in and waiting for them at the garage. Laurie's heart jumped when she saw him. He showed her a smile she hadn't seen before, knowing and intimate, that made her blush for the second time in an hour.

They had fifteen songs on the set list now, an hour's worth, and with stops and starts they made it from top to bottom in two hours. They took a break and then played it again, this time in an hour and a half, with the tape deck rolling.

"Don't Make Promises" chilled her as they sat on the dirty carpet and listened to the playback. The lyrics now seemed prophetic: songs that were all about tomorrow, people telling lies in their sleep.

She left when Skip did, and this time Gabe didn't move to stop her. She had to hurry to catch up to him on the driveway. "So," she said. "You want to come over to my place?"

His smile seemed tired, but she dismissed the thought as paranoid. "Sure," he said. "Why not?"

Once on the freeway, he kept disappearing from her rearview mirror. The first couple of times she slowed until he came roaring up behind her again. The third time she decided he could find his own way to her apartment. He'd done it before.

He pulled up as she unlocked the front door. She waited for him and let him walk in first. Inside, with the door locked, she turned to him, her breath caught in her swollen throat. He came to her in four pounding, cowboy-booted steps, tangled one hand in her hair, and kissed her.

On the drive home she'd made herself a promise, and now, with the last of her fading will, she went through with it. "Uh, listen," she said. "Don't you think we should be, um, using a condom or something?"

"No," he said. "I hate those damned things. They're not natural."

"Well, have you ever been tested?"

"Yeah." He took a step back. "I've been tested. Heterosexual AIDS is a myth. Men don't get it, not from women, not doing the things you and I did."

The past tense and the tension of his shoulders made her wish she'd never said anything, but it was too late now. "Women do," she said. "From men. And I wasn't implying you might have gotten it from sex. Hetero or otherwise."

"What's that supposed to mean?"

"Needles," she said. "I was worried about needles."

"I don't know what the hell you're talking about."

"You're saying you've never shot heroin?"

"That's what I'm saying. Who the hell told you I did? Gabe, again?" When she didn't answer he said, "Maybe we should just skip it." He looked at the door but didn't actually move toward it.

"I didn't mean to make you mad," she said. "A girl can't be too careful, you know."

"Of course she can. It's easier to be too careful than anything in the world."

"Hey," she said. "So you've been tested. So I'm satisfied."

But satisfaction proved not to be so simple after all. Skip had lost the mood and she was unable to coax it back.

"It's late," he said at last, reaching for his clothes. "I should go."

"Don't," she said. "Please. I don't want to fight. Can't you just stay with me? I don't care about the rest of it."

The miniblinds above the headboard broke the glow from the street-light into stripes across his bare chest. He shrugged and turned away from her. She got up to brush her teeth and when she came out of the bathroom she saw him quickly shut his eyes.

She lay with her back to him, her brain buzzing with thoughts of her aging car and the rent she could not pay, of the meals she'd missed in the last six months, of the long hours wasted at Mazola Mike's coffee shop, of the clothes at Nordstrom's that she couldn't afford to try on, let alone buy. For a second or two, listening to the playback of that night's rehearsal, she'd let herself believe her life might change, but she saw now she'd only been kidding herself. She couldn't even cry properly, or so much as reach for a Kleenex, because there was someone next to her in bed that she didn't want to be there. It was a situation she'd promised herself she'd never let herself get into again, and yet here she was.

Around three o'clock—she'd been watching the second hand crawl around the lighted dial of her alarm clock for an hour—Skip said softly, "You awake?" She didn't answer or turn to look as he dressed in the dark and let himself out.

When she heard the Mustang roar away, she got up and locked the door and put on a T-shirt to cover the body that no one wanted, and, finally, fell asleep as the sun crawled out of the darkness.

DOUBLE LEAD

Practice was scheduled to start at seven. She made herself wait to leave the apartment until 6:55, just to show them, then chewed her fingernails all the way to Whittier as she tried to anticipate how Skip would react when she finally walked in.

In the end it was an anticlimax of the mildest sort. Skip was fully present, neither flirtatious nor distant. Once Laurie got past her nerves she felt like a key turning in a lock. Everything meshed, especially between her and Skip: the double lead on "Neither Are We," the duet on "Don't Make Promises," the words Skip had written for "Fool's Cap."

They broke for coffee and played the set again, and there were long seconds at a time when she didn't seem to have an existence separate from the others. When the last notes of "Carry On" died out, Gabe looked at Laurie and said, "We're ready."

Everyone was a little giddy, Laurie included. She felt like she might start laughing at the smallest thing and be unable to stop.

Jim nodded. "I'm going to make some calls, follow up on that demo."

"Yes," Laurie said. "Yes, I want to play somewhere."

Everyone looked at Skip.

Skip popped his guitar strap loose and laid the guitar in its case. "Go ahead and book some things."

"Does that mean we can count on you?" Laurie said. She hadn't meant anything beyond the most immediate context, but in the sudden quiet she could see that the words sounded much worse than that.

Skip straightened up slowly. "Don't worry about it," he said. They looked at each other for a second or two as Laurie wondered how she was supposed to take it. Don't worry because yes, he would be playing? Don't worry because the band was going to break up any minute so the question was irrelevant?

Jim said, "You want to work on some more tracks tonight?"

The elation from the set was already fading. "I'm tired," she said, and it seemed true once the words were out. "Maybe tomorrow."

She was the first one out the door. It's come down to this, she thought. Searching every word, every act, for signs and portents. If he speaks to me before I get to the end of the driveway, it means he loves me. If I step on a crack we're doomed.

She walked straight out to the LBD, low heels clacking on the damp pavement in a brisk, no-nonsense rhythm, in case anyone was listening. Guitar and amp into the trunk, not turning to look behind her. Unlock the driver's door and get in. No fair peeking in the rearview mirror. Count to three, start the engine. Nothing to hold her here. Let the brake off, ease away from the curb, now check that mirror for cars.

No cars, only Skip. Stopped in the middle of the misty midnight street, hands palm out at his sides. She rolled down her window and looked back.

"In a hurry to get somewhere?" Skip asked. He had a half smile on his face, bowed legs, the boots, the big silver buckle on his belt.

"Depends," she said.

"Give me a ride to my car?"

His car was all of thirty feet away. "Sure," she said.

He put his guitar in the back seat and got in next to her. When she glanced over at him his eyes were closed. He looked years older that way.

"Suppose," she said, "we could drive two blocks and be anywhere in the world. Where would you be?"

"Home." He didn't open his eyes.

"No unfulfilled desires to see Katmandu or Mount Kilimanjaro?"

"Well, actually . . ."

"You've already seen them."

"Sorry."

She pulled away from the curb. "So which way is home?"

He opened one eye. "We're leaving my car, I take it?"

"You tell me."

He shrugged. "It's just a car. Go west on the 72 and get off in Hollywood."

GALLERY

It wasn't what she'd imagined the apartment of the legendary Skip Shaw
to look like, though it made perfect sense once she'd seen it. The building dated from the early sixties: white brick, concrete slabs, aluminum
and louvered glass, thin straight lines intersecting everywhere, the whole
of it buried behind oleanders and dying palms.

He'd furnished the inside to match, with a Naugahyde sofa, a curtain
of wooden beads between the living room and the kitchen, and an assort-
ment of mismatched chairs and tables. A bookshelf made of boards and
bricks, stuffed full of battered paperbacks, covered one wall. The air smelled
of old cigarettes; years of them had left a yellowish haze on the walls.

What completely surprised her was the art. There were two or three
prints on each wall, all of them matted and expensively framed. They
were the kind of prints that named the artist and the picture and the
gallery, and she hadn't heard of half of the painters: Fernand Khnopff,
Arnold Böcklin, Egon Schiele, Max Ernst, Max Beckmann, Jean
Delville. They all had people in them, they were all more or less realistic,
yet were all at the same time very painterly, full of intimations of doom
and allegory.

She stopped in front of Edvard Munch's *Madonna*. Sperm swam in a
red border around a naked woman, dark, with the contours of her head
and body receding into the background.

"Beer?" Skip called from the kitchen.

"No thanks."

He came out with a long-necked bottle of Bud and stood next to her, looking at the print. "When you're on the road," he said, "you can stay in the hotel and get wasted, which God knows I did my share of. You can do the tourist thing, which ends up reminding you that you don't belong there. Or you can find yourself a hobby. I used to go look at pictures. When the tour guides would come around I would always walk away. I just bought whatever made me feel something.

"I used to be a tough guy about shit like this. You know, the whole 'I'm just a yarn spinner' kind of crap, like writing songs isn't fundamentally different from making furniture. Except it is. It's more like what these guys do, which makes you cut off your ear or jump off a bridge."

"Do you not write at all anymore?"

"A line or two, maybe a snatch of melody. Mostly I don't bother to write them down because the pieces don't ever fit together they way they used to. One line doesn't lead to the next, you know?"

She pointed to the *Madonna*. "So what does this make you feel?"

"I think it's sexy. Nudity and death and conception and responsibility. Not silicon-and-airbrush sexy—real-life sexy."

She turned to him to see if he had something in mind besides the painting. Evidently he did.

Later they lay in bed by the reflected light from the front room and smoked a joint, her head resting in the curve of his left shoulder. She asked what he did all day and he told her about the jingle factory in Van Nuys.

"What commercials are you on? You have to tell me."

"By the time I get out to the parking lot they're gone out of my head."

She turned to audit his expression. "I don't know if I should believe you or not." Only after the words were out did she remember Gabe and his newspaper articles.

He didn't seem inclined to take offense. "Hell, what else am I going to do? Flip burgers? Sell encyclopedias door to door? I'm too old to get hired for a real job. There was this guy I knew in my bohemian days. He'd sold some short stories to the *New Yorker,* wrote this one novel that got great reviews, but somehow he never made a living at it. He didn't know how to do anything else either. Ended up writing educational comics. Learned to do his own lettering too, which made him a kind of a double threat in the educational comics marketplace."

"Was he happy?"

"Happy? Writing educational comics after being the toast of New York? He was a fucking junkie, when he could afford it, and he sure as hell didn't talk about his day job."

The conversation was headed places she didn't like, so she changed tracks. "You don't even own a stereo, do you? I didn't see one anywhere."

"No," he said. "Playing's one thing. Listening to somebody else . . . it just makes me frustrated."

"Because you could do it better?"

"Because I could be doing it. Instead of listening to it."

"Let me guess. You don't dance."

"No," he said. "I don't dance."

He reached for a pair of tweezers on the bedside table to hold the roach. She asked, "What were you like as a kid?"

"Intense. I hated being a kid. All I wanted was to grow up so nobody could tell me what to do. My dad walked out when I was four. I remember him mostly from photographs. He used to eat Butter Rum Life Savers and I remember that smell. I grew up with this fantasy that he would simply show up one day and take me away with him. We used to move a lot, my mom and me, and it drove me crazy because I thought my father would come looking for me and not be able to find me. He died when I was thirteen and it turned out he'd been living in Florida with a new wife and kid and he hadn't been looking for me after all. I wanted to go to the funeral and my mom wouldn't let me because we didn't have any money. After that, well, after that I put my head down and slogged it out because I knew there wasn't going to be any rescue."

"Where did you live?"

"A long string of middle-sized California towns. Bakersfield, Fresno, Atascadero. Mom was a seamstress. We were so poor we lived out of the car sometimes. California always had good roadside rest stops, with showers and barbecue grills and everything.

"The first few weeks in a new town were always the worst. Mom would be trying too hard to impress everybody we met, and I'd be going to a new school and getting into fights."

He was quiet for a long time, and finally she said, "Where'd you go off to?"

"I was remembering my first day in third grade at Bakersfield. Christ, I haven't thought about this in years. There was this fat kid named Chuckie Welch who sat in the back of the room and played with these little-bitty toy cars all through class, and I hated him because he didn't get in trouble for it, the way I knew I would have. Then during lunch I got in a fight with this other kid and he threw me down on the playground and I skinned up my elbow and tore one knee out of my new Levi's. And I started crying in class, and everybody thought it was because my elbow was all bloody, but it was because I didn't know how I was going to face my mother and tell her I'd fucked up my brand-new jeans that were going to have to last me the rest of the year."

As she listened, she realized she had no idea whether he was lying or not. She wanted it not to matter, the way it didn't matter if a song or a short story was strictly autobiographical. But the only time it didn't matter was when they were playing music or making love.

As she drifted off to sleep she called up one more time the memory of how good the band had sounded, regardless of the previous night's disaster with Skip. Despite all her premonitions of doom, her ears lulled her with comforting messages, reassuring her that sleeping with Skip would not affect the band after all.

No, she thought. Don't get your hopes up. You've got too far still to go.

A DAY AT THE BEACH

Catherine and Shannon were in the driveway getting into their tidy white Accord when she got home the next morning. It was only nine o'clock and she'd thought of nothing but going back to bed since she'd left Skip's apartment, but when Catherine said, "We're going to the beach, want to come?" Laurie found herself saying yes.

No need to bring a bathing suit, Catherine told her. The water wouldn't be warm enough for swimming until June, two and a half months away. So she went as she was, going inside only long enough to drop off her guitar and amp, change her shoes, and use the bathroom, not even checking the answering machine to see if there was yet another call from her landlady. And somehow, just sitting in the passenger's seat instead of driving, discussing with Shannon the unlikely trio of Barney, Beavis, and Butthead instead of arguing music with the band, all of that combined with the knowledge that she was for the moment utterly un-reachable, made her feel as if she'd stepped sideways out of her own life, as if she were watching an autobiographical film.

"Little did she realize," she said aloud, watching the highway unroll in front of her, "that tranquil spring morning, how soon she would become a prisoner of her own global fame."

Catherine looked over at her, laughing. "What?"

"In those days she could travel in an ordinary passenger car, and walk on the beach without fear of being recognized."

"Aunt Laurie," Shannon said, "you are being a very silly person."

"Soon she would look back upon those times with a nostalgia that bordered on the melodramatic."

"Should I start looking for the nearest mental hospital," Catherine said, "or is this a side effect of your staying out all night?"

"Yes," Laurie said. "Both. Either. None of the above."

"Are we going to the Wedge, Mommy?" Shannon's interest had al-ready moved on.

"We'll have to ask Aunt Laurie that, Sweetie. But first she has to tell your mommy who she was out all night *with*."

"I'll tell you everything once we get there."

The Wedge was a scrap of beach south of Marina Del Rey where a stone jetty and a sharp drop-off combined to create waves up to eight feet high, lurching up alarmingly only to crash moments later into the hard-packed sand. The water was muddied to the color of weak cocoa from the violence of the assault, while a hundred yards north it was a limpid turquoise. Surfboards were outlawed and only pathologically fear-less body surfers, wearing wet suits, goggles, and small yellow plastic rud-ders strapped to their hands, would get in the water.

The repeated explosions of wave against beach were loud and dra-matic and irregular enough to keep Laurie, who had more than once thought of herself as leisure-impaired, from becoming restless and long-ing for something constructive to do.

While Shannon assembled alien landscapes from sand and kelp and leaves and sticks, Laurie talked about Skip. When she was done Catherine said, "Sounds like somebody I'd fall for."

"Ah. That bad?"

"You tell me. Where do you see it going?"

"It's hard to fit a happy ending on this particular chassis," she admitted. "On the other hand, I don't see me married to a doctor in Darien, Connecticut, ten years from now either."

"God, I could. Let him be rich and very, very busy."

Laurie watched a heavily tanned man in his forties, his graying hair in a thin braid down his back, fight his way out past the break, catch a monster wave, and get slammed into the beach. When the tide pulled away he was on his hands and knees. He shook himself off, ducked under the next wave, and paddled out again.

"What does it take," she said, "to make you want to do something like that?"

"You mean," Catherine said, "as opposed to what you do?"

They were home by three o'clock. As they pulled into the driveway Laurie saw a badly dressed woman with thinning brown hair pin a note to her front door. No chance to hide out at Catherine's either; the woman had already spotted her.

"I've been calling all week," she said as Laurie climbed the driveway toward her. "Didn't you get my messages?"

"I'm sorry, Mrs. Donnelly," Laurie said, "but I don't have any money. I can't pay the rent." She was still beside herself and listened in amazement to the words that came out of her mouth. "I don't know what happens next."

Mrs. Donnelly let the silence stretch painfully, then said, "What about tea?"

"Pardon?"

"Do you have any tea, then? Since you don't have money?"

Laurie let her in and got iced tea for both of them.

"Since you were honest with me," Mrs. Donnelly said, "I'll be honest with you. It's a lot of trouble to evict somebody. Maybe we can make a deal."

In the end Laurie wrote her a hundred-dollar check, leaving herself with a not entirely reliable bank balance of $7.36, and promised her another hundred the following Thursday, and every Thursday thereafter until she could pay the rest of what she owed, including late charges. Which meant that out of her two hundred a week from the Duck she would have a hundred left to buy gas for the LBD, feed herself, and pay all her bills.

And yet the longer she went without a job, the more her life expanded to fill the space the job had formerly occupied. As, for example, when Jim called an hour later, before her hair was dry from her shower, to tell her the studio and Dennis were available if she wanted to work.

THE RINGER

They did drum tracks for "Carry On" and "Midnight Train" because she wanted to play something that rocked. "Dinner?" Jim asked when they were done. Dennis had already retreated to the kitchen to begin his intense nightly study of the *Times*' sports page.

"Rhythm guitar?" Laurie said. It was idiotic for her not to agree to food, both bank-account-wise and hunger-wise, since she hadn't eaten all day, but she didn't want to lose the groove. "On 'Carry On'?"

Jim hesitated. "You mean, you want to do the rhythm part yourself?"

"I am the rhythm player, aren't I?"

"You're the lead singer. And the songwriter. And, really, a very good guitar player."

"But . . . ?"

"But we do have Skip available. He's done more session work than any other ten guitar players I know. And every time that brand-new reel of tape passes over those analog heads you lose fidelity."

"You're saying I shouldn't play my own guitar parts on my own record."

"I'm just saying—"

"—that Skip could do it better, faster, more reliably. Too bad. It's my record, I'm playing guitar on it. You've already told me I should give up on landing a major label or getting any money out of it. If all I'm doing this for is the record itself, I'm not going to listen to somebody else play my guitar parts."

"Okay, okay," Jim said. "Really. It'll be fine."

She considered the song. Each chord in its necessary and inevitable place, its name and its shape. She made everything that was not the song go away. No hunger, no pain in her back, no anger, no consciousness of the tape or the microphone or Jim waiting for her to either prove something or not. In her headphones Dennis clicked off the beat and she played the song correctly and passionately, exactly the way it unfurled in her mind, start to finish.

"I apologize," Jim said. "That was perfect."

"Thanks. Now how about 'Neither Are We'?"

She got it in two takes, and the only reason she needed three for "Midnight Train" was that it was getting on toward seven o'clock, time for their regularly scheduled practice, and she couldn't keep Skip from jumping her carefully constructed mental fences.

Gabe got there first, so they laid down his parts on "Carry On" and "Neither Are We" while Jim and Dennis ate bologna sandwiches. Laurie could smell the meat across the studio and it made her faintly sick to her stomach. After "Neither Are We" there was a scratching at the door and Molly stuck her head in. "Jim? There's some guy here looking for Skip."

She stood aside. From the dark hallway Laurie saw a heavy-duty gray airline-proof guitar case edge into the light, followed by an emaciated man in a black leather jacket. "This is weird," he said. "Skip didn't tell you I was coming?"

"No," Laurie said, startled by the open hostility in her voice. As was Gabe, who turned to look at her.

"He said something about learning his guitar parts? That he might need me to sub for him at some live gigs?"

"This is the first I've heard of it," Laurie said brightly.

"Gosh," he said. "This is kind of awkward."

"Isn't it?" Laurie said. She was trying to remember the last time she'd felt such instantaneous dislike of anyone. Part of it was physical—he could have been any one of the look-alike, big-haired, lethally tanned, scarecrow-thin, lightning-fast, scale-regurgitating, lite-metal guitarists that had ruined pre-Nirvana MTV for her. The rest of it was misdirected anger at Skip, who had inflicted this walking disaster on her and done it behind her back.

"Well, it's not your fault," Jim said, and held out his hand. "I'm Jim."

"I'm Mitch," he said. "Mitch Gaines."

Laurie wrinkled her nose. An odor had followed him into the garage: incense, maybe, or patchouli oil.

"I thought so," Jim said. "You were in the house band at the China Club for a while, weren't you? You're really good."

"Yeah, thanks, man, that was a nice gig."

"This is Laurie. She's the real talent. She writes the songs and sings lead."

"And plays guitar," she said, wanting to be a grown-up but watching herself act out anyway, wondering when this bizarre detachment would pass, and how much more damage she would do in the meantime. She forced herself to shake his skeletal hand.

"Um, Skip told me he'd be here," Mitch said. "Is it okay if I wait a little bit?"

"Sure," Jim said, motioning toward the ratty sofa. "Have a seat. We were about to listen to some playback."

Now she was misdirecting her anger at Jim, for being nice to Skip's ringer. "Are you sure it won't grind too many molecules off your tape?" she asked him.

"I think we can afford it, just this once." He went behind the board and played "Carry On," rhythm, bass, drums, and Laurie's scratch vocal, at substantial volume. Laurie watched Mitch out of the corner of her eye as he bobbed along to the music; she was sure he'd practiced in a mirror to get the most effect from his big hair.

"Nice guitar sound," he said afterward. "Is that Skip?"

"No," Skip said from the doorway, "just Skip's amp."

Laurie cringed. Her tiny practice amp had no tone or sustain, so she'd talked Jim into letting her use Skip's Fender Twin. She'd meant to find a better way to break it to him, and now she would have to face the reper-cussions. Skip gave Jim a look and then said, "Mitch, how the hell are you?"

Skip and Mitch shook hands like they were arm wrestling. That ap-parently wasn't enough, so they had to grab each other's shoulders with their left hands at the same time. "Lookin' good, bro," Mitch said. It made Laurie glad she'd used Skip's amp. She wished she'd blown it up.

"So, have you met everybody?" Skip asked him.

"We've met," Laurie said.

"Jim, if you could dub off one of our rehearsal tapes for Mitch, he

could be working on it in case we ever need him." Jim nodded, put a
fresh cassette in the deck, changed out the big reel.

"Skip, could I talk to you outside?" Laurie asked.

"No. If you've got something to say, say it."

"Okay, fine. What I wanted to know is, is this the Skip Shaw Band
now? Because if it isn't, I think the rest of us get a vote on who's playing
in it. No offense, Mitch."

"No sweat," Mitch said. "None taken, man."

Skip locked eyes with her. "Mitch can do the work, learn it fast, and
step in without rehearsing. You got somebody else can do that, bring 'em
on. If not, we should get started. It's late."

Laurie turned away and picked up her guitar. Before she'd slept with
him, she thought, she could never have hated him this much.

Mitch sat on the couch and played through a pocket-sized amp and
headphones, inaudible over the band, looking at Skip and never down at
his instrument. Laurie led them through the set twice, with only a ten-
minute coffee break in between, and what her performance lacked in
empathy it made up in raw power.

At the end of the second set Mitch took the rehearsal tape from Jim,
packed up his guitar, and left with Skip in tow. Everyone else adjourned
to the kitchen table.

Jim said, "He didn't seem that pissed off about us using his amp,
really, did you think?"

"Jim, for God's sake," Laurie snapped. "Can't you see what's happening?"

"Skip said from the start there'd be gigs he didn't want to play," Jim
said. "We all agreed."

Gabe cleared his throat. "I think Laurie may be concerned that Skip's
getting ready to quit."

Jim said, "Oh come on, he—" He stopped and thought.

"If he never shows up again," Laurie said, "he doesn't have to deal
with his conscience, because he gave us this . . . this *Mitch* to supposedly
take his place."

"What have you got against Mitch?" Jim said. "He's actually a very
good player, you know."

"He looks like some eighties hair band refugee. People will laugh
at us."

Gabe and Jim looked at each other. Gabe said, "Have you been getting enough sleep lately?"

"Yes, thank you, and I'm not having my period, either." At that instant she had a sensation over the entire surface of her skin as if she'd just dived into cool water. For two or three seconds she was completely and perfectly in two places at once: Jim's kitchen on a spring night in California, and the boardwalk at Fiesta Texas, outside San Antonio, on a fall afternoon. She smelled rain and felt a breeze tug at her hair.

"Laurie?" Gabe said gently. "What's going on?"

"I'm fine," she managed to say. It was very peaceful there on the boardwalk and she didn't want to come back.

Distantly she heard the rattle of Dennis's newspaper, and then his voice saying, "She needs food."

"Is that right?" Gabe said. "When was the last time you ate?"

The sensation faded. There had been words in her head, possibly important, and they were gone too.

"I don't know," she said. "Yesterday?"

Jim's chair squeaked on the linoleum. "How about scrambled eggs? You like eggs?"

"I'll be okay in a second," she said. "You can stop humiliating me now."

"You're not driving until you eat," Gabe said. "We'll take your car keys away if we have to."

"You and what army?" she mumbled. She suddenly realized she didn't have enough strength to stand up.

Jim put a glass of orange juice in front of her. "Drink this," he said, "and tell us why you stopped eating."

All she wanted was to find Fiesta Texas and the smell of the rain again. She didn't know where it had gone. She picked up the orange juice glass with both hands and drank. Then she told them about her landlady and her last ten job interviews, and barely stopped herself from going on to Skip and Grandpa Bill and the kitty she saw run over when she was seven and a half.

Jim gave her a plate. Eggs scrambled with cheese and hot sauce, a couple of flour tortillas. He opened her hand and put some pills in it. "Vitamin C," he said. "Now eat."

She ate, and at the taste of the food she started to cry.

"Too much hot sauce?" Jim said. Then, "Oh. Sorry."

Gabe handed her a Kleenex. "Would you all stop staring at me, for God's sake?" she said.

Jim ran some water in the skillet and sat down again. "First things first," he said. "Your landlady's right. It would take months to evict you."

"Second," Gabe said, getting out his wallet, "I want you to have this." It was the hundred-dollar check she'd written him in January for playing on the demo tape, now creased and stained.

"Come on," she said, pushing it back toward him. "You earned that."

"Give it to me when we get our record contract," he said, and tore the check to pieces. "Right now it'll buy some groceries."

"Third," Jim said, "can you type? Also, you might want to slow down a little, with an empty stomach and all."

"Okay," she said, crying more now because of Gabe, "and yes, I can type okay."

"I may be able to get you some part-time clerical work at a place I know."

"That would be . . . that would be great. But couldn't we just start getting some paying gigs?"

"I talked to Art Fein, who books Club Lingerie, and he's pretty interested. I'm also working on the Teaszer. So that's going to happen, maybe pretty soon. But it's no money. We'd be getting a split of the door after they pay the sound man and the guarantees for the headliners. We're talking five or ten bucks apiece if we're lucky."

"Classic Ronnie Reagan supply-side economics," Gabe said. "The clubs get all the breaks. People got to be in three or four bands to get any work. You get a virtually endless supply of goods, in this case bands, who have to take whatever they can get. It's a real inflation-stopper."

"Thanks," she said, blowing her nose on her napkin. "Get me depressed enough and I stop crying every time."

"So," Jim said. "You want me to check into that job or what?"

"Yes," she said. "I guess maybe you'd better."

"One more thing," Dennis said. "Cheer up, will you?"

TEMP

And so it was that she started word processing at Sav-N-Comp, a service bureau that operated out of a storefront in Glendale, thirty hours a week at eight dollars an hour, and her life was once again transformed. She was suddenly free of the guilt of sitting in her apartment without making money and yet, at the same time, she was frozen in a reverse metamorphosis, halfway between the band she'd nearly imagined into reality and a regression to the quotidian caterpillar existence her mother had always pushed her toward, where one hour of no creativity followed another.

Five days a week she got up before eight, pulled on jeans and a T-shirt, knotted her hair, grabbed a muffin and a glass of juice on her way out the door. She got to the office by nine and then typed, proofed, and poured text into templates until three. Mondays, Tuesdays, and Thursdays she drove from there to Jim's house to work on the album until six, sat down to dinner with Jim and Molly and Sam, then practiced with the band until midnight or so. Wednesday night for laundry, Friday to collapse and put herself back together for her Saturday gig with Summer.

From "Angel Dust" right up until Sav-N-Comp she'd been writing steadily, at least a song every week or two, and if only one out of four gave her the little chill that made her want to play it again, at least she was productive. Not even waitressing for Mazola Mike had kept her from it. Now she didn't dare let go of her emotions long enough to see where they might venture on their own. She opened her guitar case on Saturday nights at the Duck or in Jim's garage, and some nights she didn't bother to take it home from Whittier.

As for Skip, he'd been a model of responsibility ever since the Big Hair Incident. That had happened on a Thursday, and the following Sunday Skip was early, diligent, and left a half hour before Laurie did. When she went outside she found him lying on the hood of her car, smoking. He said, "You want me to go away, you just say so." Only much later did it occur to her that she could actually have said it, and by then they'd already been to bed and Skip was curled in sleep with his back to her.

By mid-April of 1995 they had three finished tracks in the can, half a dozen more nearly there, and the rest with at least drums and scratch vocals. They'd had to replace two cover songs in the live set to keep it from going stale, and it was going stale anyway. They were becalmed.

Laurie arrived for a Tuesday recording session to find Jim even more obsessive than usual, adjusting mike stands, shuffling tape boxes, leaping up to empty Skip's ashtray or carry out a half-finished Pepsi can.

When Laurie refused to take "Nothing" for an answer, he finally admitted that Art Fein had called an hour before. "We've got a gig. A week from tomorrow, Club Lingerie. We're opening, Estrogen second, Caustic third."

The inside of her brain lit up like a pinball machine. "We're ready," was the first thing she said. Then the bells began to go off, bing-bing-bing. "This is fantastic. Great! Is Skip going to do it? Do you think anybody's going to be there on a Wednesday? Club Lingerie. This is so great."

"Art's got this cable TV show he does called *Art Fein's Poker Party* and I asked him about us doing that, but he was, uh, noncommittal. He goes for cult bands, rockabilly types, people even I've never heard of. I get the feeling he thinks we're a little mainstream."

"Is that bad?" She cared less for her credibility than she cared about finding a place to play. The sooner the better.

"Not necessarily. Maybe we are going to be mainstream. Maybe we're going to be big."

She felt big, bigger inside than out, as if she'd swallowed the future and it was expanding inside her. "Can we work?" she said. "I really want to work right now."

Later, over dinner, Laurie said, "What if it did happen? What if we did get big?"

In her peripheral vision she saw Molly set her silverware on the table and look at Jim. Sam, following the action, put his own silverware down and looked too.

"We've talked about it," Jim said carefully. "If something actually did happen, I'm old enough and smart enough now that I'd know what to do with the money. And some real money would be nice. It'd be worth the effort."

"You been waiting a long time," Molly said. She reached across the table for his hand and he stretched it out to her. "You deserve another shot."

"Another?" Laurie asked.

"I was supposed to be big back in the eighties," Jim said. "I was with this band called Harm's Way, and we were hot stuff in Jacksonville, Florida. Headlining clubs, winning talent shows, getting played on the local radio. We'd gone as far as we were going to get locally, so we threw everything we had in the van and drove the entire length of Interstate 10, Jacksonville to LA, in two days. This was back when 'Money for Nothing' was on MTV every fifteen minutes. Live Aid, the Jacksons' Victory tour, Hall and Oates. We all had short hair and skinny ties and played Two-Tone ska bands in the van all day and night.

"We'd been putting money aside for two years to get out here. All five of us lived together in this crummy garage apartment in East LA, which wasn't too bad except we couldn't leave anything in the van overnight and once a month somebody would shoot one of its windows out. We hustled our demo all day, played auditions and open mike nights and went to clubs every night. And it never happened.

"Later we found out our manager had no clout at all, was kind of a laughingstock in the business. On the other hand, she had a couple of big names and *they* were working. So maybe it was her, maybe it was bad luck, maybe we weren't really all that good. Anyway, we stuck it out for four months, then the other guys went back to Florida and broke up."

"Why'd you stay?"

"I had a job, for one thing. And LA had started to get under my skin. And I'd met Molly and I thought maybe I was in love."

"You *were* in love," Molly said. "It was nearly tragic to watch you."

"Did you try to start another band?"

"I didn't have the heart for it. Or the time, by that point, between work and chasing after her."

"Did you miss it?"

"Did he ever," Molly said. "He was a wreck. I wanted him to get another band, just to shut him up, but he didn't want to do it. I wonder how I managed to put up with him sometimes."

"It was easy," he said. "I'm hysterically funny when I'm bitter."

"Was that when you started the studio?" Laurie asked.

"Eventually. I spent a couple of years not playing at all and that almost put me in a rubber room. I guess it was like an alcoholic trying to dry out."

"No," Molly said. "It was like somebody with a brain-chemical imbalance going off their medication. Wasn't any twelve steps or higher power would have helped you. You weren't healing up, you were getting worse and worse."

Behind the kidding Laurie could see old wounds that had scabbed over but never healed. Even so, she envied them, envied the two hands clasped together, brown and cream on the green Formica. She wanted to picture herself sitting like that with Skip—not married and living in the suburbs, necessarily, merely openly affectionate—but her inner eye refused to go even that far. "After all that, you're ready to go out again?" she asked. "You're not scared?"

"Sure I'm scared. Molly's scared too. But it's different now. I need to play, but I don't need the fame, not the way I did then."

"The way I do now."

"Yeah."

"But you're not going to big-brother me and try to talk me out of it?"

"I'd be wasting my breath."

NERVES

Instead of sleeping that night she agonized over what she was going to wear, over the set list, over whether Skip was going to take the entire band down in a phosphorescence of self-destruction.

Wednesday night she practiced guitar instead of doing laundry, searching for the gist of Skip's lead parts. Nothing flashy, nothing she might fumble under stress, no more than a musical life vest to float her through a show if Skip should happen to founder.

Thursday afternoon the new *Weekly* hit the street and there she was, "Laurie Moss," in the Club Lingerie ad, "And Band" a few points smaller underneath. She took five copies and left one folded open on the seat as she drove to Whittier, so that it could provide peripheral comfort and reassurance.

That afternoon she ran the boards while Jim laid down a cheesy organ part for "Carry On" with a borrowed mid-sixties Farfisa. Then they sat together at the console and mixed it onto a DAT master that already contained "Neither Are We," "Angel Dust," and "One to Go." In playback the sound quality was so pristine that they could hear the catch of the pick as it first hit a guitar string, hear the ridges of a cymbal as a drumstick brushed across them, hear the air subside after a bass note.

After dinner Molly stuck around to help address FedEx waybills to a dozen independent record companies. "FedEx is just to get their attention," Jim said. "It doesn't mean they're actually going to be in any hurry to get back to us."

"Okay," Laurie said.

"They get approximately one million tapes a day. And just because I know these people, that doesn't mean they want to listen to a tape I happen to be on. In fact, a couple of them are probably going to feel like I've betrayed some kind of a trust by making them do it."

"Okay."

"I just don't want you getting your hopes up too high, you know?"

"I know," she said.

"So it turns out a guy I've worked with at Matador is going to be in town next week, and he told me he's coming to the show. Because he's coming, a guy from Alias Records said he'd come too, and a guy from Cargo." Jim was deadpan, as if trying to deliver bad news in the least alarming way possible.

"That's good," Laurie said. "Isn't it?"

"I don't want to scare you, but this is kind of an important window for us. People in this business are very jaded, and the things that get their attention are either old established bands with track records, or brand-new bands that might possibly be the Next Big Thing. So I've been working hard to get a buzz going about this gig. If we don't get noticed right away, it could take years. We become familiar and they lose their sense of urgency about us."

"Okay," she said.

She concentrated on her pen strokes, holding everything inside her like an explosion at the bottom of a mine shaft, watching for tremors. She opened up a hairsbreadth at practice and was barely able to make herself quit playing; afterward she took a cassette dub of the four finished songs and drove half the night with it, past Riverside to San Bernardino and back, out to where the mountains and the desert reclaimed the right-of-way and stars burned fiercely through the smog.

She understood that hope and common sense were the green and red lenses of the glasses that would give perspective to her career. She closed first one eye, then the other, as she drove.

Saturday night Summer was cool and distant and Laurie knew she'd seen the Club Lingerie ad. Summer's hurt and anger and Laurie's guilt seemed to provide as solid a foundation for the music as the joy they'd started with. If the audience was quieter and more introverted, beer sales nonetheless continued to climb.

Afterward Summer went to Brad's office to collect their money. She was gone a long time. Laurie sat at the bar while waitresses stacked inverted chairs on tabletops and herded the last of the customers out the door.

"Here," Summer said, snapping her out of a fog of exhaustion with a damp stack of tens and twenties.

"Sit down?" Laurie asked.

"I don't think so."

Laurie sighed. "I don't like this. It's no fun anymore. I don't want us to be like this."

"What do you want us to be like? Do you want to split up?" Before Laurie could answer, she said, "I know you need the money. I talked to Brad just now and he can give you at least one night a week, solo, a hundred guaranteed, but you'll probably end up closer to one-fifty. It's a pay cut, but you've got your straight job now, so you don't have to use that as an excuse to keep playing with me."

"What if I *want* to keep playing with you?"

"You just said it was no fun anymore. Make up your mind."

"It doesn't matter what I say tonight, does it?"

"You don't have to decide tonight. Take your time. *I'm* not going anywhere." She picked up her guitar and left.

Brad had clearly been watching through the one-way mirror behind the call brands. When he came out he said, "She's in a lot of pain."

"Oh, please. Even if it's true, can't you find another way to say it?"

"She's a brilliant songwriter, but she's not moving to the next level. Everyone takes her for granted. Meanwhile you come in and overnight you're playing at Club Lingerie."

It was the very pitfall Jim had pointed out to her on Thursday. Brad should have understood this already, and Laurie saw it was inappropriate for her to tell him so. "Actually it's been almost a year," she said, "but who's counting? Look, Brad, I think Summer's great too. She doesn't need me to carry her. And I've worked for this. I can't remember the last good night's sleep I got. I've missed meals, I've worn the same week's worth of clothes until I'm sick of the sight of them, I've driven my car into the ground, I—"

"What if she did?"

"What?"

"What if she did need you to carry her?"

"What are you saying, that I should give up the band to play with Summer?"

"Not give it up, just . . . put it on hold for a while."

"This band can't wait. They may not last until Wednesday. This could be the only shot *I* get. They're the greatest band I've ever heard, but my guitar player's psycho, my keyboard player's afraid to leave his family, and I'm already afraid to tell anybody how old I am because it could hurt my chances with a major label. And you want me to *wait?*"

She was halfway to the door when Brad said, "See you next Saturday?"

"I'll be here," Laurie said.

Skip was drinking rum and belligerent at Sunday night's practice. Monday he didn't show up at all.

At eight o'clock Jim said, "Let's call Mitch. If we're going to end up with him Wednesday night, we should at least get a couple of rehearsals."

"No."

"Laurie—"

"Be reasonable," Gabe said. "This is, like, really important. We need him."

"He's got—"

"Laurie," Gabe said, "if you say one word about his hair, I swear to God I will strangle you where you stand."

She looked to Dennis, who shrugged. "At least," she said, "let's try a couple of songs without him. Maybe Skip'll show."

They went to the garage. Laurie put on her guitar and blew into her curled fingers, which had suddenly gone cold.

"What are we supposed to play?" Gabe said.

"The set," Laurie said. "Play the set."

They started "Get Ready," and instead of chords Laurie played Skip's part, a tricky double-stop lead that was supposed to sound like horns and strings combined. She'd been practicing it for days, and she got it close enough to right to see Jim and Gabe trade amazed looks.

Unfortunately it went downhill from there. She fumbled the jazzy solo on "Brighter Day" and ran out of ideas halfway through the lead to "Angel Dust." After that she tried to regroup, sticking mostly with rhythm and salvaging a nice melodic line on "Neither Are We," but it was too late.

They put down their instruments in unspoken consensus and trudged into the kitchen. "If Skip isn't here by seven-thirty tomorrow," she said glumly, "you can call Melvin."

"Mitch," Jim said.

"Whatever."

"Look, you impressed hell out of me," Gabe said. "You were great on 'Get Ready.' I don't think any of us realized how good you are. You could play lead guitar in a lot of bands."

"But not this one."

"Even in this one," Jim said. "We could rework the arrangements, practice the hell out of them."

"Meanwhile," Gabe said, "the gig is Wednesday. Day after tomorrow."

"I already gave in," she said. "You don't have to rub my nose in it."

"You're missing the point," Gabe said. "You're a really good guitar player, but this is supposed to be a band. You're not responsible for every single thing. If Dennis was to accidentally crush his right foot—"

"Which could happen," Jim said. "He could mistake it for a badger or something."

"Thanks," Dennis said. "Thanks a lot."

"—it wouldn't be up to you to play his bass drum and still play guitar and sing too. You can't control everything. Hello? Laurie? Is any of this getting through to you?"

They gave up at ten o'clock and Laurie drove straight to Skip's apartment. She felt much like she had when Jack smashed her guitar; she could hear rushing water in her head and the world looked floodlit and pale.

The entrance to the building was locked, but an open window

looked into Skip's living room from the front porch. As she reached up to slide the screen out of its aluminum frame, Laurie saw that her hands actually seemed blurred due to their slight but violent tremors. A bookshelf blocked the lower part of the window, and she methodically stacked the top row of books onto the concrete slab of the porch and then climbed inside. Let him be in bed with somebody, she thought. I could burn this thing to the ground.

She walked into the bedroom. Skip was naked except for a pair of black-framed reading glasses. He had Mick Fleetwood's autobiography open in one hand and with the other he was eating Hydrox cookies out of a package that lay next to him on the bed. His head jerked up and for a satisfying second she saw real fear on his face. Then, without her being able to say what specifically had changed, he was staring at her with annoyance.

"What the hell are you doing? You about scared me to death."

"We were supposed to practice tonight," she said.

He nodded slightly, as if impatient for her to get to the point.

"You didn't show up. You didn't call. And I'm sick of it. We don't know if you're going to show up on Wednesday or not, we don't know if your name's going on the album, we're all just sitting around waiting on your fucking pleasure, and I don't feel like waiting anymore."

He smiled. "Are you kicking me out?"

"If you want out of this band you're going to have to quit. Personally I don't care, go or stay, as long as you make a decision and stick to it."

"Well," he said. She seemed to be amusing him, and that only made her more furious. "I've come this far. I guess I want to see what happens Wednesday night."

"'I guess' isn't good enough."

"Okay. You have my word. I, Skip Shaw, being of deteriorating body and infantile mind, do solemnly promise to attend, play, and sing with Laurie Moss and the Mossbacks on Wednesday, the twenty-sixth of April, Year of Our Lord Nineteen and Ninety-Five."

"And the rehearsal tomorrow?"

"And the rehearsal tomorrow. Is that good enough, or do you need it in writing?"

"That's fine," she said, turning away.

"Hey," he said.

She stopped, but didn't turn. "I have a name."

"Hey, Laurie."

She faced him. He still had made no effort to cover himself, still had his reading glasses on. She saw that one earpiece was attached with a safety pin. "As long as you're here," he said, "and I'm already naked and everything, do you want to fool around?"

"I don't think so," she said. She left the screen off his window and the books on his porch and slammed his front door on her way out for good measure.

SOUND CHECK

Skip was on time for Tuesday's practice, as if nothing had happened. Laurie forgot the words to "Carry On," which she'd been singing in public for seven years, started "Neither Are We" in the wrong key, and hit herself in the upper lip with the microphone on "Say Goodbye."

"You're getting it all out of your system," Jim said kindly. Laurie glared. Skip disappeared as if by magic between the time Jim shut everything off in the garage and the time everyone else arrived in the kitchen.

"How are we supposed to move everything?" It was approximately the fifteenth increasingly desperate question she'd asked in a row.

"I've got a van," Dennis said. "You've probably seen it? Parked outside?"

"Go home, Laurie," Gabe said. "Pretend to chill. Take some Xanax if you got any."

Skip was parked at the far curb when she pulled into her driveway. She crossed the street to his Mustang, self-consciousness lending an inadvertent sway to her walk, and he rolled his window down. "Hey," he said.

The streetlight turned his crow's feet into stark black slashes. The lean fingers of his left hand gripped the chrome that surrounded the window and his right hand held the wheel. He was Skip Shaw, living legend, and he wanted her. A puff of wind brought her the smell of jasmine and caressed her with a lock of her own hair. She gave herself a long moment to catalog the desire in his eyes and then she said, "Why don't you come inside?"

She opened her eyes at seven on Wednesday morning and knew she was awake for good. While Skip slept she tiptoed around the apartment, making coffee, reading, playing through the set with an unplugged guitar. At ten-thirty he sat up on the edge of the bed and coughed for five minutes or so, a morning ritual. Then he lit a cigarette and padded naked into the bathroom.

When he came out she handed him a cup of coffee and began trying on clothes for the gig. Black seemed her last best hope. Skip quickly tired of being asked his opinion and said, "I'm out of here."

"Sound check's at six."

"Did I promise to do the sound check too?"

"Skip . . ."

"Kidding. I'm kidding."

She parked around the corner from Club Lingerie at five-thirty. She'd been there three or four times since she'd been in LA and knew a little of the history: It had been the Red Velvet in the sixties, when the Knickerbockers had been the house band, and then it was Souled Out in the seventies. It hadn't changed its name since 1979, making it a venerable institution by LA standards. Its biggest exposure came when Walter Hill dressed up the interior as a redneck joint in *48HRS.*, leaving little to recognize beyond the long red-brick wall behind the bar.

She carried her guitar and amp over to where a friendly-looking white-haired guy was filling a beer cooler. "I'm Laurie Moss," she said. "I'm early."

"I'm Dominic," he said, and shook her hand. "I own the place. Ace'll be along in a while—he's the sound man." He looked at his watch. "You got a bit of a wait, if there's anything else you need to do. You guys'll be up last, probably not until eight, eight-thirty."

She appreciated his not hammering home her naïveté. Of course they would be up last; their amps would go in front of the other bands' and they would make do with what little of the stage was left. Dominic gave her a Snapple and told her to make herself at home. He looked twice at her amp as she carried it and her guitar to a table near the bar, but he was gentleman enough not to make fun of either her or her equipment.

It had the ancient odors of any nightclub in daylight, old smoke and older beer, with a hint of Lysol from the open doors of the bathrooms. Tonight, she knew, it would instead smell like perfume and sweat, like wine and electricity. There would be moments of highly charged possibility, moments in which spirit would transcend flesh through chemicals artificial or hormonal, and moments when the music, all on its own, would seduce, batter, or sweep someone away from causality and dread for at least one infinite fraction of a second.

It was seven o'clock before Caustic was set up and miked and the slow ritual of sound check began—each instrument, each drum, each vocal mike auditioned in turn, notes and levels scrawled on masking tape on the mixing board, and then only a minute or so of driving, horn-fueled ska before the music passed briefly through chaos on its way to silence again. Laurie loved the process the way she thought a surfer would have to love the distant sound of breaking waves, for the sheer promise it held.

Despite an undercurrent of nerves, she felt honed and ready, alive in the moment. Her senses and emotions were resonating theatrically to everything around her. As Caustic cleared the stage, the front door opened on the last incandescence of the sunset, silhouetting a man with an amp and a guitar. Though she could see it wasn't Skip, it still felt to her like it should have been. A pang of loneliness played in her head like distant violins.

The man with the guitar was heavyset and vaguely familiar-looking, with straight, shining black hair and copper skin. He stopped at the bar for a beer and then glanced at Laurie, taking in the equipment next to her chair. "You want anything?" he asked.

"I'm fine."

He brought his beer over to the table and said, "I'm Dan Villanueva, the token boy in Estrogen."

She offered her hand. "Laurie Moss."

"Ah, the mysterious opening act."

She nodded. "I saw you guys at a Monday night at the Whiskey last fall." Monday was no-cover night on the Strip and the Whiskey would sometimes shoehorn in six or seven bands. "You were really good."

"Thanks," he said shyly. "We're way better now. Are you solo or are you a band?"

"I'm a five-piece," she said.

"And that's your amp?"

He took her up on stage and let her plug into his new Fender Blues

Deluxe, which sounded so sweet and soulful that she hated not having one just like it, hated her financial condition that forbade the slightest thought of it.

"You might as well use it," he said. "It's going to be sitting up here anyway."

"This is truly kind of you."

He shrugged. "We're all struggling, right?"

When she got down off the stage Jim and Dennis were carrying in Dennis's drums. Her emotions were still running high and it was all she could do not to tell them how ridiculously glad she was to see them.

Gabe and L'Shondra came in, carrying either end of Gabe's speaker cabinet, and, unexpectedly, L'Shondra gave Laurie a hug. "I love that dress," she whispered. "Am I allowed to wish you luck? Or do I have to tell you to break a leg or something?"

"Luck is good," Laurie said. "Luck is fine."

She was too restless to sit during Estrogen's sound check, barely noticed what they sounded like. Jim brought her another Snapple from the bar. "He'll be here," he told her.

"Why does he have to do this?" she said. "This is such bullshit."

"I'm not arguing with you," Jim said. "Want me to call Mitch?"

"That is so far from funny," Laurie said.

Estrogen finished and Laurie introduced Dan to the rest of the table. "Are you the same Jim Pearson that produced that Random Axe EP?" Dan asked.

"Nominally," Jim said. "They were pretty clear as to what they wanted."

"That was good work, man. A lot of the buzz around them now is because of the way that record sounds. I wish we could afford you."

"It's easier than you think," Jim said. "Some canned goods, a share of your T-shirt revenue . . ." He passed Dan a business card from his wallet. "Give me a call."

Laurie's attention focused on Ace, the sound guy. He was young and good-looking in his sweat pants, running shoes, leather jacket, and ponytail, and he was positioning mikes around Dennis's drums. Any minute now he would be finished and ready for the rest of the band. Ready for Skip.

He's fired, she told herself. Even if he shows up this second, he's still fired. I can't take the stress.

"Okay, we got everybody?" Ace asked.

Laurie opened her mouth to make an excuse but before the words came out she heard Skip say, "Let's do it."

She turned around. He was somehow ten feet behind her, the massive Twin Reverb amp in his right hand, his guitar case in the other. "You're late," she said.

Skip shrugged and smiled. "Apparently not."

She plugged in to Dan's amp again, switched it off standby, and felt the serious amplification bring the guitar to life in her hands. The difference from playing in Jim's garage was absolute and qualitative. At this volume the guitar seemed to emit light and heat as well as sound. When she turned from side to side she could hear the change in air pressure through the speaker. Trailing one finger lightly up a string sent rasping squeals to the far corners of the big room.

The truth of the electric guitar is that the electricity is contagious, passed from wall outlet to guitarist to audience if the emotional humidity is right. Laurie was too filled with her power to hang on to her anger with Skip, her money worries, anything, in fact, beyond the sound.

To her right Jim had the DX-7 at the lip of the stage. Laurie was in the middle with Gabe, Skip on her far left. It was the same configuration they'd been using in the garage for the last two weeks. Skip was duct-taping his effects box to the floor. Gabe was screwing in earplugs, and Dennis was stomping on his bass drum pedal with evident satisfaction.

"Hey, Dennis," Jim yelled. "How can you tell if the drum riser is level?"

"I don't know," Dennis yelled back. "Who cares?"

"No," Jim said, "it's a joke. The answer is, 'If the drummer is drooling out of both sides of his mouth.'"

"That's not funny, man."

"Sure it is," Jim said. "Trust me."

Laurie walked to the center stage microphone and said, "Test, one, two." Her voice boomed across the empty club.

Skip crossed in front of her. "Nice amp," he said.

She wondered if he might be jealous, and found she liked the idea. "I've always depended," she said, "on the kindness of strangers."

Skip made a face and hit his low E string. Jim, like Pavlov's piano player, answered with a low E from the keyboard and Skip tuned up. Ace got his levels and suddenly, finally, it was time to play.

Laurie turned to Dennis. "'Get Ready,'" she said.

"I *am* ready."

"Dennis, I swear to God . . ."

Dennis counted off. Laurie turned to the mike and laid into the opening chords.

The band sounded thin at first, and the monitors seemed comatose. Laurie didn't care. She knew how the song was supposed to go. The greater danger was that people would think her simpleminded due to the idiot grin stretching her face. She remembered exactly how it felt to be an awkward fourteen-year-old at the Sunken Gardens in San Antonio, in love with a sound, and now that she was making that joyous, inexorable sound herself it was everything she'd known it would be. It was over too soon, leaving her out of breath as she looked into the darkness and said, "Need a little more?"

"That's plenty," Ace said. "Sounds good, guys. See you tonight."

She realized she'd been hoping for an excuse to go on, dreaming that Ace, who heard a couple of dozen bands every week, would be so blown away that he would ask for a personal encore. She laboriously shifted gears, put Dan's amp on standby, and unplugged her guitar.

As she climbed down from the stage Skip said, "You were rushing it a little."

She turned to look at him. His hair was disarrayed and not especially clean. His once-black pearl-snap Western shirt had faded to a darkish gray except for the sweat stains under the arms. He held her eyes for a moment and then popped his guitar strap loose and laid his battered Gibson in its case. She thought about the different stages Skip had played on, from the Royal Albert Hall to the Hollywood Bowl, and for the first time it didn't intimidate her.

This is the best band he's ever been in, she thought, and he knows it.

"I'll try to watch it," she said. "And if I don't? Just see if you can keep up."

OPENING NIGHT

It was the first official Band Dinner, all of them out together, so they took the van to the Rock and Roll Denny's just down the street. Spirits were high, even Skip's, right up until nine o'clock when they returned to an empty club for their nine-thirty start time. Not entirely empty—there were a dozen or so bored and listless drinkers at the back of the room—but no entourages, no expensive leather jackets, no AmEx cards waving in the smoky air.

"Don't panic," Jim said, unconvincingly. "These guys are notoriously late to everything."

"If they're much later," Laurie said, "they're going to miss us entirely."

"Well," Jim said. "We did what we could."

Laurie went outside to sit on the curb and watch traffic on Sunset, trying to clear her head. The sound check had been great with no one there. What difference did it make who was in the audience now?

All the difference, of course. It made all the difference.

She didn't notice Gabe standing behind her until she stood up and dusted herself off to go inside. "You all right?" he said.

"Yeah. Emotions running a bit high and fluttery tonight."

"No shame in that. I wish Jim hadn't said anything about those industry people. They're a bunch of damn vultures is all. They never get onto a scene until it's dead. They're probably all out at some plastic punk club trying to find the next Green Day."

"So who needs 'em?"

"Not us," Gabe said. "We're Laurie Moss and the Mossmen."

The dressing room was the size of the guest room in a very cheap apartment, with dark paneling and dark, damaged carpet to make it look even smaller. There seemed to be a single twenty-five-watt light. At nine-thirty, Ace knocked on the door and said, "Ready when you are."

Dennis led the way, Gabe and Jim behind him. Guitar strapped on, holding its neck high to make it through the narrow door, Laurie followed them toward the stage, Skip bringing up the rear. It took a long time. She could hear her footsteps on the carpet, hear her own breath in her mouth. She tried again and again to swallow, though her constricted throat seemed to have forgotten how. Her eyes focused on Gabe's short dreadlocks and the sheen of his gray polished cotton shirt; in the edges of her vision she saw empty tables and cavernous space.

They climbed onto the stage and she went straight to the red glowing light on Danny's amp, found the jack at the end of her cord, ran it through her strap, and plugged it, with stiff and uncooperative fingers, into her guitar. When she looked up she saw Jim run his fingers silently over the keys of his DX-7, then rub his hands together with glee.

She turned to look at Gabe, his legs a shoulders' width apart, fingers already poised to hit the first note, smiling, utterly calm and motionless. Even Dennis was eerily silent, the first drummer in her experience who didn't make a nervous clatter at the start of a show. They all watched her, all waited for her, Skip included, and it became real to her for the first time that she was a second or two away from playing her own songs at one of the top clubs in LA, backed up by the band of her dreams, who were even now tuned, aligned, fueled, and ready for her to turn the key. Nothing else matters, she thought. Not right now.

She nodded to Dennis, and walked toward the mike as he clicked off the tempo. "How ya doin'?" she said to the empty house as Jim and Gabe dug into the first two irresistible bars of "Get Ready." Dennis led into the third bar with a perfect Motown drag roll and she laid her guitar part squarely on top of the drums. Then came Skip with the string part, played Albert-King-style, hard and stinging. A spotlight hit her in the face and she opened her mouth and started to sing.

The words were laid out in her head like crossties, the music like rails, and she rode them for all she was worth, Skip, Gabe, and Jim throwing the weight of their voices behind her on the chorus until she no longer knew if it was in her power to stop, or to want to stop.

Skip played the sax solo on anguished guitar and together they roared into the final verse, into the final chord, and finally into the inevitable silence afterward, broken by applause and even a few whistles.

"Thanks," Laurie said. "I'm Laurie Moss, and this is my band, the Mighty Moss-Tones." A flurry of applause erupted from a table near the front of the stage. She squinted into the lights and saw Catherine, Molly, and L'Shondra with three or four friends. She was giddy, and she realized that if she wasn't careful she could turn into the Medicated Elvis and not be able to shut up. So she stepped away from the mike and nodded for Dennis to count off "Brighter Day."

MARK ARDREY

After the lead in "Carry On," the last song, it dropped down to bass and drums, quiet enough for Laurie to introduce the band. When she got to Skip—carefully qualified as "sitting in with us tonight"—there were yelps of recognition from the audience, and a couple of requests for "Tender Hours."

Skip stepped reluctantly up to his mike and said, "Not tonight. Tonight I'm just a Moss-Tone." He nodded to Laurie and they started the build-up to the last verse and the end of the set. The applause was substantial, but by the time they'd said their thank-yous and unplugged, it was over.

The first thing Laurie noticed after she got off stage was the return of self-consciousness. She caught herself wondering, Am I okay? Am I bummed that it's over? She wouldn't have asked those questions with the set actually in progress. But now that they'd come up, the answer seemed to be that she was fine. Suddenly, deeply tired, at the same time that she was buzzing with the pleasure of what she'd done.

They loaded the van while Estrogen's drummer set up, the *Best of Blondie* blaring over the sound system. Okay, she admitted, an encore would have been nice. She knew an opening band getting an encore at a club would have been a miracle slightly more astonishing than raising Lazarus, but then, when did desire ever stop to figure the odds?

"Okay, that's it," Jim said, and Dennis waved and drove away down Sunset. Laurie stashed her practice amp and guitar in the dressing room and sat down at the table where Jim and Gabe had already joined L'Shondra and the others, adding a second concentric ring of chairs around the outside. Skip, apparently, had simply disappeared.

"You were incredible," Catherine said, eyes shining. "You were good with Summer, but this . . . this was like a whole other level."

"Thank you," Laurie said, surprising herself yet again with sudden regret that she hadn't invited Summer, with a completely unreasonable wish that Summer could have been there to share this.

L'Shondra reached across the table to squeeze her hand. "She's right. Gabe's played with about a hundred bands, but this is the best ever."

"Thank you," Laurie said. She smiled at L'Shondra and then couldn't stop herself from looking behind her. "Did Skip just take off? Is Dennis coming back?"

Jim and Gabe gave each other a look that Laurie recognized. "All right, what's going on? What is it you're not telling me this time?"

"Dennis has another gig, down at the Teaszer," Jim said.

"What, you're saying Dennis is in another band?"

"It's not a big deal," Gabe said. "You've got your Saturday night thing with Summer, Dennis has a couple of other bands he plays with."

The fact that they hadn't told her upset her more than anything else. Don't let this spoil things, she pleaded with herself. Please. "How many exactly?"

"It depends which week you ask," Jim said. "This is LA. One band breaks up, the guitarist starts a second band, the bass player starts a third."

"What happens if we have a gig?"

She could see Jim and Gabe both searching for the perfectly reassuring answer, but before either of them could get it out a voice behind her said, "Is this a bad time?"

Laurie turned and saw what she at first took to be a plainclothes cop. He was medium height with short dark hair, black-rimmed glasses, black slacks and shoes, pressed white shirt, black knit tie. "I was wondering," he said calmly, "if I could talk to you for a minute."

A surge of panic sent her down a chain of associations: police, Skip, heroin, evidence accidentally in her guitar case, bungled trial, prison, despair, suicide. She noticed the man was holding out a business card and took it in suddenly clammy fingers.

"Mark Ardrey," he said, offering his hand. She shook it limply, trying to read the card in the attenuated light. Gradually she began to realize that the logo behind his name consisted of a G and an R crushed together to form a circle.

"General Records?" she said. "For real?"

"For real," he said. "Can I buy you a drink?"

Now that she had a moment, he looked less like a cop than a shoe salesman from 1959. If he'd looked the way he was supposed to—silk shirt, mousse, unstructured jacket—she was sure she would have been falling all over herself. As it was, she couldn't seem to take him seriously. "Sure," she said. "Pull up a chair."

Laurie had been reading *Rolling Stone* since the age of twelve and she knew the history of General Records the same way she knew about Hank Williams or the Moog synthesizer. General had been a bona fide major label through the early sixties, then gone under, as so many had, in the wake of the Beatles. Warner's had bought their back catalog in 1965 and then, in the late eighties, revived the name as a boutique label under the Warner/Elektra/Atlantic umbrella.

"Jim," she said, "Gabe, this is Mark . . ."

"Ardrey," the man said, leaning across the table to shake hands. "General Records." To Gabe he said, "I've seen you around town. You're really good." To Jim he said, "You produced the *Kindness* EP, right?"

"That was me," Jim agreed.

"So I was talking with Brett Gurewitz yesterday, you guys know Brett? Bad Religion, Epitaph Records?"

"I know him," Jim said.

"Well, he told me he was going to be here to check you guys out tonight, only he never shows up. I kinda feel stood up, here."

"You and me both," Jim said.

"I mean, I feel like I'm missing the boat, you know, that these guys are all off at some A-list party and they didn't tell me about it."

"Sorry you got stuck listening to us," Laurie said. She'd let the words out thinking they'd come off as mildly ironic and amusing, but she'd apparently misjudged. The high from playing was slowly receding, the train disappearing down the track without her. She could barely hear its whistle.

"No, hey, you guys were terrific. I didn't mean it like that." He signaled to a waitress, who ignored him. "Have you been playing out much?"

"This was our first gig," Gabe said.

"You're kidding."

"We've been holed up in a garage in Whittier for four months," Laurie said.

"Whittier? No kidding. I live in Whittier. How long have you been together?"

"Laurie's been with us since January," Gabe said. "The original stuff is all hers. The rest of us have been jamming together off and on for a couple of years."

"Including Skip?"

Gabe looked at Laurie and said, "Off and on."

"Where do you know him from?"

"I met him at a jingle session," Gabe said. "We got along and I brought him over to Jim's."

"What's he like?" Ardrey asked. He was leaning forward now, elbows on the table, genuinely interested.

Discussing Skip had fallen off the list of things for which Laurie was in the mood. She excused herself and went over to the table where Dan Villanueva was selling Estrogen CDs and T-shirts.

"When are you guys up?" she asked him.

"Any minute. I caught the end of your set. You guys are hot."

"Thanks. Your amp made a big difference." She picked up one of their CDs. The cover art looked like it had been thrown together in a couple of minutes in Photoshop. "Do you guys sell a lot of these?"

"Couple of thousand in the last year."

"Wow, that's good."

"Not exactly major label numbers, but the profit margin's better. We made back what they cost in a couple of weeks. I can give you all the info if you want." He looked over at her table. "Speaking of major labels, is that Mark Ardrey over there?"

"You know him?"

"He hangs around the scene a lot. He never signed anybody that I knew personally."

"But he's for real?"

"He does A&R for General, at least this week. The word on the street is they're looking for an excuse to get rid of him. Just thought you should know that. I mean, the fact that he's here tonight shows how out of it he is. Everybody else is at the Viper Room to hear Random Axe."

"You were talking about them earlier."

"Yeah, everybody says they're going to be the next Green Day."

"Which explains what happened to everybody who was supposed to come hear us."

"This business sucks. I love playing, but the business sucks." He looked at his watch. "Sorry. My wife was supposed to be here fifteen minutes ago to run the table while we play."

Laurie wondered if he'd brought up his wife to distance her. She was embarrassed that he might have thought she was coming on to him. "Got any kids?"

"Two. Makes it hard sometimes, but I wouldn't trade 'em for anything. Ah, there she is." He got out from behind the table and then paused on his way to the stage. "Don't take my word on this Ardrey business. Maybe he can help you. He sure can't hurt, as long as you don't get your hopes up too high."

"I don't know," Laurie said. "He can't even seem to get waited on."

Laurie went back to the table. As Dan had promised, Estrogen was indeed "way better now." Without talking or looking at each other they segued crisply from one tight, disciplined song to the next.

After ten minutes Ardrey said, "I like these guys. They got a lot of heart." It struck Laurie as an unusual thing for him to say. "You guys were better, but they're good."

"We're not better," Laurie said. "Not yet."

"I actually don't know a lot about this business," Ardrey said. He'd moved closer to her to talk into her ear, almost shouting to make himself heard. "Which is okay, because nobody does, and the people who say they do are lying. But my point is this: There is only one universal currency in this business, and that is melody. It's the great unsolved mystery. It doesn't translate into any other art form. You can't write about it, you can't paint it, you can't sculpt it. Nobody knows where it comes from, or why one pattern of notes will lock into your brain and another one just blows away. Whatever the hell it is, you've got it."

Laurie couldn't shake the feeling that the man was a flake. He dressed badly, he was in bad odor with his own record company, and he was simply too free with his sincerity. "Then you should sign us," she said, standing up.

Ardrey shook a mock-reproving finger. "Now, now. Doesn't do to get pushy. When are you playing again?"

"Who knows?" she said. She was suddenly so tired she wondered if she could make it to the LBD, wondered if she had willpower enough to force it up the steep slope of the Hollywood Hills and down again to her apartment. She managed a costly smile. "G'night, everybody. Y'all were great."

She stopped for her guitar and amp, and on the way out the door she saw a slender redhead slide into the chair next to Jim and lean over to hug him. The woman looked to be in her mid-thirties, pretty, expensively dressed in a black blazer and half-unbuttoned silk blouse.

I don't want to know, Laurie thought. I've had enough for one night. She walked out of the club unrecognized and unmolested, breathing cool, clear air, still hearing the low throb of the bass guitar through the wall behind her.

T H E   L A S T   D A Y S   O F   S U M M E R

She showered the smoke and fumes off and sat up for an hour or so letting her hair dry, watching ancient sitcoms on Nickelodeon and drinking water to wash the last residues of excitement and despair out of her aching muscles. Even then she had to fight for sleep, only to wake up at seven forty-five to a snarling alarm clock and go through the motions of getting dressed, eyes squinting against the sunlight, groggy consciousness tiptoeing around the hard questions waiting to be asked.

As soon as she got to work she called Jim, who said, "You should have hung out another five minutes."

"So I could meet your girlfriend?"

"That's okay, Molly will only kill me if you say that in front of her. Yes, I wanted you to meet Melinda. She manages bands. I've known her for years, and she wants to take us on. In fact . . ."

"What?"

"Well, she had something for Saturday night, only I know you've got your thing with Summer, so I told her we couldn't make it."

"What kind of a thing?"

"A benefit, medical care for the homeless type deal. No money, good karma, good press after."

"I can't do it, Jim. I told you from the start—"

"I know. I know. I was trying to find something that could be construed as good news to lead off with."

"Oh God, what now?"

"It's not the end of the world, but . . . both Matador and SubPop passed on the tape. Both very nice letters. Both mailed on Tuesday."

"They probably decided together, while they were making plans to ditch our show and go see Random Axe."

"Both of them said it's a very professional, very commercial demo and it ought to be on a major label."

"Anybody's label but theirs?"

"Maybe they're right. Maybe we should be on a major. That guy Ardrey last night said—"

"Dan was telling me about him. Nobody expects him to be at General next week."

"I've heard the rumors too, but he's there today, and he did like us. It's a start. Look how far we've come since January. We've got a master tape almost done. We've debuted at a major club on the Strip. We've got a potential manager who thinks she can get us work, and we've got, as they say, 'major-label interest.'"

Laurie said, "We've got a guitar player who can't decide if he wants to play with us, an audience who'd rather hear him than me, and a handful of rejection letters. My landlady could change her mind and evict me any day, and if I'd actually been free to play this benefit thing, I wouldn't have a proper amp to play through. You said yourself that if we don't get noticed when we first come out of the gate it's going to take years. On top of all that I'm fighting to finish an album that nobody wants."

"I take it you won't be over tonight to work on the vocal tracks?"

She sighed. "I don't think I can face it right now. I'm sorry. When we're actually playing, everything is great. Especially last night, when we had a real audience to play to. It's the best feeling I've ever had. It's just . . . everything else. The real world. I can't stand the inside of my own head anymore."

Jim was quiet for a long time. "So do we go with Melinda?"

"Go with Melinda," Laurie said. "Tell her any night other than Saturday."

She went straight home after work. Summer's VW Rabbit was parked on the street across from the apartment, and Laurie's first thought was, Please, not tonight. She contemplated driving on past, but no, Summer was on the porch, was standing up to wave at her, the breeze pulling at her brown flannel shirt.

Laurie pulled into the driveway and parked. As soon as she got close enough to see the creases around Summer's eyes and the flat, forced smile that kept dropping away and returning to her mouth, Laurie knew that whatever this was, it was not going to be easy.

"You okay?" Laurie said.

"Sure," Summer said, then quickly, awkwardly, reached out to hug her. Laurie, already turning toward the door, recovered as best she could and patted her keys against Summer's back.

"Come on in," Laurie said, unlocking the door, turning on lights, throwing her purse on the table by the door. "You want something to drink?"

"No. No, thanks. You go ahead. I mean, if you want to."

Laurie stopped halfway to the kitchen and turned to face her. "Summer, what in the world is wrong with you?"

Summer sat on the couch, sank into the cushions, then scooted forward, forearms on her knees. "It was very sweet what you said about me last night."

"Last night?"

"When you introduced 'Tried and True.'"

Laurie couldn't remember what she'd said. Something about Summer being one of her favorite songwriters, she imagined. "How did . . . Oh. I get it. You were there."

"I left at the end of the set. I couldn't face you last night. I'm not sure I can face you now."

"Why not? Will you tell me what's wrong?"

"Knowing you were playing with them wasn't the same as seeing it. It was like actually running into Fernando with his wife or something. I guess you knew that, which is why you didn't invite me and I had to read the ad in the *Weekly* like everybody else."

"I thought you didn't want to hear about—"

"It doesn't matter. Really, it doesn't matter. What I saw last night . . ." Her eyes had turned red and puffy.

"What exactly did you see last night?"

"I saw your future." She looked straight at Laurie for the first time since she'd come inside, and the tears were now overflowing and running down her face. "I'm not in it."

Laurie sat on the couch and took one of Summer's hands in both of her own. "Summer, that's not true. The rest of the band knows that our Saturdays are strictly off limits—"

"That's ridiculous." Summer wiped her eyes on her shirtsleeve and seemed suddenly in complete control. "You can't be in a working band

and not be able to play Saturday nights. How many gigs have you already given up because of me?"

"None," Laurie said, but it sounded like a lie even to her own ears.

"Even if that's true, and I don't believe you, and it wouldn't stay true for long in any case, what about me? Am I just supposed to sit around and wait for you to get tired of me holding you down?"

"You're not—"

Summer started crying again. "We should split up now." Then, barely a second later, she was back in control. "The longer we wait, the uglier it's going to be. I already talked to Brad. He wants two weeks' notice, tomorrow night and next week, so he can push the farewell concert angle. He's not happy, but he understands."

"Understands *what?* Because I don't understand this at all."

"That I'm going to be playing the Duck and places like it for the rest of my life. And that he's going to be booking people like me as long as he's there. And that he's only going to get talent like you on your way up."

"Or on my way back down?"

"It's way too early to think about that."

"I can't believe you talked to Brad before you talked to me."

"That's what I'm trying to tell you. This isn't about you anymore. It's about me protecting myself."

"How did we end up where we have to protect ourselves from each other?"

Summer, to Laurie's relief, didn't answer. Instead she got up and went to the door. "I love you, you know," Summer said.

"I love you too," Laurie said. "I don't want you to go."

"I know that," Summer said, and went.

And so, two nights later, they played their next-to-last duet together. Summer talked too much between songs, about Laurie's new band, about the songs themselves, about, for God's sake, the weather, and the audience loved her for her lack of self-control. It made Laurie seem sullen by contrast, even to herself, though she was sure she hadn't started out that way.

Sunday she went to Whittier to work on the album. "I knew you'd come around," Jim said. "What is it you guys say in Texas? Get back on the one that threw you?"

" 'Throwed,' " Laurie said. "The word is 'throwed.' "

When she hadn't heard from Summer by Thursday night she called and got her answering machine. The same on Friday. Saturday night Summer was sitting on the edge of the stage when Laurie walked in the Duck. "Hey," Laurie said. "I tried to call you."

"I know," Summer said. Laurie couldn't yet tell if her smile was more than superficial.

When Laurie left Jack it was over. She'd never had to see him again, let alone do something as intimate as this: get up together on a stage in front of two hundred people, blend one voice into the other, move in rhythm, let all defenses down. "Are you sure you're up for this?" she asked.

"I'm a professional," Summer said. "So are you."

" 'Professional.' A perfumed word to cover a myriad of ills."

"That's just your guilt talking," Summer said. "If you have to, remind yourself that this was all my idea, first to last. Let's both try to live through it."

In the end it was anticlimax. There was a whiff of the perfunctory about it, more wistfulness than true regret, more professionalism than epiphany. When it was over Summer collected her guitar and her two hundred dollars, kissed Laurie, promised to call, and melted into the crowd.

A H Y P O T H E T I C A L   Q U E S T I O N

After Laurie's father moved out she'd spent months remembering every time he'd ever been disappointed in her. Her mother had sensed it and used her own disappointment as a weapon throughout what was left of Laurie's childhood.

She sat up late Saturday night imagining she had Aladdin's magic lamp on the table in front of her. On this hand, a record contract with General Records. On the other, the ability to go through the rest of her life without ever disappointing anyone again.

Which do you choose?

Of the Same Name (2)

It was three months and one week from the time Laurie decided in a February panic that she had to have a finished master tape to the afternoon in mid-May when she recorded the last of the vocals. After that final session Jim took Laurie to her first major league baseball game, then they worked on the mix until five Saturday morning. Laurie crashed in the guest room until ten and then they started again.

It was like mixing on her Tascam four-track except for the size of everything involved. It took both of them to work the faders on Jim's mixing console, sometimes colliding as their hands moved from one channel to another. It seemed to Laurie that for every song there was a single true and correct mix. She knew exactly how each instrument should sound at any given point in the song—how loud, how much reverb, how much treble and bass, where exactly it should sit between the listener's ears.

Saturday afternoon, as they took a breather, Jim said, "Estrogen seemed to move a lot of CDs at Club Lingerie."

It sounded like a tentative step toward something Laurie herself had been considering. She answered carefully, not wanting to frighten him off. "Dan said they made back their investment in a couple of weeks."

Jim nodded. They rehearsed their moves for "Linda" and then Jim said, "I guess they put, what, about fifteen hundred in it initially?"

"I made a couple of calls. It's around that. For a thousand CDs and five hundred cassettes."

Jim nodded and they tried a take using the master, dubbing it down to its own individual digital audiotape cassette. When she listened to the DAT Laurie shook her head. "The bass should be going *pooom, pooom,* like this monstrous explosion halfway across town."

They tried again and listened again. Jim said, "If you've been making calls, you've been thinking about this."

"About what?"

"About us doing the record ourselves."

Laurie shrugged. "I wake up at five A.M. sometimes. It's that or relive childhood embarrassments."

"So what were your thoughts?"

"That we wouldn't have to listen to a lot of asinine opinions if we did it ourselves. We'd only have to listen to five."

"You're leaving Molly out?"

"No, I was leaving Dennis out. Drummers aren't legally *allowed* to vote, are they?"

They made two more tries on "Linda" and then still one more, the fifth, where they caught it perfectly, volume up, swaying unselfconsciously, hands crawling like independent robots over the alien landscape of faders and knobs.

They took the finished song from DAT to standard cassette and then took the cassette to the kitchen, where they played it through Jim's jam box. "Fifteen hundred dollars is a lot of money," Jim said.

"Nobody's looking at you on this one. You've already paid all the recording expenses so far, not to mention feeding me."

"Who else is there to look at?"

"I don't know that yet. But I don't know that I'm ready to pursue this yet either. I mean, I'm not Bob Dylan, with basement tapes and trunks of unpublished songs lying around. This record is five years' worth of work for me, and I'm not sure I'm ready to throw it on the self-published scrap heap."

"The one doesn't necessarily mean the other. I mean, if we should happen to consider this seriously at some point. Industry people don't like to listen to tapes anymore. A CD, with nice art, would actually get listened to. And if we did get a label deal, we could include a rerelease of this record in the contract."

"If we did happen," Laurie said, "to talk seriously about this. And if fifteen hundred dollars should happen to land in one of our laps."

But the idea had seized her. A CD now, with her name on it, and a record deal later. An hour or two later she asked, "Who do you know that's an artist?"

"Believe it or not," Jim said, "Dennis is pretty good." He got a CD down from the shelf behind them. "He did the cover." It was a mixture of collage, pencil, colored pens, and type, striking and confident. "Makes sense, really. Visual arts and coherent speech are usually mutually exclusive."

They finished at twenty minutes after midnight Saturday night. Jim

put together a cassette copy of the finished album and Laurie sat at the
kitchen table for ten minutes, just looking at it.

"Are you okay to drive?" Jim asked.

"Yes."

"Then go home. Sleep."

She drove back to Studio City with the tape in her left hand. The
album was complete in her head and it never occurred to her to put the
tape into her deck. When she got home she lay down in her clothes and
slept for twelve hours.

The finished tape was still unplayed on Sunday night when, after a
long bath, with clean sheets on the bed and the apartment at least tidy,
she made her weekly calls home.

Her mother first, for conversation that was perfunctory at the same
time that it was reassuringly familiar: Corky still out of work, the San
Antonio heat already in the nineties, when was she coming home?

Then Grandpa Bill and a chance to brag about the album. "Will you
send me a copy of the tape?" he asked.

"Of course, but . . . I don't know if you'll like it."

"That strikes me as a particularly foolish thing to say. I'd love it for no
other reason than that your voice is on it. Add to that the fact that you
wrote the songs—"

"Most of them."

"Even if it was only one. How could I not love it?"

He seemed to expect an answer. "I don't know, Grandpa. I guess,
being who you are, you'd just have to love it."

"Much better. Now, you said something about putting it out yourself. What would that cost? "

"Grandpa, no. That's not why I told you about it."

"It's a simple question. Surely you can answer a simple question."

"Well, I said I'd looked into it . . ."

"So you must already know the figures."

"It'd take about fifteen hundred dollars."

"And you'd have to sell how many to pay me back?"

"A hundred or so."

"From everything you've said, it sounds like a perfectly reasonable investment to me. Why don't I send you a check?"

Part of her had hoped for just such an offer, but now that it lay in front of her she felt deceitful, manipulative, and hideously guilty. "Wait, wait. Let me talk it over with the guys. If I can feel okay with this and you still want to do it, I'll get a firm quote, okay?"

With the help of a woman named Janice, the art director at Sav-N-Comp, Laurie picked up enough Photoshop and Quark to lay out the CD and cassette labels and inserts. She brought Dennis in one weekend in early June and they tweaked the album art until they were both happy with it, and added the titles: LAURIE MOSS and OF THE SAME NAME. That Monday they FedExed a DAT master and a zip disk of the art to EvaTone in Florida.

All this time Melinda, true to Jim's word, had been finding them work. None of it amounted to more than double figures for the entire band, but their third gig got them a mention in the "Critic's Choice" column of the *LA Reader*.

"*Laurie Moss and Band*. Whatever happened to Skip Shaw? A legend in the early seventies and several times nearly an obituary by the end of the decade, Shaw has suddenly surfaced again as, of all things, a lead guitarist. He's backing a young songwriter with powerful hooks and a distinctive voice who looks to have a bright future; catch them Friday opening for the hot ska-funk of Save Ferris at the Teaszer."

She kept a copy on her bedside table for days. Half the time her heart would start to pound at the words "powerful hooks" and "bright future," and she would think, This is it. It's happening. The next time she wished she'd never met Skip, or that she'd had the foresight to walk away from him, to take Gabe and any of the others who'd been willing, and start fresh without him.

On Thursday, June 22, they played the Casbah in San Diego. It was the anniversary of the day she'd met Summer at the Silk and Steel, a year and three days since she'd first entered the greater Los Angeles city limits. She'd tried to reach Summer on the phone, hoping they could celebrate together, and gotten her inevitable answering machine instead.

SLAMM, the San Diego music paper, worked the same ground as the *Reader:* two-thirds Skip ("a living—but God knows how—legend of the seventies" who "regrettably played none of his own songs") and one-third Laurie ("infectious tunes and a joyful energy on stage").

You asked for this, she told herself. You made a deal with the devil.

With Skip in the band she had probably shaved two or three years off the time it took her to get noticed. And back when she was still in San Antonio, mopping the kitchen floor, she would have lost her mind to think she'd one day be playing with Skip Shaw. Let alone sleeping with him.

Not that she was sleeping with him that often. Playing out, which they did about once a week, seemed to energize his libido—provided Laurie was not overly aggressive herself. His rules were clear and Laurie was left to take him or leave him.

Usually she took him, her postcoital bouts of self-disgust notwithstanding. Some nights she felt like a screenplay that had been optioned but never bought, stuck in a relationship that never developed while off limits to potentially higher bidders. Other nights, when she looked over from center stage to see his eyes half closed, his fingers working the guitar neck with passion and tenderness and restraint, when she heard his raspy voice flow into and around hers, then her forces retreated in disarray and she settled for whatever terms he offered.

Some nights they would sit up and Skip would smoke and they would talk. "What was it like," she asked him once, "when you were starting out? Were there bands underfoot everywhere you went, like now? Were club owners put out because you wanted to play there?"

"It was different, and it was the same. There weren't so many places to play, and a lot of the places we had weren't used to electric instruments, so they were always trying to get us to turn down. There was a lot of hitching rides in the rain, sleeping on floors, missing meals. All the same, though, I knew where I was going and when I look back now it's like it was this straight line from nowhere to a record deal."

"Did you always know? That you were going to be famous?"

"Yeah. Always. My mom couldn't take a picture of me when I was a kid without me trying to set everything up—dramatic lighting, moody expression—I was a prima donna beyond my years."

"Me too. I was always thinking how something would look when they filmed it for the movie-of-the-week about me. When I'd come out of a door into the sunlight and a flock of birds would take off and I'd hear this dramatic music in my head. Laurie Moss, based on a true story."

"That's what you should call the second record. After you're famous."

"Am I?" she said. "Going to be famous?"

"I knew it the first time I laid eyes on you. You've got the looks, the talent, the need. Whatever it is that famous people have, you've got it. In spades." He crushed out his cigarette and turned off the light. "Now go to sleep, for Christ's sake."

In July the finished CDs arrived. Laurie had moved to full-time, eight-to-five Monday-through-Friday, so she'd had the order delivered to Sav-N-Comp. She brought the first of the cartons back to her cubicle, where she cut the tape and lifted out a cellophane-wrapped CD. She'd spent so many hours working on the art, staring at printouts cut to size and stuffed into a CD jewel box, that she could feel the emotion of the moment only obliquely, like a memory of the future.

That Friday they were back at Club Lingerie for a record release party. They'd sent advance copies to the *Weekly,* the *Times,* and the *Reader;* the *Weekly* had put them in their "Pick of the Clubs" section, saying they were "the alternative to alternative" and how the "distinctive twang and churn" of Skip's guitar "permeated" the album.

Full-time work meant the cacophony of an alarm every morning before six o'clock, fewer practices, lapsed housecleaning, too much fast food and too little songwriting. It also meant paying her rent again, and meant her very own Fender Blues Deluxe, which Fernando had sold her at his employee discount. Summer had patched things up with Fernando when she and Laurie were still doing their weekly duets; when Laurie had gone to see Summer at the Duck in June, the three of them had sat together during the breaks, and if it was awkward, it was better than silence.

Summer returned the favor that Friday night. Fernando and Catherine were there, as was a booking agent named Sid "the Shark" Modesto, drawn by the chum of publicity in the water. Sid looked to be about sixty, with fringes of white hair at each ear, aviator-style bifocals, and a blood-red terrycloth shirt. He handed out cards to everyone at the table, including the waitress.

Also on hand was Mark Ardrey from General Records. Laurie had seen him half a dozen times since April, once at Tower Records, the others at her shows. He'd waved and smiled and she'd waved back and hurried away in another direction.

They were third on a bill of four bands. They played for over an hour, plus encore, and while it was happening Laurie forgot the long work week, the growling in her stomach, the precarious feeling of a thousand CDs and five hundred cassettes that no one might actually want to buy. She came off stage soaked and exhausted and had to sit for a minute in the dressing room before she could go out onto the floor of the club.

"Everything okay?" Gabe asked.

She nodded. "It's just the transitions."

When they finished the load-out Ardrey was waiting for her. "So," he said, "are you giving out promos of this CD to industry heavyweights like me?"

"What's the matter, Ardrey, doesn't General give you an expense account?"

"I don't understand," he said, giving her a dejected look that she was unsure if she should take seriously. "Why is it you don't like me?"

"It's not that I don't like you," she said. "I don't trust you. I don't believe in you."

"You don't believe in me? What am I, God? I can think of a few people who'd be surprised to hear me say this, but that particular pair of shoes doesn't really fit me."

"No, you're the Easter Bunny. I'm supposed to believe that if I'm a good little girl you'll leave me a basket of gold records. Only I don't think it's going to happen. I don't think you're seriously interested in this band at all. I don't think we're 'alternative' enough or 'techno' enough or 'punk-pop' enough or whatever-adjective-you're-looking-for-this-week enough for you to actually have the guts to sign us."

"Hey, now, what did I ever do to deserve this?"

"Nothing," she said. "Nothing is exactly what you've—"

Jim walked up with a copy of the CD. "Hey, Mark," he said. "Hope I'm not interrupting." He gave Laurie the kind of look she'd seen him give his son that meant there would be a lecture later. "Have you got one of these yet?"

"No, in fact I was just—"

"Great, well, here you are. First printing, going fast."

As Laurie walked away she heard Ardrey say, "She doesn't seem to like me, and I don't know why."

L'Shondra had the CDs at a table near the stage. "Eight CDs, three tapes," she said. "That's good, isn't it?"

"Yes," Laurie said, relieved. "It's good."

At the band table, Skip was signing a beat-up *Tender Hours* LP sleeve for a balding man in his forties wearing jeans and a polo shirt. "So," the man said, "uh, writing any new stuff these days?"

"I write a rent check once a month," Skip said. He looked up and saw Laurie. "There's the songwriter in the group."

The guy nodded at Laurie, clearly not wanting to offend, and returned nervously to Skip. "Is it, like, okay if I hang out for a minute?"

Skip shrugged. It meant, Laurie knew, he was trying to think of a way to say no that wasn't blatantly offensive. The guy misread it and sat down. "So," the guy said. "What was it like? Smoking dope with Dylan and jamming with Lennon in Toronto? I mean, how heavy was that?"

Skip was literally squirming. He was unable to look at the man's face and his mouth spasmed between a scowl and a death-mask rictus. Laurie was so embarrassed for the stranger's sake that she would have stepped in had it not been for the immense quantity of Skip's attitude that she'd swallowed over the last six months. The moment stretched agonizingly until Skip finally managed to say, "Uh, yeah. Yeah. Unbelievable." He looked at Laurie with utter desperation in his eyes.

She relented. "Listen, Skip, we've got that thing . . ."

"Oh, yeah, yeah," he said, leaping to his feet. He patted the guy awkwardly on the shoulder. "Take it easy, man."

"Okay," the guy said, holding up the signed album and smiling radiantly. "I will!"

They stopped by the dressing room for their guitars and Laurie nearly had to run to keep up with him as he shouldered his way to the street. Hands reached out to slap his back as he passed and he didn't seem to feel them. On the sidewalk he turned to Laurie and held out his keys. "Can you drive a four-speed?"

"Sure," she said, startled by the intimacy of the offer. Skip led her around the corner onto Wilcox, where they put their guitars side by side in the trunk of the Mustang. She got in and reached across to unlock the passenger door. Skip, hugging himself, was looking off into the distance and she had to knock on the window to get his attention. "Your place or mine?" she asked as he got in. "I can't believe I just said that."

"I don't care," Skip said.

She started the engine and then nearly killed it again as she pulled away from the curb, fighting the weight of the clutch. The brakes and the steering were both manual and she had a bad moment where she thought she'd have to let Skip take over. But Skip didn't seem to notice and within a block or two she found the hang of it. That left her free to worry about leaving the LBD overnight—though she had to admit, as attached as she was to the car, it was insured. Skip, on the other hand, was nursing the single most extreme and melodramatic mood she'd ever seen in him.

"Are you going to tell me what's going on?" she asked.

"I should never have done this."

"Let me drive, you mean?"

He glanced at her as if only a lunatic would dare to distract him with jokes, then his eyes dulled into a thousand-yard stare that she could see reflected in the passenger window. "The band," he said. "Playing in public. I should never have come out of the studio."

"All the guy wanted was a brush with greatness," Laurie said. "I don't see the life-or-death issue here."

"*What fucking greatness?*" he yelled. Laurie nearly put the Mustang into a street lamp. "Show me the fucking greatness," he said, in a more reasonable tone, then lit a cigarette and sucked the smoke deep in his lungs. "I live in a one-bedroom apartment in a crappy neighborhood, I haven't written a new song in twenty years, most of the people who've actually heard of me assume I'm dead, and the rest I owe money to. I don't have a single record in print, I haven't toured since Nixon was in the White House, and out of the eight million oldies stations in the world they're all playing the same hundred and fifty songs, and not one of them is mine."

It was an Everest of self-pity she'd never seen him scale before, and it left her with nothing of merit to say. After five minutes or so he went on, "I heard this guy on the radio the other day talking about how third grade was the best time of his life. And I thought, You pathetic schmuck, that is really sad. And then I started trying to figure out what the best time of my life was. And you know what?"

He waited for an answer until Laurie finally said, "What?"

"There wasn't one."

"Come on."

"It's the truth."

"What about *Tender Hours?*"

"It came out two weeks before Dylan's *Nashville Skyline. Nashville*

Skyline went to number one. *Tender Hours* peaked at number fifty-one. I
was twenty years old. I thought I was as good as Dylan. I thought
Nashville Skyline was shit. And all anybody could talk about was how brilliant and innovative Dylan was to rip off a bunch of tired old C&W licks
that those Nashville guys tossed out in their sleep. It was the 'new direction' everybody was looking for, despite the fact that the Byrds and
everybody else had already been there and back again. I got left in the
dirt."

"You're saying there was never any time in your life when you
thought, This is it, I'm happy, this is what it's all about?"

"In bed, maybe, for ten or fifteen minutes. The rest of the time I was
always living in the future or the past. Things would start to move for me
and I'd get into this adrenaline frenzy, I'd get so worked up I'd have to get
high to cool out. Getting your first record deal is such a rush, your head
is on fire with all these possibilities. Then the possibilities don't come true
and you pay for all that emotional energy you borrowed against your success, the success that didn't happen. Or didn't happen as big as you
needed, or as big as they promised."

His evil mood worked its way into her system like a contagion. If
Skip Shaw—Skip Shaw!—feels this way, what hope is there for me? Why
do any of us do this to ourselves?

He'd turned away again, looking out the window. He had both hands
against the glass, his long, thin fingers arched like spider legs, the cigarette
still burning between two of them. Then he pushed his face against the
glass like a five-year-old, and Laurie saw the driver of a car in the right-
hand lane double-take as he passed them.

When Skip finally tired of that he slumped down in his seat, eyes
level with the dashboard, and said, "Other than sex, I guess I was happiest
when I was shooting smack."

"You told me you never shot heroin."

"When did I say that?"

She knew perfectly well when he'd said it; he'd said it when she asked
him to use a condom. She was unwilling to bring that conversation up
again, and she wondered if he was taking that reluctance for granted. "I
asked you and you said no."

Skip shrugged. "Maybe you misunderstood. You ever try it?"

"No."

"Don't. Because if you like it, you'll spend the rest of your life think-ing about it. Knowing it'll kill you, one way or the other, and trying to decide if you care." Just talking about it, Laurie thought, seemed to cheer him up. "That's what really happened to the sixties, you know. It turned out that the only reliable way to get the peace and satori and oneness that everybody wanted was to shoot poison in your veins. Which you bought from criminals, and which you needed God's own worldly goods to pay for."

"Tell me what it would take," Laurie said. "What would it take to make you happy?"

He was quiet again for a while, then he said, "Sorry. I guess the time I could even process that question is long gone. It's like asking me what it would take to make me a fifteenth-century Chinese woman."

She shook her head. "All of this is because some guy wanted you to sign his album?"

"He wanted me to ride the mystery train again. He wanted me to be a star so bad that it made *me* want to be a star all over again. And I can't do it. I don't have the heart for it."

"So what exactly do you have the heart for?"

He looked at her and the whole naked moment sank into the LaBrea Tar Pit of the Skip Shaw persona. "You, baby." He smiled. "I got the heart for you."

You do tonight, Laurie thought. And tonight would do.

M Y S T E R Y   T R A I N

The next weekend they packed a box of CDs and all their equipment and drove all day to play San Francisco on Saturday and Berkeley on Sun-day. Skip insisted on following behind in his Mustang; Laurie, who was not in the mood for him, stayed with the others in the van. Lately it seemed to her that he was hugging the fine line between charm and bull-shit, between tortured genius and depressive loser, and small variations in her own body chemistry could make the crucial difference.

The band—minus Skip—did their first radio interview at Stanford's KZSU, an awkward affair punctuated by questions like, "Laurie, how did you convince Skip Shaw to come out of retirement and play with you?"

and "How many Skip Shaw classics are going to be in your set tonight?" When Laurie tried to get the DJ to cue up "Carry On" from the CD she'd brought, he said, "Whoa, is this the Tim Hardin 'Don't Make Promises'?" and played that instead.

After the Berkeley show they loaded out and got on the road for LA. Laurie arrived home at nine in the morning, showered, and made it in to work by ten-thirty.

When the phone rang after three it caught her nodding off in front of her terminal. It was Jim. "Did you not give Ardrey your work number?" he asked.

"No," she said. "Why?"

"He's been calling you at home all day and he finally gave up and called me instead."

Something in Jim's voice alerted her and she swallowed the cynical remark that had been sitting on the end of her tongue. Her heart, which had slowed after the initial shock of the ringing phone, began to race again. "Why?" she repeated. Her voice came out thin and reedy.

"Because," he said, "General Records wants to offer us a contract."

THE TOUR

THE FIRST TIME

Music magazines don't like first person. I hate the clunking contrivances they insist on instead: "this reporter" or "when asked about . . ."

I can't talk about *Of the Same Name* without talking about who I was when I first heard it, and who I am when I listen to it now. Life is not a hypothetical question, and when the tree falls in the forest it doesn't sound the same to the raccoon it falls on as it does to the logger who cut it down.

I first heard Laurie Moss on Stanford's KZSU in early August of 1995. I was driving into San Francisco on the Junipero Serra and "Neither Are We," with its jazzy-but-distorted chords and Laurie's hurt and weary vocals, simply blindsided me. I turned up the radio and tried to fix the details of the song in my mind, afraid the DJ wouldn't back-announce and this music would pass out of my life without my ever knowing what it was.

One reason it hit me so powerfully was the refrain—"My heart and my mind/They're not talking to each other/But then again/Neither are we." My wife Barbara and I were not, at that time, talking to each other. The only thing holding us together was Tom, then three years old and starting to spend mornings in day care.

After Tom, the thing that most defined the marriage for me was the fact that Barb was chair of the Department of Psychiatric Medicine at Stanford, pulling down a six-figure salary, and I was a writer and house-husband whose income ran to a couple of very significant figures less. Barb has sworn to me that she never once held that difference over my head. From where I stood, there was little that didn't remind me of it.

Barb has five siblings (her preferred term), all but one of whom are driving fast-track careers: Her oldest brother is a broker on Wall Street, her little sister is a hospital administrator in Houston. The one exception is her next-to-oldest brother, who dropped out of college, worked for two years in a used bookstore, then hanged himself. The not speaking comes from her side of the family—on any given day you need a score-card to know whether or not it's safe to pick up a ringing phone.

When Bobbi D'Angelo or Brad from the Duck talks about damaged people, they don't have to draw me a picture. Barb is on Prozac, with Ritalin to ease a tendency toward compulsive behavior and Xanax to smooth out the peaks. The easy answer is to say that her father, an obses-sive small-town real-estate czar, pushed all of his children relentlessly toward success, and I've used that answer more than once. Another is to say that her genes have prepared her to function perfectly in some kind of bizarre high-stress environment that doesn't happen to exist in the real world just now.

Barb's first reaction to anything is anger, shading occasionally to rage. Mine, though we're not talking about me at the moment, is to feel sorry for myself, and it turns out the two don't mix well. Before Tom was born we swore we would never fight in front of him, and of all the betrayals and broken promises, I hate that one the most.

I ended up calling KZSU to ask about the song, and they told me it was self-released and that Laurie had left the CD at the station when the band had been through town the week before. I finally tracked down a copy at Neurotic Records in the city and didn't take it out of my stereo for a month.

I won't pretend that it was the music alone. There's a special feeling of possession that comes from discovering a brand-new artist on your own, a bond you just can't form with an established act in the top ten. The CD folder included photos of the band and I spent much too long studying Laurie's picture for the signs and portents she always talks about. I liked the obvious intelligence in her eyes and the challenge in the angle of her head, but it was her mouth that fascinated me: sensual lips that were amused and vulnerable at the same time. I read life histories, entire worlds into that mouth. I was prickly from lack of physical affection, I was worried about a career that was subsiding without ever having reached a peak, and I was at least two-thirds in love with Laurie Moss.

G E N E R A L   R E C O R D S

Meanwhile Laurie was preparing herself for her first meeting with General Records, scheduled for Monday, August 14. Expectation management was an ongoing battle that she and Jim fought together over the phone.

"We're going to get there," Laurie said, "and they'll have never heard of Ardrey."

"No," Jim said, "Ardrey will be bigger there than we'd ever dreamed, only he won't have told anybody else about us. And he's going to get run over by a truck tonight."

"Too dramatic. This will all turn out to be a stunt that Ardrey pulled in hopes of rallying support for us at the label. We'll get in there and Ardrey's boss will have to apologize to us."

"No, no, they'll all know about us, only they won't be able to look us in the eyes. There'll be some smothered laughter. Then it will come out they're only hiring us to do backing tracks for a posthumous Liberace album."

A week before the meeting Jim told her that Skip would not be attending. "There's a small matter of an advance that Warner's paid him in the seventies. He never turned in an album and never gave them back the money. General goes through the Warner accounting department."

"What if they won't sign us without Skip?"

"I happen to know Melinda already told you about this. She told you General had offered you a solo contract and it was you who said it had to be for the whole band. Thank you, by the way."

"Did I say that?"

"Yes, you did. The point is, General only cares about you."

"But the contract is for the band."

"With a clause that says any of the original members, excepting you, can be replaced on terms acceptable to the remaining original members."

"I swear to you, if Skip screws this up . . ."

"I talked to him, and at least on this one I think he's right. There's a better chance of him screwing things up by being there than if he stays home."

"It also keeps him from being committed to anything."

"What difference does it make? Since there's going to be a virus in their computers that's going to wipe out any trace of our existence anyway?"

"You're right, of course," she admitted. "What was I thinking?"

They'd agreed to a forty-thousand-dollar advance—chump change by superstar standards, yet a lot of money compared to the independents. At least it seemed that way at first. Once Melinda's fifteen percent came off the top, and they repaid Grandpa Bill for what they'd already spent to press the CDs and tapes, and reimbursed Jim for his recording expenses, Laurie estimated she would make seventy-eight hundred. Out of that at least a thousand had to go toward her back rent and God knew how much she'd have to put into the LBD to get her long-overdue California plates and inspection sticker.

She bought a new outfit with her VISA card anyway.

"I only tried cocaine once," she wrote me in e-mail. "It was in high school, and I felt like I'd had way too much coffee and something great was just about to happen to me. As opposed to feeling cozy and sleepy, tucked into bed after something good has already happened, which is how I'd prefer to feel. At any rate, I felt the same way walking into the General Records offices as I did on cocaine."

General Records was scattered across one wing of the Warner's building in Burbank, a two-story, earth-toned, heavily landscaped island in a sea of concrete. They rode there together in Dennis's van and met Melinda in the parking lot.

"Did you talk to them about the album?" Laurie asked her. The band had decided they weren't ready to go back into the studio yet, and that they wanted General to release *Of the Same Name*.

"Not yet," Melinda said. "This could be a hard sell. I want to wait for the right time, which is almost certainly not today." She looked Laurie up and down. "'Kay?"

"I guess," Laurie said.

"Cheer up. This is a pack of cruel, heartless bastards who are guaranteed to be nice to you at least until you've signed the contract. Which also isn't going to happen today."

Once past the Warner's reception area it seemed to Laurie that there were twice as many people as the building had room for—those at the bottom of the food chain had their desks in hallways and closets and cul-de-sacs, with memos and artwork taped to virtually every inch of every wall. Laurie had expected steel and leather and glass and instead found wood, threadbare carpets, and chaos.

After a quick tour, the receptionist left them in a conference room where a magnum of champagne sat photogenically in a bucket of ice. At five places at the table sat black folders with the General Records logo stamped in gold. Laurie opened one of them and saw a thick sheaf of paper headed "Exclusive Recording Agreement." It ran to over forty pages, with subheads like "Engagement and Term" and "Lender's Master Delivery Obligations." She felt like a fairy-tale princess, about to sign away her firstborn for the privilege of having her straw spun into some-one else's gold.

Ardrey came in five minutes later to put the lie to at least half the scenarios she and Jim had agonized over. Jim looked at her and mouthed the word, "Unbelievable." Laurie giggled and Ardrey turned on her.

"What?" he said. If he was a little paranoid, Laurie thought, he was overall happier than she had ever seen him. She wondered how long it had been since he'd actually signed anyone. "Do I have toilet paper stuck to my shoe?"

"You're perfect," Laurie said. "We're glad you're here."

There were two men with him, one in his fifties and wearing a pin-striped gray suit, introduced by Ardrey as Ross Claybeck, a senior vice president at General. He had thick white hair, combed straight back from his forehead, and manicured fingernails. The other, a publicist named Dave Rosen, was young and dressed in a Lakers sweatshirt and a Dallas Cowboys cap.

Eventually they settled at the table. Claybeck adjusted his left cuff and said, "We don't have any special agenda today. This is just to feel each other out about what directions we might want to take, what we can do for each other, that kind of thing. Dave is looking for handles he can use to promote the group. I'm basically interested in getting to know you."

She imagined the band sprawled on Claybeck's tasteful living room furniture, feet propped on his glass-topped coffee table, drinking his im-ported beer, watching an Angels game on a big-screen TV that had ap-peared in the teak-paneled wall by remote control. No, she thought, you don't want to know us.

"There's copies of our standard contract for each of you," Claybeck went on, "so you can take them home and look them over, and we can answer the hard questions next time."

Melinda said, "I've already looked, and this is the same boilerplate I've seen before. You already know what I think of it." Claybeck opened his mouth and Melinda waved the entire topic away. "We'll go over all that later."

"Of course," he said, and Laurie felt herself losing her grip on consequence. She'd worked for ten years to get into this room, and now the whole thing—General Records, the contract, the very idea of a music *business*—suddenly seemed irrelevant and unreal to her. Irreal.

"Now, I understand you just put out an album yourselves. What kind of backlog of material do you have? How soon would you be ready to go into the studio again?"

"Well," Laurie said. She looked at Melinda, who raised one shoulder in the slightest of shrugs. "I don't understand why you guys can't release the record we just made."

Claybeck smiled at her like she was slightly retarded. "Well, for one thing, the difference in sound quality between a garage recording and the work of a professional studio is enormous."

"With all due respect," Jim said, "it *was* recorded at a professional studio." Echoing Melinda, he held up his right hand. "We could argue about it, which is not what I meant to do, or we could listen to the CD together. If there's anything on there that's not up to General's sonic standards, you can tell me."

"This is very unusual," Claybeck said.

"Not really," Melinda said. "It's getting to be pretty common practice in the rest of the non-General universe."

"It's not our practice to release home demo tapes," Claybeck said.

"It's not a demo," Laurie said. "It's a fully finished album. It's the reason you signed us in the first place." She wondered masochistically if Claybeck could name a single song from the record. Fighting to hang on to her good mood, she looked at Ardrey, who reluctantly cleared his throat.

"She's got a point, Ross. It's not like we still had our own studios and producers and all that. They've got a finished album that's already paid for, which means that much less to recoup. There's a good business case for it."

Claybeck shifted only his eyes in Ardrey's direction while the rest of his body remained rigid. He did not convey warmth. Laurie realized that Claybeck was simply too old for this business, that he was tired of younger dogs nipping at him. She also saw that his accumulated money and power would let him take the company down with him if he chose.

Claybeck changed the subject, conceding the point without having to agree to it. Eventually Dave Rosen opened the champagne and they all stood up for a toast, and then everyone was moving around the room and clumping into individual conversations.

Laurie turned and almost ran into Ardrey. "Thanks," she said. "For sticking up for us."

"Hey," he said. "I know what people say about me behind my back. They say old Ardrey's on the way out, old Ardrey's got no clout, old Ardrey's never on to anything till it's over. But who came through for you?"

"You did, Mark." She couldn't help flinching.

"Look," he said, "you guys earned this contract, it's not like it was a favor I did you. I don't expect you to fall in love with me for it. But is there some reason you couldn't at least *like* me a little?"

"Think about it," she said. "Would you have said what you just did, about me falling in love with you, if I was a guy?"

"Maybe," Ardrey said, grinning. "You never know what I might say. You think you know me, and you don't know me at all."

If he'd said it with Skip's dramatic self-pity she would probably have walked away. Instead she offered him a raised eyebrow.

"I've got kind of a goofy history," he said. "I try not to make a big deal about it, about the way I dress and everything, but people always think I'm weird anyway. See, my parents are Friends."

She pretended to misunderstand as a way of keeping her distance. "That's more than I can say. Mine can't stand each other."

"As in Society of. You know, Quakers? They founded Whittier, where your band practices. Named for John Greenleaf Whittier, the Quaker poet?"

"Okay," Laurie said. "So you guys are against war and everything, right?"

"First of all, I'm not a Quaker. I grew up with them, and some of it rubbed off. I like plain clothes, I don't like violence. Which makes it a little hard to sign bands in LA, as you might imagine."

"I just seem to have this immunity to organized religion. Everyone around me can have it and I never seem to come down with it."

"Not to quibble again, but the Friends aren't organized. A lot of meetings don't even have anybody in charge. They believe in the 'inner light,' which I always kind of liked. I mean, there's a few gray areas, but most of the time it's not that hard to know what to do. Share what you've got. Don't have sex with children or rob people at gunpoint. Pick up after yourself." He gave her a sidelong look. "Admit it. You're warming to me."

"I'm thawing a bit. It's true."

Melinda and Claybeck appeared at Ardrey's side. "Where have you been?" Claybeck said to him. "Melinda is breaking my kneecaps, here. Help me."

"I'm on their side," Ardrey said. "Artists and repertoire. It's my job."

"I only want one more thing," Melinda said. "We need to put this band on the road, and I want some money to make that happen."

"Not out of the advance, I assume?"

"That would be correct. Now, Jim talked to a booking agent who thinks he can get them into some clubs in Arizona and New Mexico starting in three weeks. With any luck he can keep them on the road for at least six months after that. But not without tour support."

They'd talked about a tour in the abstract but these were the first dates Laurie had heard. Three weeks? Six months? It meant getting out of her lease, quitting her job, doing something with her car and the rest of her possessions. Could she handle six months on the road with Skip? Could she talk him into going in the first place?

"Which agent?" Ardrey asked.

Melinda wrinkled her nose in disgust. "Sid Modesto."

"Sid the Shark?" Ardrey said. "Well, he's got a few character problems, but if anybody can put a tour together that fast it's Sid."

"Character problems?" Melinda said. "The man is pond scum. But I don't have his contacts."

Claybeck said, "We can't possibly fit an album by a baby band into our schedule for six months, maybe longer. There's no point in touring before there's product. You don't want to go roaring up to the intersection just to sit and wait for the light to change."

"I'm betting you can get the record out in three months, maybe two," Melinda said.

"Either way," Laurie said, choosing to ignore for the moment that nobody had told her about the consultation with Sid the Shark, "we need the tour."

"Okay, okay." He looked at Melinda. "Call me tomorrow, we'll work something out." Then he turned to Laurie and held out his hand. "I believe we have a deal. You're a very impressive young lady. And quite a talent."

Laurie told herself he didn't mean to condescend. She took his hand and smiled bravely. "Thanks."

Then Claybeck was gone, with a magisterial wave, and Laurie said, "Three weeks?"

Melinda nodded. "Start packing."

PATRICE

Laurie signed the General Records contract on August 16, two days later, in Melinda's office in Venice. Dennis voiced concern because it was the anniversary of Elvis's death, but cooler heads prevailed. Gabe and Jim were also there; Skip and Ross Claybeck were not. Skip's signature, however, was already on the contract. Ardrey was there and Melinda took pictures of him with the band and the contract in the fond hope of getting one into *Billboard*.

With Ardrey was a Frenchman named Patrice who spoke almost no English. He was about fifty, with long gray hair combed behind his ears, blue double-knit pants, and a leather jacket. After the signing, the photo op, and the requisite champagne, Ardrey introduced him around. General had hired Patrice, Ardrey said, to direct their first video.

"Everybody's agreed to 'Angel Dust,' like you wanted, for the single," Ardrey said. Laurie had an involuntary pang of delight at the word "single." "Though I still like 'Don't Make Promises.'"

"But we settled that, correct?" Laurie said. "Because it doesn't really represent the album? Being kind of old and folky and countryish and not written by Laurie Moss and having Skip singing on it?"

"Except for one thing. Chemistry. That song has chemistry to burn, as Wernher von Braun used to say. But that's okay. Poor old washed up Mark Ardrey doesn't get to pick the singles anymore."

"Spare me," Laurie said. "Patrice is going to shoot 'Angel Dust.'"

Ardrey opened a catalog from a Guggenheim exhibit of Patrice's black-and-white photos. They were mostly of street kids in early adolescence, grainy and full of desperation. Ardrey said, "We thought we'd turn him loose in Hollywood, let him shoot the kids here."

"You'd be doing their parents a favor," Laurie said. She plunged on past Ardrey's puzzled look to ask, "Didn't Soul Asylum already do this in 'Runaway Train'?"

"This is different," Ardrey said. "We're going to hire some of the kids, put them in the audience with you at a club, give it more of a story."

Jim was still looking at the pictures. "I like this," he said, pointing to a photo of a boy of thirteen or so crouched on a surfboard on a brick street in a French resort town. The boy, in baggy shorts and no shirt, had bent his legs as if riding a wave, the board upside down with the fins sticking up. Laurie could see the ocean behind him, and she could see the rich kid that he and his friends had taken the surfboard from, standing off to one side looking frightened and angry at the same time. The friends were laughing and clowning, and the kid had a cigarette burning in one corner of his mouth. The defining detail, however, was the expression on the face of the girl, also maybe thirteen, who had turned away and was now walking toward the camera, hurt and disgusted and lost, clearly sick of the kid and all his smart-ass friends.

"There's a whole movie here," Jim said.

Laurie looked at Patrice and pointed to the picture. "I like this too. It has a lot of heart."

Patrice tapped his right fist twice on his chest. "Thank you. I think the same about your song. I make you a video with a lot of heart, okay?"

"Okay," Laurie said.

Ardrey and Patrice left and Gabe said, "Hey, babeee. I make you the feeelthy vee-joe."

"Don't complain," Laurie said. "I just got you into pictures and you didn't even have to sleep with me."

Immediately she wished she hadn't said it. Gabe, Jim, and Dennis all looked embarrassed in declining order of intensity. Laurie sighed audibly. "Okay, now that I've so tactfully conjured the absent Skip, has anybody told him we're touring?"

"He's been informed," Melinda said.

"Do we know if he's coming?"

Melinda shrugged. "If we knew which side of the deck he was going to end up on, he wouldn't be a loose cannon, now, would he?"

Laurie sighed again, more quietly. "I'll handle it."

Jim said, "Maybe I should . . ."

"Nope," Laurie said. "Not this time."

CELEBRITY BOWLING

She got to Skip's apartment before eight. The sun was still up, the air cool and sweet, the way it was in Texas once a summer, the way it was in Hollywood almost every night. It finally hit her that she was about to leave LA. She sat on the curb and watched palm trees turn to silhouettes as the sun went down behind them.

Saturday would be her fourteen-month anniversary. It seemed like no time at all when she tried to conjure it as a single entity. When she thought about the moments, though, there seemed to be more of them than in the rest of her life put together. The way she'd always thought true love would be.

She heard the whisk of one denimed leg against another, and then Skip was sitting next to her. "You said eight o'clock," he said.

She nodded. "Here I am."

Skip was barefoot, in jeans and a white T-shirt. His hair was in his face and he hadn't shaved in a while. He combed through his hair with his fingers and lit a cigarette and the two of them sat and watched the deep, lacquered blue of the coming night.

"I'm going to miss this place," Laurie said.

"Everybody wonders why it's so crowded out here. Then they come out themselves and they don't want to leave either."

She let the peaceful moment stretch as long as she was able, and then she said, "You're not going to tour with us, are you?"

"Why do you say that?"

"I don't know. I guess I've been waiting for you to let me down ever since this whole thing started."

"Just don't forget who was the first to tell you I would do it." He took a deep drag and blew the smoke out his nose. "Melinda called me this afternoon."

He seemed to be waiting for a response. "Yes?" she said.

"Ardrey had just called her. Very apologetic. He'd fought and argued and done everything he could do."

"About what?"

"My share of the advance. Your pal Clay Dick's got a long memory and loves a grudge. He got the lawyers to dig up some fine print in my old Warner's contract that lets them keep anything I make off this record until that old advance is paid back. With interest."

"You're kidding."

"Kidding? I don't think so."

"Can't you fight them?"

"Sure. I could pay thousands of dollars I don't have to some shyster of my own to take on the entire legal department of Time-slash-Warner. What do you think my chances are?"

"I can't believe they'd do that."

"Believe it. This is still fairy-tale time for you. What you haven't seen yet is that the fairy godmother and the wicked witch are one and the same."

The temperature seemed to have dropped ten degrees with the sunset. Skip didn't seem to notice, though Laurie had to cross her arms to keep from shivering.

"So," Skip said. "Who told them I was in the band?"

"What do you mean, 'told them'? Ardrey's been following us for months. How could he not know?"

"There's a difference between being a sideman and getting a full cut as part of the band. Who put it in the contract that I was part of the band?"

"All I did was set it up so we'd all get an equal share. Now, wait a minute. Are you blaming *me* for—"

"Back when this whole thing started I made you promise me something. I made you promise that anything I did beyond playing—like having my name on the record, I specifically remember mentioning—had to be in my own way and in my own time. Remember?"

She did remember, and it was a cold, hard lump in her stomach. "Are you telling me you wanted me to cut you out of the money?"

"I told you not to get me involved in any legal bullshit without asking me first. That seems pretty clear to me. As for the money, I'd have to ask you: What money? I'm sure as hell not going to see any of it now."

Despite her chill, Laurie could feel the sweat start under her arms. "This is ridiculous. You're just looking for somebody else to blame because you pissed away your own career. You're the one who took that advance and didn't deliver. You dug this grave with your own two hands."

Skip shrugged, stood up, dusted off the seat of his jeans, and started back toward the apartment building. He was halfway there when Laurie finally called after him. "Skip?"

He turned around without speaking. She stood up and tried to find something to do with her hands. "I'm sorry," she said. "I felt so goddamned noble, writing the contract that way. I didn't think . . ."

He nodded once, very slightly.

"I have to know," she said. "If you're not coming on the tour, I have to find somebody else."

He let her twist for a few seconds and then he said, "Here's the deal. Take it or leave it." He started counting off with his left little finger. "First, if I come, I'm not sleeping on somebody's floor. I'm not going to have some fool kid's parents come home and throw me out in the middle of the night. Either we do Motel 6 or we get a bus we can sleep on. Two. I bring my own car. I'm too old to have to ask somebody for the keys to the van if I want to go drive around by myself. Three. As long as I make the sound checks and the gigs, the rest of my time is my own. I don't have to do interviews or radio jingles or celebrity bowling."

Three seemed to be it. She hadn't heard anything she couldn't live with. "Does this mean you'll do it?"

"I got no choice," he said. "I need the per diem."

Guilt tortured her all the way home. She felt unclean and went straight to the shower, scrubbing herself to a bright red glow. By the time she got out, she'd calmed down enough to call Melinda at home. "When

Skip signed the contract, did he say anything? Like wanting to be left out
of it or anything?"

"No. He just asked what I thought his share might come to. Why?"

"Nothing," she said. "Just Skip."

The relief was only temporary. She lay awake half the night hearing
"Don't Make Promises" over and over again in her head.

S T R U G G L I N G

Even before Laurie's signing I'd tried to pitch an interview to the usual
editors. I'd done an Internet search on her name that turned up nothing
beyond outdated club listings and I wanted to know more.

"What's your angle?"

"I don't know," I admitted. "I haven't talked to her yet."

"What do you know about her?"

"She made a great record. You should hear it."

"The cutout bins are full of great records. Call me when you've got a
story."

Such is the sensitive world of rock journalism. In the end I decided
they might be right: I'd built an obsession out of a few songs, a photo-
graph, and the sudden hole in my life that came from Tom being in day
care.

Day care was Tom's decision, not mine. It constantly amazed me how
he'd come with parts of his personality fully formed. He'd been fascinated by animals, for instance, since his eyes had first learned to focus. I
used to take him to the park in his plastic carrier when he was only a few
months old, and as he sat beside me on the park bench he would reach
out to dogs and squirrels with a kind of desperate yearning that he never
showed toward humans. By the time he was three it was easy for his
friends to lure him into preschool and away from his old man with siren
songs of stuffed toys and the teacher's pet kitty.

It left my mornings free to write again, though the writing itself
wasn't going well. I'd spent most of a month working on a piece on
comics for *Spin* that, by the time two different editors were finished with
it, had lost its focus and was twice its assigned length. They'd put it out of

its misery and I'd had to settle for a kill fee instead of publication and the money I'd contracted for.

Then there was the book proposal I'd had going around for a couple of years. It was called *Struggling,* and it was about musicians who'd had minor hits over the years without ever getting beyond cult status, people like Gary Myrick and Dwight Twilley and Marti Jones, who'd been from label to label doing brilliant, deeply personal work, and were still playing the same clubs they'd always played, when they could afford to tour at all.

I tried to explain to one editor how the second half of most rock books was deadly dull. "It's like Tolstoy said in *Anna Karenina*—all successful bands are the same. The drugs, the writer's blocks, the concert riders for no brown M&Ms, the inevitable breakup."

"Tolstoy said that?"

"This, on the other hand, is just the good parts. The first guitar, the first gig, the first single on the radio."

"You're not getting it," he told me. "The bigger the act, the more books you sell. These people, they got no coattails your book can ride on."

I was a few months away from my fortieth birthday, a bad time to have to ask one of the all-time hard questions: What's your second choice for what you want to do with your life?

SHOOT

The band was shooting the "Angel Dust" video the day after *Billboard* came out. To Laurie's amazement Skip drove up as they were carrying the equipment into the Whiskey at seven in the morning. "I never did a video before," he said, and that was nearly the last thing he said all day.

The shoot introduced her to a level of tedium she could never have imagined. They went into makeup at eight and at ten Patrice started shooting master footage. They played along with the CD eight or ten times under blinding lights, then Patrice said, "I want some pictures of the guitar player singing?" Though Laurie tried to explain that Skip didn't sing on "Angel Dust," in the end it was easier to play "Don't Make Promises" a couple of times to shut him up. Afterward came three hours of close-ups, no more than a few seconds of the song at a time, until Laurie prayed the single would tank so that she would never have to sing it again.

At four o'clock Patrice brought the kids in, and the band began playing the song all over again. At one point a carefully rehearsed moment happened in the audience that brought handheld cameras swarming in on it. Patrice's attempts to explain were incomprehensible and Laurie was too tired to care. Finally, at six, it was time for the Whiskey to start sound checks for the night's real bands. Patrice and his crew disappeared down Sunset on the trail of the extras, leaving the band to load out by themselves.

As they sat on the sidewalk afterward, too exhausted to move, Gabe said, "This would be a good time to talk about getting a roadie for the tour."

"Okay," Laurie said.

"We know somebody," Jim said. "His name's Chuck Ford."

"I've done tours with him before," Gabe said. "He can run sound and lights and he can do guitar tech stuff. And he's very calm. He'll work for an equal share."

"Okay."

"We need him," Jim said.

"Okay," Laurie said. "But I have to meet him."

Gabe said, "He doesn't have Big Hair, if that's what you're worried about."

Laurie closed her eyes and leaned her head against the outside wall of the Whiskey. "This could be a long tour."

LAST WEEK

On Wednesday Patrice decided he had to film a rehearsal. He'd come up with some ideas, Ardrey said, and needed a little more footage. To no one's surprise it took the entire evening.

Thursday night another photographer came to Jim's for pub shots. She was tall, about forty, with fluorescent red hair. Skip, to no one's surprise, failed to show. The rest of them posed with and without instruments, individually and in all their possible permutations and combinations. Laurie was relieved at not having to take her clothes off. "But then that's only because we're not shooting a cover for *Rolling Stone,*" the photographer said.

Skip also failed to show for a round of interviews on Friday. His absence, Laurie was fairly sure, had cost them getting "Angel Dust" on *CMJ New Music Monthly*'s CD, since their interviewer had brought a copy of *One More Lie* to get it autographed.

Chuck Ford came to rehearsal on Sunday. He was six feet tall, forty years old, with graying hair and beard. He had glasses and an easy smile and the voice of a late-night DJ. He shook Laurie's hand and said, "I love your record."

"Great opening line," Laurie said, and listened with amazement as he fiddled with the mixing console and in the space of five minutes cleaned up and sweetened the band's sound. When he was done he sat on the battered sofa with a stillness that Laurie envied. At the end of the set she turned to Gabe. "If he can lift an amp," she said, "hire him."

Monday the 28th began her last full week in LA. She'd given notice at work and left word on Summer's answering machine. She'd told her mother, who, for the first time in Laurie's memory, accused her of being stupid. "You finally get a real job and you don't even try to keep it. I don't know what's going to become of you."

On the other hand, her landlady had seemed pleased. "You'll lose your deposit, of course, but I won't file a bad credit report. This place was more than you could afford, that's all. And now I can rent it to some out-of-town screenwriter for an extra two or three hundred a month and not feel guilty about it." She sighed. "On tour. The very words sound exciting, don't they?"

"I don't know," Laurie said. "Ask me again in six months."

She had only one thing left to do, and that was to say goodbye to the LBD. Even with the small fortune it had cost her in repairs, the mornings it had refused to start, the stale dusty smell it had developed, the shimmy that started at exactly fifty-two miles an hour, it was harder than she ever would have imagined to let it go. It had taken her away from Jack and brought her to her first band practice. She'd watched fireworks drip from the Disneyland skies inside it, listened to the band's first demo in its cassette deck, and slept on its cracked vinyl seats more than once. It had given her freedom in a world of struggle and uncertainty, and she would be inexpressibly diminished without it.

She called the *Times* Monday afternoon and placed the ad. The following Saturday evening she sold it for nine hundred dollars cash to a seventeen-year-old boy and his father, and cried as she watched it drive away.

On Tuesday night, September 5th, she finished cleaning her apartment by nine o'clock. She carried two boxes out to the curb that held everything she intended to leave in Jim's attic, and two suitcases that held everything she meant to bring in the van. She locked the door, put the key in the mailbox, and sat on the porch to wait for Jim to pick her up and take her to his house for the night.

The perks of success, she thought. Three weeks ago I signed a record contract with a major label and tonight I'm homeless. She was too excited to cry, too terrified to be happy, too amazed at what she'd done to consider hedging her bets.

She saw Jim's headlights climbing the hill and went out to meet him.

L'ENVOI

Wednesday morning Dennis pulled into Jim's driveway with an eight-foot former U-Haul trailer hitched to his bumper, now painted a peculiar shade of lavender through which Laurie could see jets and lettering touting the Air Force Academy in Colorado Springs. Chuck Ford was riding shotgun, and as soon as he'd said hello he started loading equipment. For her part, Laurie had been up since seven, sitting in the death-camp atmosphere of Jim and Molly's kitchen. Sam had gone off to day care in tears and Jim and Molly had been sitting in despondent, red-eyed silence ever since.

As Chuck closed and padlocked the trailer, Skip pulled up to the curb with Gabe in the passenger seat. He sat idling while Dennis went out to the street to talk to him. Jim went into the house to say goodbye and came out with his glasses in his hand, wiping at his eyes with his shirtsleeve.

"We ready?" Dennis said, walking toward the van.

Gabe showed no inclination to offer up his seat, and so Laurie's fantasy of a romantic ride through the desert with Skip, whom she hadn't seen except at rehearsal since his blowup about the contract, withered on the vine.

"Ready when you are," she said. Jim's pain was not her pain, she told herself, and neither was Skip's. Nothing lay ahead of her but six months of hanging out with her friends and playing music. First stop Tempe, Arizona, for interviews and an in-store promotion during the day Thursday, followed by second slot on the bill Thursday night. She couldn't repress a smile as she got in the back seat with Chuck, and she looked at her watch to fix the time: 11:08 A.M., Wednesday, September 6th. So it begins.

THE ROAD

Near Indio Dennis pulled into a truck stop the size of a small city, complete with bunks, showers, restaurant, gift shop, pay phones with seats, pornographic video rental, and all the diesel you could pump. Skip waited for them under an awning, having sprinted away and left them within a mile of getting on the freeway in Whittier.

"You want to change vehicles?" Skip asked her as she stood in line to pay for her Coke and powdered sugar donuts.

In fact she did. Jim's taste in music ran to Kansas and Alan Parsons; Dennis had Kiss, Judas Priest, and various guitar instrumentals from Dick Dale to Pell Mell; and Chuck, well, Chuck didn't own any tapes. "To tell you the truth," Chuck had apologized, "I don't own much of anything at all." That was the point where she realized just how little she knew about the people she was going to spend her next six months with, most of that time in a space smaller than a jail cell.

"Do you think people would talk?" she said.

"It's their talk I'm trying to avoid. Gabe spent the whole drive out here telling me I ought to be nicer to you."

"Did you agree?"

"Hell, you know I never listen to advice." The road seemed to suit him. He was wearing a blue work shirt and black jeans, and his hair looked clean and windblown. The dry desert wind had brought out crinkles around his eyes and mouth, where a smile rested comfortably.

"Let's risk it," she said.

Once they were moving, the thunder of the V8 engine and the roar of the air conditioner made it easy enough not to talk. Twice Skip switched on the AM radio, twisted quickly through the dial, and turned it off again.

His guitar and amp took up the back seat. The longer Laurie looked at them the more fragile seemed his connection to the rest of the band, until she finally said, "Skip? If your heart's not in this, you don't have to go through with it."

He'd been quiet so long he had to clear his throat before he could speak. "Darlin', when you say shit like that it just makes me feel old."

"I'm serious."

"Of course you are. Your heart's in everything you do, and I don't expect you could imagine a life where you didn't feel that way."

"Are you patronizing me?"

"No, I promise I'm not. And I promise, the instant I don't want to do this anymore, I'll let you know."

That afternoon he didn't seem world-weary and self-pitying as much as isolated and abandoned, the calf separated from the herd that keeps blundering on, head down, in the wrong direction. She wondered if it would be possible to seduce him as they drove, convince him to pull over and take her out into the desert with a blanket and a canteen. Some sixth sense warned her not to try.

When they got to Tempe, Skip took one of the two room keys and shut himself up with his guitar and amp. Laurie stood in front of the closed door for nearly a minute, then walked three doors down to let herself into the second room and throw her suitcase at the bed.

"On tour for seven hours," she said to the walls, "and already set to wreck my first motel room." Then, as if the walls had actually heard, she said, "Just kidding. I promise I won't wreck you."

She stretched out on one of the beds to take her emotional temperature. She seemed a few degrees low: annoyed and hurt by Skip, tired from the drive, restless at the thought of another full day ahead of them before they got to play. She dozed off before she could work up a proper snit.

She woke to Dennis pounding on the door and yelling, "Let's eat!" All six of them crowded into the van and spent an hour in futile search of the Ching Hai Vegetarian House, which Gabe remembered from a previous tour. They finally ended up at a hole-in-the-wall Mexican place where the food tasted like Patio TV dinners, then went to check out the club.

Whoever named it the Egypt Club had a vivid imagination that let them see beyond the cinder-block cube on an orange dirt lot dotted with low-to-the-ground weeds. Chuck bent over one of the weeds to pluck an off-white, double-pronged thorn which he showed to Laurie. "They call 'em bullheads," he said, and in fact it did resemble a miniature cow skull. "Careful. There's poison on the tips that makes them really sting."

"How did you know that?"

"Pop was in the Air Force. We moved a lot. What I most remember about this area is that I could never ride my bike. I couldn't make it down the block without one of these bad boys taking out a tire."

At the door Jim attempted to explain to the manager that they were Laurie Moss.

"You're tomorrow," he said. He was thin, irritable, at least forty.

"We just wanted to look around," Jim said.

"Cover's three dollars."

Laurie paid. The walls inside were black, the floor pale linoleum, the stage a small triangle in one corner. "Well," Laurie said, "the stage is sort of shaped like a pyramid."

"That must be it," Gabe agreed.

They took over one of the room's two tables. There were four other people in the room; Laurie didn't know if they worked there or had paid to get in. It's okay, she tried to tell herself. We start small and work our way up. The first band took the stage and started an odd, fast, country-tinged song in the tradition of local heroes the Meat Puppets. Skip quietly slid his chair back and went out the front door.

Gabe and Jim looked at her with alarm when she got up too. "I just want to see what's going on," she said.

Skip was just hanging up a pay phone under a streetlight next to the highway. "Hey," she said. "What's the deal?"

"Calling a cab. Going back to the room."

"Were you going to tell anybody?"

"I didn't want a discussion. And I don't answer to anybody, remember? As long as I make the sound checks and the gigs. Or have you forgotten that already?"

"What got into you all of a sudden?" Though, truth to tell, she didn't remember him saying a word since they'd left the motel.

"I'm pissed at myself for not bringing my own car."

"Why'd you come with us if you didn't want to be here?"

"I thought I did. I thought it might be fun, all of us out together. It just turned out that I don't have it in me tonight to listen to one more aspiring band."

"Fine," she said, suddenly tired of him. "Suit yourself." As she walked away she listened for her name, for an apology, for an invitation to his motel room. All she heard was the groan of an eighteen-wheeler on the highway as it climbed painfully up through its gears.

B L U E

The next morning at eleven she showed up at a local AM station with Gabe and Jim. The station, as it turned out, had a show devoted to new music that only ran on Fridays and Saturdays. Their interview would run for the first time while they were in Flagstaff and again while they were in Durango, Colorado.

At the record store they set up in the parking lot: no Skip, stripped-down drum kit, vocal mikes run through their amps. They played five songs, plugged the gig four times, sold two CDs to people in the audience, and a third to the store to put in inventory.

They'd barely loaded in the equipment at the Egypt Club when the trouble started.

"Just so we're clear," the manager said. "We charge three bucks at the door, first hundred goes to the sound guy, the rest gets split between the bands."

Jim straightened up from where he'd been duct-taping his volume pedal to the floor. "We drove out here from LA to do this. We've got a guarantee of two hundred."

"You got a contract?"

"Right there," Jim said, pointing to the briefcase next to the bass drum.

The manager raised his eyebrows, as if to say, Who knows what the future has in store? Gabe looked at Skip and said, very quietly, "Trouble."

Skip nodded.

They'd never been cheated in LA, but Laurie suddenly realized that both Melinda and Sid the Shark were four hundred miles away. She could see from the stiff, ritualized way the men moved that hormones were pumping: Male Pattern Boldness, she'd called it once. "Maybe we should just pack up and go?" she asked.

"He didn't say he wasn't going to pay," Jim said. "If we play, he's legally obligated to do it." He studied her face and said, "Don't worry. It's going to be okay."

The opener was a predictable three-chord three-piece, crisp and well rehearsed. When Laurie took the stage at eleven there were less than a dozen people in the club. She said goodbye to the idea that the place would miraculously fill up and obviate any problem about money.

"Hey there, Tempe," she said. "I'm Laurie Moss and these are the Mossmen and this is a song called 'Carry On.'" They'd changed the set list at dinner, losing the Motown and Marley and putting in everything loud and fast they could think of. "Carry On" was as loud and fast as they got, and when they finished Laurie was sure she could hear crickets outside.

They soldiered on. Halfway through the set they lost the end of "Fool's Cap" in the roar of motorcycles. Five large male bikers and one substantial female came in and stood by the bar while the band played "Angel Dust." Afterward the biggest of them came up to Laurie and said, "Do you guys know 'Born to Be Wild'?"

"Sorry," she said. She was on the stage and he was on the floor and he was still taller than she was. "I don't think—"

Jim said, "Laurie?"

"One second," she said to the biker, and leaned over the keyboard.

"The rest of us know it," Jim said quietly. "If you'll just trust me on this, I suggest we play it."

She turned back to the biker. "It would be our pleasure," she told him.

Skip sang lead. Laurie managed harmony on the choruses and all in all it was credible for a first attempt. What Laurie was not prepared for was the sight of a single tear rolling unashamedly down the big biker's cheek. Another lesson, she thought, about prejudices musical and otherwise.

After the set, when her guitar was in its case and Chuck was winding cords into tidy bundles, she looked up to see the big biker standing over her again. "You guys are real good," he said. "Can I buy you a beer?"

"Make it a lemonade and it's a deal," she said.

The big guy's name turned out to be Blue. She didn't get any of the other names because the majority of her attention hung on Jim and Chuck at the bar.

"Sorry, fellas," the manager was telling them, "but I can't do it. You can see the turnout we got tonight. If you want to wait around till after we close maybe things'll pick up and I can do something for you, but as it is I'll be lucky to pay the sound guy. I can give you a few beers for your trouble."

Jim slammed his briefcase on the bar and hauled out the contract, settling in for the long argument. Chuck walked to the stage and picked up Laurie's mike. "I know y'all are looking forward to the next band," he said, an easy smile just visible behind his beard, his voice calm and intimate. "And we'd like nothing better than to pack up and get on our way, if we didn't have this slight problem. We had a contract to play here tonight, but the manager's decided not to pay us. So we'll just have to sit here until he either changes his mind or somebody calls the cops to sort the whole thing out."

"Is that true?" Blue asked Laurie.

"Sadly, yes," she said.

"You wait right here," he said.

The manager put his right hand under the bar as Blue walked up. Laurie would have called out to stop him if her voice hadn't failed her. Blue's friends saw the hand move as well and they all stood up and fanned out around the room. Whatever Blue said, he said it very quietly, and after a few long seconds the manager's right hand came up empty, opened the register, and began pulling out damp, crumpled bills. He held the money out and Jim took it, his hands shaking so badly he had to use both of them.

Blue said something to Jim and Jim nodded and tried to count the money. Finally Blue gently took it away from him, counted it, and handed it back. "It's all there," he said to his friends.

After the van was loaded Laurie got a copy of the CD and wrote, "For Blue—Thanks for a night I'll never forget," on the booklet, and signed it with Xs and Os. Blue laughed when she gave it to him and said, "Maybe see you again some time."

"Not in this dump you won't," she said, and he was still laughing when she walked away.

Outside she found the van gone and Skip standing next to his Mustang, Lucky Strike in hand, hair blowing in the diesel wind from the highway, grinning.

Now it was Laurie that shook, shivers not just in her hands but all over. Six more months of this? she thought. Playing to empty rooms and risking her life to get paid? She hugged herself and stared at Skip. "What's so funny? Did you get a big charge out of that scene in there? Did it give you a thrill to see that asshole back down?"

"Nah. I wasn't even thinking about that. I was thinking that tonight was the first time, in all the months we've been together, that nobody knew who the fuck I was. Or cared." He took a final drag on the cigarette and flipped it away. "I was into it."

THE FISHBOWL

Flagstaff was better, fifty people in the audience and a young guy running the club who loved the band and wanted them back. Durango was rowdy on Saturday night, and Sunday they got to sleep in. Monday was Albuquerque's Fabulous Dingo Bar, Tuesday was Santa Fe, Wednesday Roswell and all the UFO souvenirs they could possibly want. On Thursday they had a day off and went to Carlsbad Caverns.

After that first week on the road she knew each of them in ways she'd never known anyone except Jack, her mother, and her brother: bathroom habits and personal hygiene, secret abilities (Jim's card tricks, Gabe's yodeling) and sleep patterns (Dennis's awe-inspiring ability to fall asleep literally anywhere, and stay asleep twelve to fourteen hours at a stretch, muttering quietly the entire time), vices (Laurie's stuffed Tigger toy and her secret love of lemon cream pie) and virtues (Chuck's absolute inability to take offense).

They were circumscribed by their private jokes and imaginary characters: Ken S. Masmacho and Alfred Lord Tennis-Anyone; Mama Cass Sanders, doomed to sing the truth when no one would listen and then choke to death on a piece of her uncle's fried chicken; the ancient Chinese arts of Do Zing and Tu Ning; the Sirens of the Highway; Anno Dominos. They acquired nicknames: Dennis was "Sticks," Jim was "Ivory Joe," Skip was "Dingo" (which he clearly didn't like), Gabe was "Snark," Chuck was "Spud," and Laurie was "Crunch," a name she secretly liked so much she never wanted to be called anything else ever again.

They argued endlessly over each other's top ten album and movie lists, debated the significance of first concerts attended and first albums bought, then got into the serious business of Most Embarrassing Moment and First Sexual Experience—in Jim's case one and the same—finishing with the game that never grows old, Who Would You Kill With One Week to Live and Six Bullets?

En route to Durango, on the improbably named Highway 666 between Gallup and Shiprock, a sandstorm suddenly darkened the afternoon sky, swelling the sun to a dim orange ball. Towers of rock faded to silhouettes on the horizon while tumbleweeds came hurtling at them out of the darkness. Jim put a moody album called *Sunsets* on the tape player and they all sat in awed silence while waves of sand washed up against the windows.

In Carlsbad Melinda had sprung for a motel with a pool, so after getting up at six-thirty to be the first into the caves, they spent the afternoon lying in the sun, surrounded by screaming children. Skip and Dennis drank themselves into an early night, and Laurie got sunburned on the tops of her feet. The next morning, only minutes away from Texas, they turned north again to the Bluebird Theater in Denver, then on to Boulder; Bozeman, Montana; and Moscow, Idaho, home of the Karl Marx Pizza.

By the second week patterns had formed. Skip and Dennis anchored one room, Gabe and Laurie the other. Jim and Chuck alternated. Chuck always slept on the floor; one night in six each of the others slept on a rollaway.

In each new room, Gabe unpacked his travel alarm, his own pillow, a baseball-sized carving of a cross-legged man with his head and hands buried in his lap that Laurie called the "Navel Observatory," and a picture of L'Shondra in a plastic frame. Then he set up a Discman and his carrying case of Coltrane and Miles Davis CDs, and while he was waiting for his turn for the shower, or waiting to go to the gig, he would sit perfectly still under the headphones with his eyes closed.

Her twenty-seventh birthday fell on an off day, the Tuesday before the Moscow show. Laurie pretended to sleep late while Gabe and Chuck got up, stumbled in and out of the bathroom, and finally dressed and went out for breakfast. None of them had shown any sign of remembering that it was her birthday and she told herself it was better that way. The day seemed fraught with significance. Jim Morrison and Jimi Hendrix and Janis Joplin had all died at twenty-seven, and Laurie's major label debut was still at least two months away.

She called her mother and then Grandpa Bill, washed the homesick tears away, dressed in jeans and three layers of T-shirts and tank tops, and went down to the coffee shop across the street from the motel. There she found the entire band—except for Skip—sitting around a lemon cream pie loaded with candles, which they proceeded to light while singing a hideously out-of-tune "Happy Birthday."

Laurie was unsure if there was more to Skip's avoiding her than one of his moods, nor could she tell if anyone else was complicit in their separate sleeping arrangements. During that second week on the road she moved from wondering what she'd done wrong to a simmering anger. On the drive from Moscow to Eugene, Oregon, she commandeered the shotgun seat of the Mustang and asked for an explanation.

"We're in a fishbowl," Skip said. "There's no privacy."

"It could be had, if you wanted it," she said, and, after a pause, amazed at herself, "So could I."

Skip licked his lips nervously and glanced at her. She was sitting sideways in her bucket seat, legs tucked up under her.

"Goddamn," he said.

It turned out that in the back of his trunk, behind his suitcases and dirty clothes, Skip kept an old sleeping bag, allowing him to fulfill her blanket and canteen fantasies almost to the letter. They were an hour late getting in to Eugene, and when she climbed in the van to go to the club she was shocked at how guilty she felt, how far out of kilter the band's equilibrium suddenly seemed.

Phone Call from Olympia

I read about Laurie's signing in the August 21 *Billboard* and my heart
leaped. It was as if Laurie's good fortune held out hope for my own stag-
nant career. The story had no details and no photo, only a mention in
passing at the end of a paragraph where Claybeck talked about landing
Random Axe, a band he predicted would be "the next Green Day."

That mention was enough to give me the opening I needed. I went
back to my editors with a fresh pitch, and *Pulse* went for it. With that
commitment I talked to Ardrey and then Melinda and finally Laurie.

She called me collect from a pay phone at a Vietnamese restaurant
called Mini Saigon in Olympia, Washington, on September 23. It was still
early in the tour—when I go back to our taped conversation now I hear
only a trace of exhaustion behind the bravado and excitement in her voice.
Still, she sounded unsure when I told her how much I loved the album.

"I'm sorry," she said. "I've gotten a lot of enthusiasm from people
that I don't think have ever actually listened to the record. I don't know
who to believe at this point." When she paused I could hear the rain
pounding down outside the restaurant on the other end of the phone.
"I'm not supposed to say that, am I?"

"I won't quote you," I said. I told her about hearing "Neither Are
We" on KZSU and hunting down the album and that seemed to convince her. Then I got her started on Texas music and I remember a cynical side of me thinking at the time that I'd hooked her. We talked about
Sue Foley and Steve Earle and Townes Van Zandt and after that it was
easier for her to talk about herself, about where the songs had come from
and how they'd evolved in the studio, about how she liked being on the
road.

"We're getting so good," she told me, "it's scary. It's like that hand-
carved furniture where they didn't have to use any glue. Everything just
fits together and locks in place."

We'd used up one forty-five-minute side of tape when she had to go
to sound check. "Thank you," she said at the end. "I really liked talking
to you. When are you coming to see us?"

"As soon as I possibly can," I said.

"You do that," she said. "'Bye now."

THE VISITORS

From Olympia they had a little over two days to drive to Nashville. It meant driving in shifts, Laurie even piloting the Mustang for a six-hour stretch through Wyoming and Nebraska while Skip slept in the back of the van. They were into their third week on the road, an emotional no-man's land where jokes lost their punch, indigestion ran rampant, and there was not enough sleep to go around.

They hit West Nashville with enough time to spend five hours at their motel, during which Laurie dreamed of an endless highway unrolling before her. It hummed at exactly the same pitch as the air conditioner in the room. Then she and Jim and Gabe drove in the rain to Vanderbilt to spin the CD on WRVU, stopping en route to pick up two dozen Krispy Kreme donuts—even in a near coma she remembered the DJ in Flagstaff who'd complained through an entire interview about her failure to bring food.

By the time she got to sound check she was so exhausted she didn't notice that Skip was missing until they had all the gear on stage and were tuning their guitars.

"He was in the room when I went to sleep," Chuck said. "But his car was gone when I woke up."

"He'll show," Jim said. "He spent a couple of years here in the seventies. He knows his way around."

"Probably went to see some old girlfriend or something," Dennis said, then blushed purple. "Sorry."

They made it through sound check, and over dinner Jim tried to configure a set list that would work in Skip's absence. Laurie was barely listening. The headlights on the rain-streaked windows of Hardee's made her feel like the world was melting, and her with it.

Skip arrived at the club thirty minutes before they were to go on, carrying his amp and guitar. He dug a beer out of the plastic garbage can full of ice in the dressing room and took a long pull.

"You said sound checks and gigs," Laurie reminded him. "No dog and pony shows, but you promised me gigs *and* sound checks."

"Really? I said sound checks too?"

She saw then that he had been drinking for hours, that the alcohol had already reddened his eyes and subtly tilted his balance. "Forget it," she said. "Can you play?"

"What do you mean, can I play? Of course I can play." He took another drink and said, "You know I would never fuck up a gig."

"No," she said. "I don't know that one. How does it go?"

She left him there and went for a look at the house. The club had red carpeting and red velvet curtains along one wall—no windows, just curtains. It was too much red and it made her feel like a bull in an arena. It was then, when she least wanted or expected it, that she saw Mark Ardrey.

He was sitting in a red vinyl booth with three men, all of them in their forties, all in jeans and boots, all wearing various combinations of T-shirts, athletic jackets, ball caps, facial hair, and ponytails. She tried, too late, to fade into the shadows; Ardrey had spotted her and was waving her over.

The three were a producer, an A&R man, and a regional VP from General's Nashville offices. Laurie had trouble telling them apart.

"We love the record," one of them said, and another said, "I'm totally a fan." The third held up his clasped hands and grinned at her.

"Thank you," Laurie said. "This is kind of a surprise."

"Got to keep tabs on my future Grammy winners," Ardrey said. "Besides, I've got a surprise for you." He got a videocassette out of the briefcase at his feet and handed it to her.

"'Angel Dust?'"

"You got it."

"How does it look?"

"I expect an MTV Video Award at the very least. I'm completely serious. I don't want to brag or anything, since using Patrice was my idea, but this is easily the greatest video in the history of the form."

She nodded, holding the video with both hands, feeling awkward to be standing while they all sat in front of her, as if she'd been accused of something, and at the same time wanting desperately to be alone in a hotel room with the tape and a VCR.

"So," Ardrey said, "how's the road treating you?"

"It's good," she said. "We're getting really tight." She thought of Skip, drunk in the dressing room. "Really together, I mean. Wait till you see us." She made her excuses and went to tell the band.

Skip was the first to say anything. "Is Egan out there?"

She thought the VP had in fact been named Egan.

"Christ," Skip said. "Tone-deaf, brain-dead, corporate ass-kissing motherfucker. It's because of him that Clay Dick stole my advance."

"Well, that's a relief," Laurie said. "Here all this time I'd thought it was my fault." She was startled to discover what she was capable of saying when she was tired, and it made her afraid to get in front of a microphone. Nonetheless it was time. "Let's go," she said.

Skip wobbled momentarily on the steps up to the stage. Other than that, and his playing somewhat louder and more out of tune than usual, the booze didn't seem to affect him. The Vanderbilt kids, of which there were a pretty good number for a Tuesday night, didn't mind the roughness and, all in all, Laurie thought, it was not bad for the first night after a twenty-five-hundred-mile drive.

They were the final band of the evening, and the company table made enough noise to bring them back for an encore. Afterward Laurie sent Jim and Gabe to shmooze while she stayed behind to help Chuck pack. As they carried a load to the van Chuck said, "Um, I can sleep on the floor with Jim and Gabe and Dennis, no problem. If you and Skip need, you know, privacy or something."

"I appreciate the thought," Laurie told him, "but I have this feeling it won't be necessary."

It wasn't. Skip helped with the load-out one-handed, a beer always in the other, and once the trailer was full and padlocked he put an extra bottle in each side pocket of his leather jacket and started back out to the parking lot.

"You're not going to stick around?" Laurie asked, regretting the question as soon as it was out.

"The sound checks are unresolved, but even you admitted I don't have to do dog and pony shows."

"I won't be long. And if you wait I could drive you to the motel."

"I know we settled that one too. I don't have to answer to you or anybody about how I spend my free time. Or who I spend it with."

"This isn't about answering to anybody, this is about whether you're in any condition to drive."

"I'll tell you something. I've been driving drunk for longer than you've been alive, and there's a secret to it. Concentration. You can be as drunk as you want and do anything you want to. Drive, play guitar, screw, anything. You just have to focus on it and don't try to do anything else at the same time. If you're driving, don't try to light a cigarette. Playing guitar, don't try to dance."

It was as if, Laurie thought, he'd been trying to drown some nasty little scorpion creature inside him with all that alcohol, and it kept swimming up to the top. She saw there was no stopping him. "Be careful," she said.

"Why?" he asked, and walked away.

NOBODY'S ANGEL

She endured an hour or so with the industry types, despite her overwhelming desire to look at the video, despite Egan's constantly putting his hands on her, despite Ardrey's sulky complaints that she wasn't adequately happy to see him. Finally they got away, and in the van on the way to the Motel 6 in West Nashville she pulled the videotape out of her purse and told the others what it was.

They rented a VCR in a black plastic suitcase from the front desk and as they all walked to Dennis's room she scanned the parking lot in vain for Skip's Mustang. Gabe caught her looking but then wouldn't meet her eyes. I don't care where he is, Laurie told herself. It doesn't matter.

She sat on the floor in front of the TV while Jim set up the machine. The others sprawled across the beds, hitting each other with pillows and complaining about the lack of popcorn and candy, which led to an argument between Jim and Dennis on the correct spelling of Jujubes. "Shut up!" Laurie finally told them. "It's starting."

It was very grainy, and it went back and forth between color and black and white to no apparent purpose, something that had always annoyed Laurie disproportionately. It opened with footage of the rehearsal, followed by quick, extreme-angle shots of equipment sliding into the rear of the van, all intercut with street footage of a girl and three boys in their early to mid-teens. The girl wore a loose T-shirt and torn jeans and it disturbed Laurie to see Patrice set her up as an object of desire.

The video cut to Laurie starting the first verse in the passenger seat of the van, looking as tired as she must actually have been, because she didn't remember filming it.

Next came the shots of the band on stage, again looking haggard, alternating with scenes of the girl in the audience, being hit on by a sleazy businessman in a suit. During the bridge she goes berserk and attacks him, which, Laurie thought, finally explained the commotion in the audience during the shoot. For the coda the girl and her friends got thrown out of the Whiskey, and Patrice cut back and forth between the girl walking away, bloody but unbowed, and Laurie standing exhausted by the stage door of the Whiskey while on the sound track her voice sang, "Nobody's angel tonight . . . not Daddy's, not yours, not anybody's angel tonight." The very end was lost in the band's own wild applause.

After three times through she decided she liked it perhaps too much and retired to the other room to lie awake for another two hours, wondering, If I were MTV, what would I think? If I were a thirteen-year-old boy? If I were Newt Gingrich?

It was a feeling like rolling down the runway in a plane, the engines revving higher and higher, the wheels crying out to let go of the ground. Eventually she slept in spite of it.

FRAGILE ENTERPRISE

That was the high point of a week, from Nashville on Tuesday afternoon to Bloomington, Indiana, on Saturday night, that turned into an ordeal by fire. Breakage became epidemic, from guitar strings, to a bass drum head that had to mended with duct tape, to the air conditioner on the van.

Wednesday was Knoxville, a thin crowd, a surly manager, a drunken Skip who made threats in order to collect their pay and then disappeared. Laurie found her internal clock hopelessly scrambled and stepped out of her room at three A.M. to study the panorama of gas stations and fast food along the I-40 access road. Instead she saw Jim, who she thought was in her room asleep, at a pay phone at the end of the motel building, crying.

She waited for him to hang up and then she walked over to meet him. "Sorry," was the first thing out of his mouth.

"For what?"

"I didn't want to use the phone in the room because I didn't want you guys to see me . . ."

"Jim. What's the deal?"

"I miss Molly. I miss Sam. I miss the house. I miss mowing the yard, for God's sake. I miss Molly's stupid cat shoving me out of bed at night. I even miss four hours a day of printed circuit design." He dragged the back of one hand under his nose, which was leaking into his orange mustache. "I'm too old for this. My heart's not in it any more."

"Come on, you're not too old. Skip's doing it, and he's, what, three or four times older than all the rest of us put together."

"Have you looked at Skip recently? He's falling apart too. This whole fragile enterprise is crumbling all around us."

"Jim, do you want out? I don't want you to go, but I'm not going to hold you here against your will." The words took all her internal warmth with them as they left her mouth.

"I don't know," he said. "Can I sleep on it?"

"I hope so," she said. "It would be nice if one of us could sleep."

DINING CAR

Two nights later, in a theater called the Clifton Center in Louisville, the thing that had been incubating inside Skip began to peck its way free. It came late in the set when someone in the depths of the comfortably seated audience called out for one of Skip's songs, "Orchids for Your Smile."

The title conjured late nights from Laurie's childhood when she would find her father listening to the stereo as she stumbled back from the bathroom—the Beatles' *Rubber Soul,* Donovan's *Sunshine Superman,* and "Tender Hours" and "Orchids for Your Smile" by Skip Shaw—and sometimes she would lie down in the hall to listen and she would fall asleep there, waking up in her father's arms as he carried her to bed. "Go back to sleep, Little Rat," he would say as he tucked her in, because, like one of the rats that the Piper piped from Hamelin, she would follow music anywhere.

So the opening chords at first seemed like part of the memory, until she looked around and saw that the legendary Skip Shaw was actually playing one of his own songs, something she had never seen before. And he was doing it on stage, in front of her audience. Gabe, standing behind him, stared at Laurie for a clue to what he should do about it. More out of curiosity than anything else, Laurie started to play along, and the rest of the band fell in.

Skip stepped up the microphone. Instead of the restrained, conversational voice Laurie was used to hearing on "Promises," something higher and stronger emerged from the power center behind his navel, and for a second Laurie thought she was seeing double. Somehow the man with whom she'd been rehearsing in a garage, driving across the country, arguing, making, for God's sake, love, had never completely and inseparably been the same Skip Shaw on her father's stereo until that moment, and it was at that same precise moment that she knew, like she was remembering the future with perfect clarity, that they would never make love again.

His eyes were different too, red from drinking again, but also from emotion. He leaned into the microphone like he knew the whole crowd was there to see him and no one else, and when the lead part came he stepped out from behind the mike stand and stood on the very lip of the stage.

At the end of the song he said, "Anybody want to hear another one?" and the crowd, responding to his tone of voice, gave him enough encouragement that he started into "Dining Car," with the opening lines:

> Sitting alone at the bar
> In the first-class dining car
> On the train that runs from Third Street
> Straight to hell.

Wild applause came from the vicinity of the original request for "Orchids," and the rest of the band, excepting Laurie, began to play along. Skip himself looked like he'd blown a convenience store holdup and now, with nothing left to lose, meant to take everyone in the place down with him.

"Once on board," Skip sang, "you got to ride it to the end of the line." Laurie saw that the episode was not going to end well and put her guitar on its stand rather than shovel any more coal into Skip's boiler. She

walked behind Jim and said, away from his microphone, "This happen
often?"

"Not to me. Got any ideas?"

"I'll see what I can do," she said.

As Skip neared the end she picked up her guitar again, and came in
on top of Skip's last G7 with the A minor chord that opened "Carry
On." Over the applause, which was now more confused than enthusiastic,
she said, "Skip Shaw, everybody," and then, with more bitterness than she
intended, "the living legend, Skip Shaw." That made Skip turn and give
her a Look, which she ignored to plunge into the first verse:

> You there in the back of the room
> You haven't heard a word I've sung
> Right now my night is ending
> Yours has only begun.

In her peripheral vision she saw Skip stand for a second, disoriented,
then pop the strap off his guitar and yank out the cord. Laurie felt her
heart pound and she stumbled over the line she was singing, not from
fear as much as the sure knowledge that they had passed a point of no return, that unspoken agreements to look the other way, to live and let live,
to maintain pretenses, had all been rendered null and void.

She punched in the drive channel of her amp and attempted a lead,
wanting to draw the song out as long as she could because as soon as it
was over she was going to have to go outside and look for Skip and ask
him what the hell was going on.

But by the time they were through, Skip was gone and Laurie was
denied. "I'll kill him," she told Chuck. She was wired for destruction
with no target in sight.

"Calm down, Crunch," Chuck said. "Let *me* kill him. If we ever see
him again."

"We'll see him," she said. "He left his equipment."

BLOOMINGTON

By ten A.M., though, Skip still hadn't appeared, and they departed for Bloomington without him. An hour into the trip the van's air conditioner wheezed oily smoke and died, leaving them to swelter through ninety-five-degree late-September heat all the way to their in-store near the Indiana University campus. When they finally got to the club for sound check, they found Skip sitting on the hood of his Mustang near the front door, smoking a Lucky.

"I'll do this," Laurie told them. "Y'all go on inside."

She waited until they were alone before she approached him. He was wearing a long-sleeved black Western shirt and he had his arms folded across his chest. His hair looked like he hadn't washed it in days and the circles under his eyes were the dark green of old bruises.

"Sorry," he said. "It won't happen again."

"What, exactly, won't happen again?"

"That kind of showboat bullshit. If I'm going to do this it's as part of the band or not at all."

The right thing to do, she thought, would be to ask what was wrong, try to find the source of his all-too-obvious pain. The problem was she was still furious and scared and she was tired of having to break his emotional kneecaps every time she wanted an honest answer. "So that's it?" she said. "You're sorry, and we just go on?"

"You can yell at me if you want. I've got it coming. The only thing you can't say is that I didn't warn you."

"It's not worth it," she said, and went into the club.

Details and bad timing threatened to overwhelm her. Dennis left to take the van to the local Dodge dealership to get the A/C fixed. Skip followed and brought him back in the Mustang while the rest of the band did sound check. The van, it turned out, would have to stay overnight, and would be ready by noon the next day, Sunday. Neither Gabe's amp nor Dennis's bass drum case would fit in the Mustang, which meant the equipment would have to stay in the club overnight. The thought made Laurie's stomach crawl. Chuck offered to spend the night in the club, but the manager, a self-important law-school flunk-out in a hunter's green polo shirt and ironed khakis, insisted his insurance wouldn't permit it.

Inevitably, it didn't end there. Due to an "oversight" the manager hadn't printed any flyers, so they headlined for an audience of ten. Skip sulked in one corner of the postage-stamp stage, kicking at his cord, ending each song with an angry clank of his strings. When the manager tried to stiff them Skip grabbed a handful of his polo shirt and said, "Pay us what you owe us, you son of a bitch, or I'll throw you through a wall."

The manager emptied the register and Laurie agreed to settle for the eighty-seven dollars he found there. "Don't come back," he snarled, as he slammed the register drawer shut.

"We'll be back tomorrow," Laurie said, "for our stuff. Like we told you. Noon."

They left when the manager did, then had to ride to the motel in shifts. The next day the van wasn't ready until after one, and they didn't get to the club until one-thirty. The place was shut up tight, and when Jim tried to call from a pay phone across the street Laurie could hear the endless ringing through the padlocked back door.

"Fuck this," Skip said, and used a tire iron to pop the hasp that held the padlock. The door pried open as easily. It was only when Laurie saw her amp unharmed, and flipped the switches and saw the comforting ruby glow of its pilot light, that she realized how tense she'd been for the last fourteen hours.

As they finished loading out, Skip helped himself to two cases of Heineken and then propped the hasp back in place. Laurie, who'd been expecting sirens and bullets any minute, felt like Bonnie Parker, high on fear and defiance. Their eighty-seven dollars sat in a paper bag on the back seat of the Mustang. She had a powerful impulse to stitch her name on the wall of the club with a tommy gun. "Make for the state line, Sticks," she told Dennis as she climbed into the van, "and step on it."

R E D   D O T S

Skip was nothing worse than sullen and distant until the first Saturday in October, in Virginia Beach. He'd shown up for meals and sound checks, disappeared for hours at a time after every gig, and then reappeared, according to Dennis, sometime before dawn at the motel room. Laurie had begun to keep her guitar with her in the van, working on lead parts as they drove, pushing her fingers to learn years of technique in mere days.

They were second on the bill at a former Virginia Beach grocery store turned nightclub, a cavernous suburban space with a big parking lot and room for two thousand inside. By ten-thirty the place had filled halfway. The first band was quirky and professional, and Laurie hated to walk out on them, but she was due on stage in half an hour and she didn't know where Skip was. To her surprise she found the blue Mustang in the farthest corner of the parking lot, windows down, the familiar arm dangling out the window with a lit cigarette about to burn the knuckles.

The arm didn't move in the time it took her to walk over to the car and get in on the passenger side. She'd seen enough movies to fear finding him with a small hole in the center of his forehead, courtesy of the manager of the club in Bloomington. He didn't react when she shut the car door, and only the slow ripple of his faded yellow rugby shirt told her he was breathing.

"That cigarette's going to burn your hand."

"I just dropped it."

"So you're not asleep."

"Nope."

"Were you planning to come in anytime soon?"

"I was thinking about it. Thinking quite seriously."

"Do you want to talk?"

"About what?"

"About what the hell's wrong with you?"

He still hadn't moved. His eyes were still closed and his head still rested against the back of the seat. "Wrong?"

"You're drinking like a fish, your moods careen around from one minute to the next, you don't talk, we never know where you are . . . are you even listening?"

He brought up his right hand and started to rub one eyebrow. He kept rubbing it, slowly, sensually, and his stretched-out shirt cuff drooped halfway down his forearm. Laurie reached out with forced casualness and gently tugged it down farther. It took Skip a second to realize what she was doing and at that point he tried to pull his arm away. It was already too late. She'd seen three small red dots on the inside of his elbow, and the slight purplish bruise that encompassed all three.

It was like she'd grabbed bare electrical wires. She fell back in her seat, her mind, for one moment, wiped completely clean. Then she lurched forward to open the glove compartment and drag everything out and onto the floor: ragged maps, waterlogged matchbooks, receipts, envelopes, business cards. "Where is it?" she said.

"Oh, man. Don't get all weird on me. Don't spoil this."

"*Spoil* this?"

"I was flying, and now you're all in my face."

"In your face? In your *face?*" She kicked the door open and got out and slammed it after her. "In your goddamn *face?*" She couldn't seem to get on to her next line, whatever it was. Back in the dressing room she threw a beer bottle at the cheap brown paneled wall, where it failed to shatter.

"Laurie?" Gabe said.

"Skip's in the parking lot," she said. "He's been shooting up."

Jim said, "Are you sure?"

Dennis said, "Can he play?"

She wanted to start screaming at Dennis, so she answered Jim instead. "Yes, I'm sure."

"Oh my God."

"Is he conscious?" Chuck asked. "Was he talking?"

"Yes and yes," Laurie said. "Maybe we should call the cops and let him talk to *them.*"

"Maybe if he's done this before," Chuck said, "we should assume he knows what he's doing and leave him alone."

"Chuck," Laurie said, "that is the first truly stupid thing I've ever heard you say."

"I must have been overdue," he said, and shrugged. "But it beats turning him over to the cops. You want me to go talk to him?"

"And tell him what?"

"To stop," Chuck said, and was out the door before she realized that he meant it.

She followed as far as the parking lot, which had turned into a scene of its own, with kids standing around or sitting on their cars, drinking from cans and bottles in paper bags, sharing cigarettes and joints. She felt them stare at her, not because they recognized her, but because she was young and female and alone. She folded her arms across her breasts and leaned against one of the building's plate-glass windows, staring straight ahead and glancing at Gabe for no more than a second when he came out to stand next to her.

Chuck hunkered down by the driver's side door of the Mustang. From that distance Laurie couldn't see anyone's lips move. After what seemed like hours but her watch said was only five minutes, the car door opened and Skip got out. He stretched and looked around and ambled toward the front door of the club. He walked by Laurie without seeming to see her, flipping his car keys as he passed. Chuck, who was two steps behind, waited with Laurie while Skip went inside.

"So?" she said.

Chuck shrugged. "I don't know. He made it sound so good I agreed to try shooting up with him."

Laurie stared.

"Kidding," Chuck said. "Chrissakes, Crunch, you need to loosen up a little."

"Maybe another time. What did you talk about?"

"Are you sure you want to do this? You're on in ten minutes."

"Tell me."

"Okay, if you want my opinion, the guy's a junkie. Though he may go years without actually shooting up, he's still a junkie and always will be. Give him the right set of circumstances and he's going to use the shit. Maybe someday he'll age out of it, or die, or maybe he'll end up an old junkie. The one thing for sure is you're not going to do anything about it tonight, and until he's willing to admit there's a problem, you never will."

"We can all stand up and tell him that unless he quits, he's out of the band."

"So he's out of the band. Feeling betrayed, broke, and a long way from home. What's that going to do except let you wash your hands of him? Shit, I told you we shouldn't do this right before the show."

So they got up on stage and played, Skip included, though he wasn't very good. To be honest, Laurie told herself, it wasn't that much worse than a couple of bad practices they'd had in LA when he'd been distracted and sloppy, but it was a long way down from what the band had become.

She stopped him after the show as he was leaving and said, "I just want you to know you were lousy tonight."

He seemed bored by the very concept of conversation. "It wasn't so bad."

"Yes it was. And it was the smack's fault." She stood blocking the hallway so that he would have to push past her to get to his car. Which was exactly what he did.

THE FRYING PAN

Monday morning, after a gig in Wilmington, Delaware, where Laurie couldn't tell whether Skip was high or simply playing badly, Jim woke her at eight in the morning. She dressed and walked with him to the coffee shop at the nicer motel across the street from their Motel 6. She assumed it was about Skip right up to the moment Jim told her he was quitting.

The waitress had taken their order and brought coffee, and Laurie stared at the bitter steam rising from the cup. She could smell the Clorox in the sour rag the woman had used to wipe down the table and it robbed her of any desire to eat.

"Laurie? Aren't you going to say anything?"

The only question was what they would do without him, and the answer, she supposed, was that they would go on. As if reading her thoughts Jim said, "You play piano, I can leave my stuff with you and you could use it on some of the songs, wherever you think you need it. And I can hang out for another couple of days, work on the parts with you if you want. It's the least I can do."

"Not the least," she said. "Close, maybe."

"You're pissed off. I know that."

She couldn't sit any longer. The only reason for it was to make Jim feel better, and she wanted someone to make *her* feel better. Not that she had any candidates. She lurched to her feet, nearly running into the waitress, who said kindly, "Your food's here, hon."

"Leave it," she said. "He'll get the check."

Outside the air was damp and gray and exhausted. She had an image in her head of water droplets in a hot skillet, the way they would dance together for a few impossible seconds before evaporating. Laurie Moss and her Mosslings had, for a few seconds, looked like a real band, complete with record contract, tour, and van, she thought. Before they vaporized.

She stuck her fingers through the inevitable chain-link fence between the coffee shop and the used car lot next door, torturing herself with the words that self-pity loves: "never" and "gone" and "over" and "lost." Still the tears wouldn't come.

She heard the restaurant door whoosh open behind her. "Laurie?" Jim said. "Laurie, I'm sorry. What do you want me to do?"

"Nothing," she said, and turned to face him. "Take the next plane home. If you want to leave the keyboard, that would be nice." Then, because she couldn't bear the look on his face, she said, "Tell Molly hi."

"She's going to be so surprised," he said. "She's not going to believe it."

She couldn't hate him. He had a family and a life and a simple thing he could do that would make him happy. She envied him. But he was already starting to recede, as if he were standing on shore while the wind rose and carried the rest of them away.

He was packed and in a taxi in thirty minutes. Gabe, Dennis, and Chuck crowded around to see him off; Skip was missing in action again. Once the cab disappeared, Laurie unlocked the trailer, took the DX-7 up to her room, and got in half an hour's practice while everyone else packed.

GREEN, ROCKY ROAD

They got to Baltimore at one in the afternoon of that same Monday, October 9. Laurie called Melinda to tell her Jim had left and Skip was fading. "Can you get us in the club early so we can rehearse?"

"Your pal Sid the Shark got you that gig. Shouldn't you be talking to *him?*"

"He's not my pal and I need one right now, okay?"

Melinda sighed. "Okay. Call me back in thirty minutes and I'll let you know. Sorry about Jim, but I do have some good news. I kept riding Ardrey and he's got us a release date. We've got the last Tuesday in October, the thirty-first. It's quicker than I thought they'd do it, and now we won't get lost in the Christmas flood or the barrens of January."

"Halloween," Laurie said. "We may be a ghost band by then."

"Cheer up. And call me in half an hour."

Melinda set things up with the club, and the band spent three hours reworking their arrangements around the looming, Jim-shaped silence. Laurie elected to play keyboards on four of the songs; the rest worked adequately with two guitars. Skip dragged his feet every step of the way, making all of them regret the few times he condescended to actually speak. When it was over, perhaps a little before it should have been—at the moment that Skip abruptly shut off his amp and walked out—Laurie paused to search her heart for any remaining trace of tenderness toward him and came up empty.

The rest of them piled into the van and drove to the Harborplace mall on the Inner Harbor near the aquarium and the convention center. Between the early morning, the drive, the rehearsal, and their own individual regrets, they were all stumbling with fatigue. The mall seemed to them like a stranded alien space station made of glass and primary-colored steel, and Laurie found herself puzzled more than offended by the expensive toys in the shop windows.

They didn't talk much over their various ethnic food court meals. One of them might try an experimental line like, "It didn't sound so bad with just two guitars," and then the silence would rise again like a tidal wave and smother all replies. From where they sat Laurie could see the perfect blue of Chesapeake Bay and clouds of seagulls that would suddenly break apart into individual birds that soared high out over the water and were gone.

They had a new energy that night, not necessarily better, but different. Laurie concentrated on ignoring Skip and keeping her parts simple on the songs where she played keyboards. The crowd helped. Once again Laurie was struck by how disconnected she was. One town was like another to her because it had a Motel 6 and a Wendy's and a Texaco, and the radio played Aerosmith or Mariah Carey. Yet each crowd brought its own unpredictable context, whether it was too many days of rain or somebody dead in the local scene keeping the room sparse and quiet, or else it was the local sports franchise in the playoffs or a sprawling birthday party that had everyone galvanized before she took the stage. In Baltimore they applauded wildly at the first mention of Laurie's name, stayed on their feet for the entire set, and cheered every song. It was the kind of night that she couldn't help feeling was the start of something, though she knew she was usually wrong.

For his part, Skip utterly failed to pick up on the prevailing mood. His few moments of actually giving a damn coincided with Laurie's mistakes on keyboards, which nobody in the audience seemed to mind. They played two encores, and as they left, a kid jumped up on stage and gave Laurie a hug before diving back into the crowd.

In the dressing room Skip put his guitar in its case and wiped the strings down, moving as stiffly as a dog that was about to bite. "What utter shit," he said.

"Got a problem, Skip?" Laurie asked.

"Me?" He slammed the guitar case. "I don't have a problem. This *band* has a problem, but I don't. This band sucks without Jim in it, is the problem, and I can't play guitar and keyboards both."

Laurie looked at Gabe. She felt cold and lucid and unhurried, though she seemed to have misplaced her self-control. "Am I just crazy, then?" she said. "Because I thought we were pretty good tonight. All things considered. And I thought we really went over."

Gabe looked at Skip, then back at Laurie. There was a fine sheen of sweat on the cocoa skin of his forehead that Laurie couldn't remember seeing before. "No," he told her. "You're not crazy."

"So it's me that's crazy, then, right?" Skip said, at just less than shouting volume. "As fucking usual. I mean, what the fuck do I know?"

"Well," Laurie said, counting on her fingers, "you know how to feel sorry for yourself. You know how to get drunk. You know how to shoot smack. You know how to let people down."

He took a step toward her like he might actually hit her. Laurie found herself leaning forward, into the potential blow. "What?" she said. "*What?*"

Skip froze. Though nothing moved in his face, she could see his eyes slowly disconnect. She was left looking at a mask.

He turned back to his guitar case and closed all the latches. "I'm too old for this shit," he said. "Way, way too old."

Laurie watched from the wings while he packed up his amp and pedals. She'd had a boyfriend once who got up in the middle of a fight and gathered up everything he'd left in her apartment over the last month and a half—a toothbrush, a couple of books, some T-shirts, a pair of swimming trunks—and packed it neatly into a plastic H.E.B. grocery bag and then walked out without saying goodbye. Skip had the same set to his shoulders. He rolled his amp through the crowd and out the door into the night.

Laurie turned to find Chuck Ford smiling at her. "We sold six CDs and four tapes," he said. "You guys were great."

She nodded and went back to the dressing room.

"Did he take his amp?" Gabe said.

"Yeah."

"What's going on?" Chuck asked.

"I think Skip quit," she said.

"He's just strung out," Gabe said. "He'll be back."

"Not this time," Laurie said. "If he came back I'd fire him, and he knows it. He's gone."

"Hey," Gabe said. "You guys'll work it out. It'll be okay."

Suddenly she was angrier at Gabe than she'd ever been at Skip. "Will you *stop?* Sometimes things don't work out, okay? You don't have to keep crawling back and kissing up to some asshole to make them work out. You just . . . let . . . *go.*"

She went outside and got in the van and slammed the door. With her back against the side of the van and her legs stretched out across the farthest rear seat, she folded her arms and thought black thoughts. She didn't offer to help load out the equipment and during the infinitely long drive to the motel no one attempted to break her adamantine silence.

T R I A G E

She had a room to herself that night, and the worst of it was visualizing the others all together, lying in the darkness, talking about her.

She barely slept. She contemplated returning to her computer job in LA, singing with Summer at the Duck again, starting all over again from scratch. That managed to bring a few hot, thick tears out onto her pillow.

Then she pictured herself getting off a plane in San Antonio, with Grandpa Bill half walking, half running to meet her and throwing his arms around her. She could smell the starch that Slater-White Cleaners put in his shirt and feel the stubble on his chin. She'd talked to him on

Sunday before the gig in Wilmington, before Jim quit, before Skip walked out, all of, what, thirty hours ago? How unimaginably wonderful to be in San Antonio, to stay in her old room and get up only to eat real food and shower and wash her hair and then crawl back into bed again.

Instead she got up in the morning to open the door to her room and lie in a patch of sunlight on the bed while she wrote a new set list, scrapping "Don't Make Promises" and restoring "Tried and True," dropping everything that depended on guitar flash and going back to two-part harmonies and verses, choruses, and bridges.

Then, in the early afternoon, she drove the van to the Northwest quadrant of Washington, DC, while Gabe and Dennis read over the set list.

"We could do 'Walk Don't Run,' " Dennis said.

"I redid the set list because our guitar player quit," Laurie explained, again.

"Okay," Dennis said. "I can take a hint."

"He maybe quit," Gabe said.

When Laurie stepped out to the front of the stage at the Black Cat to start the show and Skip had not, in fact, shown up, she was more relieved than anything else. An hour after that, when they had somehow made it through the night and Skip had not even turned up to gloat, she felt a brief pang of loss, more for the idea of Skip than the reality. They cleared their equipment off the stage and loaded the van and went to the dressing room to get something to drink. There Laurie's knees buckled with exhaustion and she sank to the stained brown carpet of the dressing room floor.

"It was different," Chuck said. "Not horrible, we even sold a couple of CDs."

"What about tomorrow?" Dennis said. He sounded like he was afraid to hear the answer.

"Tomorrow we've got the day off to drive to Columbus," Laurie said. "But I take your point."

"Skip's not coming back, is he?" Dennis said.

"No," Laurie told him. "Skip's not coming back."

They sat in silence while, on the other side of the door, the club's PA played "God Save the Queen" and Johnny Rotten sang "no future" over and over.

"We have to call Mitch," Gabe said. "Crunch, if you say anything about his hair I swear to God I'll kill you here and now."

"I didn't say anything about his hair."

"It doesn't have to be forever. Just to get us through until we can find somebody else. He already knows the songs, he could start Thursday night if we got him out here."

"All right."

"I mean, you have to think about the rest of us too. If we're a band and not just— What did you say?"

"I said, 'All right.'"

"I've got at least another half hour's worth of arguments. Are you sure you don't want to hear them?"

"Maybe you could write them all down and I could go over them later. Do you have his number on you?"

He shook his head. "I'm sure Melinda's got it. I didn't think I was going to talk you into it."

"And if you hadn't?"

"Are you asking me if I was going to quit?"

"Maybe I don't want to know the answer to that."

"Well, the answer is no. I wasn't going to quit. But then again I probably wouldn't have had to."

E p i p h a n y

Thursday morning in Columbus. The town didn't seem to exist beyond High Street and the Ohio State campus. Everything was red and white and covered with exhortations to the Buckeyes. Alumni were already streaming into town for Saturday's football game.

Laurie woke to a phone call from the front desk telling her a FedEx had arrived for the band. She opened it in the lobby to find proofs of the General Records version of the inserts for the CD and cassette. It was Dennis's art with better reproduction, on heavier, coated stock. In her room, after the others had gone out, Laurie put the new pieces into one of their garage-version jewel boxes and fell asleep holding it.

At three that afternoon she woke to a furious knocking with no idea of where she was and the guilty conviction that she'd missed a history final or a job interview. She staggered out of bed and opened her door to see Gabe and Chuck standing on either side of a person she didn't recognize. This person had blond hair pulled into a ponytail, battered jeans, Chuck Taylors, and a Sonic Youth T-shirt with Japanese lettering.

"Hey," the stranger said. "You want alternative? I can do alternative. No sweat."

"Mitch?" she asked foggily. He grinned and held out his hand and she shook it. "Thanks for coming out," she said.

"I've been listening to that tape Skip gave me all the way out here on the plane. It may take me a couple of nights to get the fine points, but I'm ready to play."

He seemed devoid of guile or cynicism. "We're not a cover band," Laurie said, "and you don't have to play what Skip played. Just play what you feel."

"No sweat," Mitch said. "I can do that."

And so it was that Mitch Gaines became the lead guitar player for Laurie Moss and the Ticks. Laurie spent the first week gently discouraging some of his least appropriate habits: bump-and-grind theatrics, high-speed scales, shimmering chorus effects. "Sure," he'd say to whatever she suggested. "I can go with that." A limitless supply of diet Coke seemed his only requirement.

It finally came together in a place called Club Toast in Burlington, Vermont. He'd bought a cheap Boss distortion box at Advance Music, a hangout he remembered from some previous tour, and he punched it in for the solo on "Carry On." As he got toward the end he squeezed a huge, fat, blistering note out of his B string and stood there and watched it hang in the air, and instead of chasing it with a flurry of 32nd notes, he let it decay into a whoop of feedback and then he slowly took it home, making every stroke of the pick count. The crowd liked it better than anything else he'd done all night, and their applause lit him up like a pinball machine.

"Mitch Gaines, everybody," Laurie said. "He gave up a lucrative career in junk bonds to be in my band. Let him know he did the right thing."

After the show Mitch introduced them to the Waffle House tradition. There was not, in fact, a Waffle House in Burlington, but Mitch explained that even a Denny's would do in a pinch, and they found one in

South Burlington. Laurie, who had never cared for breakfast, discovered that she'd simply been eating it at the wrong time of day. Dennis got a trencherman's platter with ham and eggs and toast, Gabe got an English muffin, and everyone else, including the two Trinity College girls who'd appeared in the van, got waffles.

"That was weird, tonight," Mitch said with his mouth full, holding up his diet Coke glass for another refill.

"'Carry On'?" Laurie asked.

"Yeah. It was like I was trying to paint a portrait with a four-inch brush. My guitar teacher would have hated it."

"I don't think you need a guitar teacher," one of the girls said. She'd left the club with Dennis, then somehow ended up sitting next to Mitch. Dennis kept staring at Laurie like it was her fault.

"Yeah," Mitch said, "but the thing is, it was fun. I can't remember the last time it was that much fun."

Now that he mentioned it, Laurie thought, it hadn't been much fun for any of them for a while. Waiting every night to see what kind of mood—artificial or otherwise—Skip was going to be in, watching Jim slowly sink in despair, worried more about hassling with the managers than how the band sounded, waiting for the inevitable end.

And now the unimaginable had happened and it turned out not to be the end after all.

Laurie wound up with Dennis and Gabe in her motel room that night. As with the other infrequent nights when sex became an issue, the band seemed to mysteriously work out the details so that Laurie was in the other room when it happened. But it was happening more often as the band generated word of mouth, and soon, she thought, things might become interesting.

By eleven the next morning the girls were gone and the van and the trailer were packed. They pulled out of the parking lot and Mitch said, "So, like, where to now?"

In a week it had become Mitch's daily ritual, at first annoying and already indispensable, his refusal to look at an itinerary no more than a symptom of his ability to live completely in the moment. "Red Bank, New Jersey," Chuck said.

"Cool. Let's do it."

In another week the band had gelled around Mitch in a way that had not been possible with Skip, the Living Legend, who drove his own car and did no dog and pony shows. "No sweat" had become the band's mantra, diet Coke au van its official drink, and Laurie found herself fantasizing about waffles and syrup as soon as she stepped off the stage every night. Mitch's interests were diverse and inexplicable, and the band found themselves on outings—to the Harley Davidson plant and museum outside York, Pennsylvania, where Laurie thought of Blue; to Freebody Park in Newport, Rhode Island, where Dylan had turned the Folk Festival on its ear; to every aquarium within an hour's drive of their itinerary.

But the real difference was on stage, where the songs got tighter as the band loosened up, talking to each other and to the audience, finding the rhythm of their new composite personality. They added a couple of eighties teen anthems that Skip had always refused to consider: Bon Jovi's "Livin' on a Prayer" on odd-numbered nights, Pat Benatar's "Love Is a Battlefield" on evens. They dropped "Tried and True" and "Fool's Cap" and "September 19th" and Laurie wrote new, faster songs to replace them.

Suddenly the crowds were bigger and women were following them to the local Waffle House equivalent almost every night. If Laurie had permitted them the slightest opening there would have been boys following *her* there as well. Skip had left a bad taste in her mouth, however, that she preferred to nurse with waffles rather than something from the dessert cart. Meanwhile, in the motel rooms afterward, that which had once promised to be interesting went all the way to disruptive, and she eventually learned to sleep with a pillow over her head.

NOTICES

In York on Monday, October 23rd, Melinda faxed their first batch of reviews to a Kinko's, where Laurie read them in amazement. Out of the six, one was mixed, four were very good, and the *LA Reader* was a full-on rave:

> *Of the Same Name* doesn't defy trends, it refutes them. It's as timeless as the Band's second album or Crowded House's first, a seamless, heartfelt pop record that deserves to be popular, gigantically so.

Rolling Stone gave it three and a half stars and called it "a promising debut marred only by a certain narrative distance and a lack of cohesion among the songs." They noted that "songwriting legend Skip Shaw makes an unexpected appearance, co-writing three tracks and contributing tasteful, stinging guitar." Laurie's voice, "at its best, as on 'Carry On,' 'Neither Are We,' and 'Angel Dust,' conveys late-night weariness, wisdom, and a wealth of compassion."

At the bottom of the stack was the piece I'd written about Laurie for *Pulse*. In it I used the word "naked" to describe the emotion in her voice.

When I first typed the word, early in the first draft, I saw that I'd crossed a line. If Barb read the story she would know it too. I'd gone from journalism to flirtation, from professionalism to self-service, from faithful husband to potential cheat. I lay in bed that night and asked myself if that was what I wanted to do. Every time I said the word "naked" to myself my heart raced, and I saw that I was going to do it whatever the risk, whatever the cost.

Barb had never made it a point to keep up with my music journalism; she had ideas for any number of medical thrillers she'd have preferred me to spend time on. When my contributor's copies of *Pulse* showed up one Saturday, however, something made her open the envelope. She was reading the story when I came in from shopping and I could see the tension in her neck. I felt like I'd been caught in a lie. I put the groceries away while listening intently to her every movement in the next room. The smack of the magazine hitting the coffee table was clearly audible. I stood in the doorway and tried to seem casual as I asked, "So, what did you think?"

"What did I *think*?" she said. Her eyes were brutal. She went to her study and slammed the door.

I'd given Tom a bag of canned goods and he'd been carrying the cans, one by one, over to the pantry and stacking them in front of the door. "Is Mommy mad?" he said.

I said, "Yes," around the lump in my throat, afraid he would ask me why. He only nodded and said, "Can I have a Dr Pepper?"

Over a year later, in e-mail, I ask Laurie about "naked."

"I remembered talking to you when I read the article," she answers. "Did I think you were flirting? Yes. If you want the truth, it gave me a bit of a tingle."

I SHALL BE RELEASED

On October 31st they played a Halloween in-store at the Mad Platter in Springfield, Missouri, that pulled in over fifty costumed people and sold a dozen copies of the brand-new General Records version of the album. That night they headlined to a full house and sold another ten copies out of their own stock.

The *Rolling Stone* with their review had hit the stands and Laurie would pick it up every time she saw it and read the review again, trying to catch herself by surprise. They had a dozen copies of it in the van, and Dennis was in the habit of pointing it out to strangers in convenience stores.

They dipped into Arkansas, then back to Knoxville, Tennessee, where they played a combination bar and laundromat called Gryphon's that removed any lingering bad taste from the prior trip. After that came four dates in North Carolina. L'Shondra's brother, who programmed for Data General, met them in Raleigh and drove them around the Triangle. It was a relief to see anyone with a tangible connection to anyone they knew from their former lives, and Laurie was impressed by an entire complex of cities that was only intermittently visible through the dense growth of pine trees.

From North Carolina they had two days to get to New York City for their official corporate-sponsored record release party at the Bottom Line on Sunday, November 12th.

Mitch had a laundry list of places to see in New York, from the Guggenheim to the Apollo Theater, from the Museum of TV and Radio to CBGBs. They left the van at the Empire Hotel's garage on Saturday afternoon and stayed up most of the night. Late Sunday morning, while the others took the "A" train to Harlem, Laurie went by herself to Central Park and sat on a bench and listened to a jazz band play under a tree.

The music made her think of Grandpa Bill, and she wished he could be there to see her hour of triumph. She wasn't scheduled for Letterman and she wasn't staying at the Plaza, but last night she'd seen her album in the Virgin Megastore and in a couple of hours she would be doing an acoustic set on WNYC followed by a showcase at the Bottom Line, one of the most famous clubs in the world.

A sense of correctness filled her. She was where she belonged, doing what she was meant to do, with people she had come to love. Today was good and there was no reason to think tomorrow would be anything but better. Nothing had guaranteed her this day, and she was grateful for it. At the same time she knew she'd worked hard to earn it, and each new set of reviews told her she was not crazy to think—perhaps—she might almost deserve it.

THE BOTTOM LINE

There were eight for dinner at Virgil's, a crowded, noisy barbecue place near Times Square: the band, including Chuck; Melinda, who'd flown in for the occasion; Ross Claybeck; and the head of General's New York office, Dominick Fetrillo. Ardrey was tied up, Claybeck said, though he would be there for the show.

Fetrillo was in his fifties, heavyset, with receding gray hair in the inevitable industry ponytail, a black silk shirt, and a leather jacket. After shaking hands with everyone he sat back and said next to nothing. The noise level kept conversation to an awkward minimum in any case; Dennis and Claybeck talked pro football, Fetrillo asked if the hotel was all right, Melinda wanted to know what General was doing about triple-A radio.

They took three cabs to the club, and Laurie ended up with Gabe and Fetrillo. "It's a great record," Fetrillo said, turned sideways in the front seat. "I'm a major fan."

"Thanks," Laurie said.

"Don't worry too much about the numbers. This is the kind of record that builds over time."

"Which numbers, exactly, are we talking about?"

"The initial orders. Ten thousand is disappointing, but hey, we're all in this for the long run. Once we break some radio and get a video or two happening, it'll take off. You'll see."

In the oddly angular dressing room of the Bottom Line Laurie shook off Fetrillo's bad news. She would think about it later, when she didn't have something more important in front of her. Another of General's baby bands, a country-rock outfit from Missouri called the Hicks, was warming up the crowd. Mitch sat smiling in one corner, seemingly unaware that his hands were playing scales at breakneck speed, while Gabe sat in another, eyes closed, wearing his bass but not otherwise touching it. Dennis was reading the *Sporting News* and Chuck was fishing a beer out of the ice.

"So," Chuck said. "Exactly how stoked are you?"

"Fully," Laurie said. "Totally. I almost hate for it to start because once it starts it'll be over too soon."

Melinda came in, shut the door, and fell back against it, fanning herself. Her wispy red hair was up and she was wearing an ecru Donna Karan suit. "It's serious out there. You got Judy McGrath, president of MTV, you got the *New York Times,* the *Village Voice, Time* magazine, *Rolling Stone, Spin*, your friend Sid the Shark, and three or four van-chasing managers who are looking to do me out of my clients. Nervous?"

Laurie laughed. "You haven't heard us in a while."

They started off with Bob Marley's "Could You Be Loved." Laurie stepped back from her excitement and her *funktionslust,* her pure animal pleasure in doing what it seemed she had been born to do, and opened her heart. What came out was everything she'd felt in the last two months on the road: frustration, longing, fear, despair, joy, confidence, contentment. When the lights were right she could see the table down front where Ardrey now sat with Fetrillo and Claybeck. She imagined that she saw amazed delight on their faces.

"Thank you," she said when it was over, above the noise of four hundred pairs of wildly applauding hands, "this is the new single," and they tore into "Angel Dust." Mitch, in brand-new blue jeans and a brand-new flannel shirt, played without a trace of calculation or artifice, setting loose one flock of notes after another to circle the room and batter at the doors and windows. They did a pair of Laurie's new songs, and "Neither Are We," then went into "Fool's Cap" and most of the rest of the album, wrapping up with "Carry On."

A standing ovation brought them back to play "Get Ready" and "Midnight Train." They said their good nights and left the stage again and once more the crowd brought them back.

"Thank you," Laurie said. "I can't possibly tell you how much fun this is. But we really have to go, so we're going to leave you with my favorite song." She played the opening A to F sharp and the band fell in behind her. "This is by Tonio K." She let the music build and then started to sing about the end of innocence, the passing of an age that would never come again. "'Blow a kiss and dry your eyes,'" she sang. "'Say goodbye.'"

D O W N T H E R I V E R

They hugged each other wordlessly in the dressing room. They all knew how good they'd been. Laurie was proudest of the kind of band they'd become since Skip left, the kind of band that played best when it counted the most, a band that was not afraid of its own possibilities.

Chairs appeared for them at the big table down front. "Sit and relax a minute," Melinda said. "We'll meet and greet once you've got your breath back."

Champagne arrived and everyone drank to Laurie Moss, even Laurie Moss herself. And at that moment, before the flush had subsided, in front of two vice presidents of General Records and a room full of the most important journalists in popular music, Mark Ardrey said, "So where's Skip?"

All eyes at the table turned to Laurie.

Laurie looked at Melinda, who shrugged. "I thought he'd be back," Melinda said. "Like the proverbial bad penny."

"Excuse me," Ardrey said, "but is anybody going to answer my question?"

"Skip," Laurie said, "is no longer with the band."

"And Jim?" Ardrey asked.

"He went home to his wife and kid. Mark, what's the matter with you? Where's your sense of timing?"

"*My* sense of timing? Who waited for her showcase at the Bottom Line to inform her record company that her band has broken up?"

Laurie looked around the table. The executives all seemed to be in neutral, waiting for a clear victor to emerge.

Gabe leaned forward, batting a stray dreadlock away from his face. "I saw you sitting out here while we were playing. Did this sound like a band that's broken up? With all due respect to Jim and Skip, who are both friends of mine, this lineup here kicks the old lineup's ass, and has been kicking it every night for the last five weeks."

"And let me remind you," Melinda said, "that the contract specifically states that anybody in the band, with the exception of Laurie, can be removed or replaced without notice to the Label."

"Goddamn right," Dennis said, as if proud to be so expendable.

Laurie's heart swelled in her throat. It would have been one of her proudest moments if Fetrillo hadn't picked that moment to ask, "What about the video?"

"What about it?" Laurie asked.

"How can we run that video," Fetrillo said, "without Skip in the band? Hell, you didn't even play the fucking song tonight."

"It was the second song," Laurie said. "And Skip doesn't sing on 'Angel Dust' . . ."

Another apocalyptic silence fell over the table.

"Oh no," Laurie said.

Now everyone was looking at Ardrey. "What's with this 'Angel Dust?'" Fetrillo said.

"You didn't," Laurie said, remembering Patrice's strange insistence on getting shots of Skip singing. From the corner of her eye she saw an expensively dressed woman with chin-length brown hair start to approach the table, then think better of it. "Tell me you didn't," Laurie said.

"CMJ passed on 'Angel Dust,'" Ardrey said. "So did MTV. But CMJ was interested in 'Don't Make Promises.' Some kid there is a big fan of Dylan and Tim Hardin and Skip Shaw."

"I know," Laurie said. "He brought one of Skip's albums to an interview where Skip didn't show up."

"We looked at what we had, and there was all this great footage Patrice shot of 'Don't Make Promises.' The story line works just as well with that song, so we did a re-edit—"

"Without telling me," Laurie said.

"We just wanted to see what it would look like. Then things got out of hand."

"The contract says—"

"Let's be realistic," Claybeck said, finally entering the fray. "It's a little late for you to give back the advance and us to unmanufacture the records. You can take us to court if you want, but we think VH-1 is going to add 'Don't Make Promises' next week. You're going to have a hard time convincing a jury that getting a video on VH-1 actually hurt your career."

Laurie had never thought of herself as part of the demographic for VH-1—or Lifetime or QVC, for that matter. And the band's audience was not, in her experience, made up of forty-year-olds with cell phones and sport-utility vehicles.

"This makes sense," Ardrey said. "VH-1 is very big on women in rock. And a cover song is always a good way to break a new band. We've got this all mapped out. I mean, I can see the two of you on the cover of *Rolling Stone,* like Buckingham and Nicks or something. But we need Skip back to pull it off. Do you know where to get hold of him?"

Laurie sat for a long time trying to find words, any words, to say to Ardrey. When she absolutely and finally could not find them, she got up and walked to the dressing room.

Melinda found her there, sitting on her amp with her back to the door, winding cables into pathologically neat rolls. "Look," Melinda said, "I'm not going to tell you they're not assholes."

"That's something, anyway."

"All I want to say is that they're the assholes who have both hands around the neck of your career. This is not the plan we originally came up with, but it's not a bad plan. VH-1 sells records."

"This isn't about VH-1. I'm okay with VH-1. It's about Skip."

"He's been in the band for a year, and only out of it for five weeks. Would it be that impossible to coexist with him for a few more months? Long enough to get some publicity out of this?"

"Melinda, he was shooting heroin. He was missing sound checks and it was only a question of time before he started missing gigs. He was bound and determined to screw up, he'd invested his whole being in it. You heard what this band has turned into with Mitch. You can't expect me to throw all that away."

"I hate to be the one to tell you this. Good does not necessarily sell records."

Laurie stood up and turned around. "It's been a long night. I've been on an emotional roller coaster all day, and right now I feel totally ambushed and betrayed by General Records. This is probably not the night for us to have this discussion."

"Tonight's the night. The entire corporate muscle of General Records is out there ready to flex for you. If you can find it in yourself, you need to go out there and try to work with them."

"Don't make me do this."

"I can't make you do anything. All I can do is what you pay me for, which is to give you advice and back you up. You did notice me backing you up out there."

"I noticed. Thank you."

"I'm asking you to try, that's all. To make an effort."

Laurie followed her back to the big table down front. They both sat down. Too late Laurie realized that she felt the same way she had the night Skip quit, far beyond caring about the consequences of her actions.

"I'm sorry," Ardrey said, "that we surprised you like that."

"You didn't surprise me, Mark," Laurie said. "You sold me out. You know I didn't even want that song on the album. Neither did Skip, for that matter. So you went behind my back and made it a single, and you didn't tell me about it because you knew I wouldn't agree. And now you want Skip back in the band for the sake of the video, as if a band was made out of Lego blocks and you could just take one piece out and put another one in and it wouldn't matter. You think your professional judgment is more important than my instincts and my feelings. Guess what? You're wrong. And if you can't appreciate what we did up there on stage tonight, then you're also an idiot."

She went back to the dressing room for her guitar and her amp. She had her hands balled up into fists because she didn't want Ardrey to see her shaking. She got all the way out to the van before she started crying, and by that point she had no idea who or what the tears were for.

By the time Mitch and Dennis and Chuck and Gabe had loaded the rest of the equipment she had dried her face and blown her nose. Everyone got in the van and Dennis started the engine. For a painfully long time they sat and listened to it idle.

"So," Mitch said at last. "Where to now?"

T W O   B A D   M I C E

When Laurie was three years old, her favorite book in all the world was
Beatrix Potter's *Tale of Two Bad Mice*. She never tired of the simple story:
Two mice named Tom Thumb and Hunca Munca sneak into a beautiful
doll's house one morning, tempted by the luscious-looking food they see
there. Then they discover the food is made of plaster, and the fire is
nothing but paper, and the knives won't cut anything. All their dreams
turn out to be an illusion, a fake. At that point, Potter says, "there was no
end to the rage and disappointment of Tom Thumb and Hunca Munca."

"That was my mantra after the Bottom Line," Laurie tells me in
e-mail. "I didn't actually trash a hotel room or carve up Mark Ardrey
voodoo dolls, but the world was a different place."

She had the persistent feeling that the walls around her were made of
tissue paper, that the sky through the windshield of the van was only a
projection, that every time she spoke she was only lip-synching to a
sound track that cleverly anticipated her every word. If the one hour out
of every day that she was on stage continued to bring transcendence, the
remaining twenty-three weighed increasingly heavy. She found herself
waking up in the middle of the night, her mind roiling with things she
wanted to say to Ardrey or Claybeck, or changes she wanted to make to
the set, or panicked thoughts about Grandpa Bill, that kept her from getting back to sleep for hours at a time.

On a somewhat more positive note, VH-1 began to play "Don't
Make Promises." As a direct result the album bubbled up to number 89
on *Billboard*'s Hot 100 for the week before Thanksgiving, then dropped
off again, annihilated by new Christmas product from the Stones, Melissa
Etheridge, and Smashing Pumpkins.

The buzz, however brief, was enough for Melinda to land them an
opening slot on the Spin Doctors' tour that would start in January of
1996. And General agreed to a video for "Carry On," to be shot right
before the band joined the tour. In the meantime they finished the rest of
their scheduled gigs, winding up at the Hurricane in Kansas City on Saturday, December 23rd.

During *Billboard* Week, as the band called it, Laurie had relented and
put "Don't Make Promises" back into the set as a duet with Mitch.
Mitch's voice was a sweet tenor, very different from Skip's, yet the crowds

responded with happy recognition to the opening lines and it seemed curmudgeonly to take that away from them.

The crowd in Kansas City loved "Don't Make Promises" and everything else the band did, brought them out for three encores, and swarmed over them after they left the stage. It seemed an auspicious way to leave things. After waffles the band drove out to see the Christmas lights at the Plaza, then dropped her at the airport, sweaty and exhausted, to wait for her predawn flight to San Antonio; they planned to catch a night's sleep and head out to LA.

"I'm going to miss you guys," she said, hugging each of them. "Please drive carefully."

"No sweat, Crunch," Mitch said. "See you in two weeks."

T H E   B I G   C

Laurie's mother met her at the airport and surprised her by taking her straight to Methodist Hospital. Laurie had cleaned up as best she could in the Kansas City airport but still felt like a refugee. "This isn't what I had planned," her mother told her. "But the doctors wanted to operate today and that seemed more important than making tamales. You must be exhausted."

"Is it cancer? Why didn't you tell me?"

"He made me promise. He said I could call you as soon as he woke up afterwards. He didn't know they were going to do it while you were actually here. Yes, they think it's cancer. They're supposed to take out part of his liver."

It had been a year since she'd seen either one of them, and if her mother seemed mysteriously transformed into someone older, plainer, and less gender-specific, it was nothing compared to the changes in Grandpa Bill. He'd lost so much weight that previously hidden bones and musculature now pushed out against his papery skin. There was, in particular, a hard line around his jaw that she didn't remember ever seeing before. He seemed distracted, like he was listening to voices in another room, and Laurie realized that the science fiction metaphor had become literal, that he had been taken over by an alien being, a cancer, and that it was speaking to him in a language of pain.

"Hello, sweetheart," he said. "You weren't supposed to see this."

She leaned across the hospital bed to hug him. "And you weren't supposed to see me until I showered. Will I approve of your doctor?"

"I dearly hope so." When he talked Laurie could see the raw gums where they'd made him surrender his upper plate. It was a final, casual insult that robbed him of his dignity when he needed it most.

Nurses kept coming in and out of the room to take his blood, check his vitals, give him a pre-op shot. Laurie had been there less than half an hour when orderlies arrived to take him to the OR. Laurie and her mother walked him as far as the double doors and then, squeezing his hand one last time, they watched him go on without them.

They sat in the surgical waiting room. Laurie, in a daze, tried to consider the possibility that she might not see him alive again. It didn't seem credible.

"I knew I couldn't stop you from coming," her mother said. "I would have if I could. I didn't want you to see him like this. It would have been better to remember him the way he was."

"This isn't going to change any of my memories, Mom. This is just the way things are."

"I don't like the way things are." Laurie's mother shook her head. "Now I sound like you. When you were a little girl you would get something in your head and never let it go. I remember you used to ask me every summer why we couldn't stay up all night and sleep all day. You would say, 'Why go to sleep when it's finally getting nice outside?' I would say, 'That's just the way things are,' and that was never good enough for you. Now look at you. You finally got your way—up all night, every night. You look so tired."

Laurie's eyes fluttered shut and she willed them open again. "I *am* tired."

"I remember your senior year in high school. Up all night fooling with the guitar, the teachers sending notes home because you were falling asleep in class."

It seemed to Laurie that her mother was not criticizing but simply had come unstuck in time, floating away from an unacceptable present. She managed to avoid it for two and a half hours, asking Laurie if she remembered a former neighbor or a trip to the zoo when she was still in a stroller, never once mentioning Grandpa Bill or Laurie's father.

When the doctor came in, he looked so hesitant that Laurie's heart stopped. She felt the edge of a darkness so black that it did not seem survivable. "He's doing fine," the doctor said, though his troubled look didn't go away. He pulled up a chair and said, "I don't know what to tell you. We couldn't find any cancer in his liver. The spot is there on the X rays, but there's no sign of anything on the liver itself. I lifted it up and checked the anterior side, but there's simply nothing there."

"That's good," Laurie said. "Isn't it?"

"It might be, except that the bloodwork and all the other signs indicate the presence of cancer. If it's not in his liver, it could be anywhere. It could be systemic. We just don't know."

"What are you saying?" Laurie's mother asked.

The doctor sighed. "My opinion . . . my *opinion* is, the cancer has spread throughout his system. I had hoped that the cancer was localized in the liver, based on that X ray, and that we could get enough of it out to prolong his life."

"How long?" Laurie asked. "How long does he have?"

"You have to remember that I may be wrong. I don't think so, but he may have a number of years yet."

"And if you're right?"

"My guess would be weeks. I would be surprised if it were much more than three months." Then, almost as an afterthought, "I'm sorry."

He sat, as if waiting to see how bad the reaction was going to be. When no one started screaming he smiled uncomfortably and walked away.

They kept Grandpa Bill in the hospital for five days, and when they let him go home Laurie moved into the spare bedroom of his house. When he felt strong enough to sit up they played canasta, a game he'd taught her twenty years before, and the rest of the day they watched wildlife shows on cable. At night she would rent vintage gangster movies, from the 1932 *Scarface* to *The Godfather,* and when his eyes hurt she would read to him. For all his sophistication, he was a Texan in his heart, so she read from J. Frank Dobie's *Apache Gold and Yaqui Silver,* his favorite.

She didn't tell any of her friends she was in San Antonio, and on New Year's Eve she and her mother and Grandpa Bill watched a swing band special on Public TV and then listened to some of his 78s: Fletcher

Henderson, Duke Ellington, and his all-time favorite, Louis Armstrong. At midnight they sang along to Lombardo's version of "Auld Lang Syne," scratches and all.

On Monday, January 8th, he was scheduled to move into a nursing home where he could get full-time care. Laurie's mother couldn't afford to quit her job to take care of him, not to mention the fact that she didn't have the training. "Medicare pays for the nursing home," Grandpa Bill said, "so I'm going. And that's that."

On that same Monday Laurie was scheduled to start shooting the "Carry On" video in Los Angeles.

"We have to make a deal," she told him the Sunday before, as she waited for her mother to come take her to the airport. "You don't keep any more secrets from me. When I call, you tell me everything you know about how you are, or I'm not leaving town."

"I don't suppose I have to point out that this is blackmail. You could go up the river for this."

"Are you the one going to drop a dime on me, tough guy? I don't think so. So swear on the family honor you'll clue me in."

He held up an unsteady right hand and said, "I so affirm."

On the flight to LA she tried to read lines of words that refused to queue up properly. It occurred to her that for the first time in her life she would close her eyes if someone offered to show her the future. Time was a funnel, narrowing around her, one lost opportunity bringing on another.

H O M E

Gabe and Dennis and Mitch and Chuck were waiting for her when she got off the plane, each holding a sign with a different misspelling of her name: Lorry Mouse, Larry Mass, Leary Moose, Lurid Mess. They all went to Jim's house to eat pizza and get caught up.

At first Laurie thought it was not such a good idea. For one thing, she kept expecting Skip to come walking out of the garage at any minute. Then there was Mitch. The band he'd known had hung out at the Waffle House; it was a different band than the one Jim had been in, the one that had lived in this kitchen. Eventually Jim said, "I really miss you guys, but you don't have to tiptoe around. I made the right decision, I don't want to go back on the road. It's okay."

"It's not that," Laurie said. "We were afraid you'd want your keyboard back."

"As soon as I get over my guilt," Jim said. "That'll be any century now."

Laurie spent the night in Jim's guest room, as she had so many times before, and the next morning she got to see all the new dinosaurs Sam had added to his collection in her absence.

General had pushed for a performance video as the simplest, and therefore cheapest, solution, and had arranged for Club Lingerie for the shoot. The director, Les Michaels, was in his forties and resembled Ben Franklin, down to the hairline and the rimless glasses. Though Laurie had admired his clips for people like Sonic Youth and Angels of Epistemology, his actual work habits left her insecure, as he rolled tape without apparent purpose and included the band in so little of it. After the extras went home, at seven in the evening, he took each of the band members aside and, under the glare of a pinpoint spotlight, had each mouth the lyrics at half speed, with exaggerated expressions. Then he shot each of them sitting alone in a corner of the dressing room. He was confident of his vision and seemed to be enjoying himself, and Laurie only wished she could say the same.

THE BIG TIME

They caught up with the Spin Doctors' tour in New Orleans. The Doctors generally played only one or two shows a week, and Sid the Shark had put together some other dates to keep Laurie and Her Three Bad Mice occupied on the off days.

Opening for a band like the Spin Doctors was a continuous trade-off. Laurie had moved from small clubs to auditoriums and amphitheaters— the sheds, in the parlance of the trade—only to find the seats less than half full when she and the band came on. Most places didn't even turn the lights completely down, so the audience wouldn't stumble on the way to pick up a T-shirt or buy an extra beer. She got reviewed, sometimes enthusiastically, never for more than a paragraph.

After three weeks on tour, sales of *Of the Same Name* continued to drop. "I don't understand," Laurie said to Melinda from a pay phone at a Shell station at the Las Vegas city limits. "I thought the point of this was to sell records."

"I asked Ardrey. He thinks people are having trouble finding it."

"I still don't understand. We're distributed by Warner Communications."

"Look, this may be a little painful, okay? You're not on the charts, you don't have a video in rotation, so the people that order the records don't know who you are. If a record store sells the one or two copies of your album that they might have in stock, they probably consider themselves lucky and don't reorder. Some of the big chains have already returned you, and they're not going to reorder unless you go through the roof."

Laurie put the phone down, not realizing she'd hung up on Melinda until the deed was done. She felt like Ron Tuggle, trying to breathe from an empty tank. What would Ron Tuggle do now? she asked herself. What would he do if he looked up and saw the only thing he'd ever wanted, the thing he'd worked for since junior high school, the thing that had been just within his reach, begin to cave in around him?

Only that morning she'd been reading an article about children's books she'd discovered in a yellowed North Carolina newspaper in the rear of the van. What children wanted in a story, the article said, was to feel powerful and to be reassured that there was justice in the world. Adults too, Laurie thought. Getting up in front of a big audience with a good band and a loud guitar was more power than she'd ever known, but it couldn't make people give her record a chance.

Nor, as it turned out, could it save her Grandpa Bill.

She'd been calling her mother and Grandpa Bill on alternate days since she'd gone back on the road. On the fourth week of the tour her mother confirmed what Laurie had already heard in Grandpa Bill's voice: The cancer was back, this time in his brain, inoperable.

SAY GOODBYE

The Spin Doctors were extremely gracious about dropping Laurie from the tour, as was the rest of the band. She got on the first morning flight out of Minneapolis and took a cab from the San Antonio airport to the nursing home.

It was a low brick building, built cheaply in the seventies. The front door opened onto a dim day room containing three desiccated plants and half a dozen people in wheelchairs. The dining room, straight ahead, smelled of boiled potatoes. Grandpa Bill was in the West wing, to her right, which had prompted him to make a feeble joke the week before about not having to die in the East.

She passed an open door where a woman in a smock was making the bed. The door to the empty closet stood open and Laurie understood that someone had just died. Farther down the hall a woman screamed with a steady, demented rhythm. Laurie saw an orderly about her age standing in the shelter of a broom closet, dragging surreptitiously at a cigarette. "Can't you do anything about her?" she asked.

"What you want me to do?"

"Can't you quiet her down?"

"She don't get her drugs for another hour yet. A pillow over the face'd take care of her, but it ain't in my job description." He turned his back on Laurie to concentrate on his cigarette.

Laurie stood for a long second, her right hand firmly holding the lower half of her face immobile, hating the idea that Grandpa Bill's life might depend in any part on this callous, casually cruel man. It was helplessness that finally made her turn away and walk down the echoing hallway until she found Grandpa Bill's room.

He was drowsing when she walked in, so feverish he seemed to glow in the muted afternoon light. Laurie pulled a chair to his bedside and took the opportunity to run a brush through her hair. Another sleepless night, another hospital room. The screaming woman rasped at her nerves, and closing her eyes only made it worse.

Grandpa Bill woke up with a start and Laurie saw the lack of recognition in his eyes. "It's Laurie, Grandpa," she said. He nodded with no indication that the words held significance for him. She tried to read to him from something called *Broken Eagle,* a paperback western that had been on his desk, while his attention drifted either to the window or to her face, where he would stare intently, as if searching for something. Finally he freed his left hand, which she'd been holding, and used it to pull the book gently down.

"Why are you doing that?" he asked.

"Reading to you? I thought you'd like to hear my voice."

He shook his head. "We should talk."

She put the book on the desk. "Of course." She waited for him to tell her what was on his mind, but he only continued to stare at her. "I love you, Grandpa Bill," she said. "I don't think I say that enough."

He shook his head again. "I have to ask you," he said, and then he lay back on his stack of pillows.

"Ask me what?"

He sat up again and looked fixedly in her eyes. "What do you think my chances are?"

She was too stunned to answer. Had no one actually told him he was dying? If not, did she have that right? Would that woman down the hall never shut up?

He lay down again, the question either forgotten or no longer in need of an answer. His eyes closed and he began to snore gently. The woman's screams abruptly stopped. Laurie propped her head on her hand and was asleep herself within seconds.

She woke up an hour later as they brought in Grandpa Bill's dinner. She realized she hadn't eaten all day and remembered seeing a convenience store a block or so away. "I'll be back in an hour or so, Grandpa," she said. "Okay?"

He waved her away, nodding, with a vagueness in his eyes that made her wonder if he yet knew who she was. She walked to the Stop N Go, which actually had a table inside, and ate a microwaved pizza and an ice-cream sandwich. The sun was setting in a dingy sky, and a bitterly cold wind tossed the bare branches of the scrub oaks along the street. February was always the hardest month in Texas, the month that lured premature buds from the trees, then froze them off in sudden ice storms. It was the month where romance turned to indifference and beloved pets ran away. If it had a full complement of days, instead of twenty-eight or twenty-nine, Laurie thought no one would survive it at all.

When she got back to the hospital Grandpa Bill was asleep again. At eight Laurie called her mother to come pick her up, and a few minutes later a hard-looking nurse came in to take his vitals and give him his nightly meds. She was unable to wake him.

He stayed in a coma for two days and then, on Friday, February 9th, at two in the morning, he died without waking up.

Laurie and her mother were home asleep when the call came. They drove at insane speeds down 410 to get to Northeast Baptist, where the ambulance had taken him, though strictly speaking there was no reason left to hurry.

He was pronounced dead at Northeast Baptist, which made the nursing home's statistics look better, and Laurie and her mother were home again by five o'clock. They tried to call Corky and got no answer, so they sat sideways on the couch, facing each other, holding hands and drinking hot chocolate while the sun struggled to rise. Laurie went over her last conversation with Grandpa Bill three or four times, and her mother repeated everything the doctors had told her.

"Listen, Mom," Laurie finally said, "do you still keep a stash?"

"What? What are you talking about?"

"Dope, Mom. Marijuana. Chronic. Don't bother acting innocent, I've known about it for years. I could smell it coming out of your room at night."

Her mother sighed, waited too long to attempt a bluff, and finally went to her bedroom. She returned with a baggie and a small metal pipe. "Do you do a lot of this on the road?" She was obviously self-conscious about asking, and equally unable to stop herself.

"No, Mom. I don't even drink. It just seemed like this might be a good idea right now."

It was. Laurie felt them both relax as they passed the pipe back and forth.

"I can't believe I'm doing this," her mother said.

"It was this or lie, and you were always a lousy liar. You made me into an honest person because I was always afraid I'd be as bad at it as you."

"You're such a cipher," her mother said. "We're sitting here talking trivia and I don't even know you anymore. You're some kind of vagabond, living in motel rooms, making your living in bars, just a disembodied voice on the phone once a week. Now that Daddy's gone I don't know if I'll ever see you again." She was as stubborn about crying as Laurie, and the tears seemed to dry up in her eyes without ever falling.

"Mom," Laurie said, and put her arms around her. "I love you. I'm the same person I always was. I take my stuffed tiger on the road with me and I still read *Cosmo* and I still can't cry when I'm supposed to."

"But are you *happy*? Your grandpa always asked me that. He would call on Sunday nights after we'd both talked to you and ask if I thought you were happy."

She wished she'd known that while he was still alive. "Yes," she said finally. "When we're playing, I'm really and truly happy at least one hour a day. How many people can say that?"

Eventually, with a cold drizzle falling in the halfhearted daylight outside, they went to bed. Laurie lay awake for an hour or more and finally took a pen and notepad off her night stand and wrote:

> People die and leave you needing more
> And it's so hard letting go
> Something broke inside and I'm afraid to let it show
> And it's so hard letting go.

A few minutes later she was asleep.

ASHES

After the memorial service Laurie and her mother and Corky went to Brackenridge Park. They had Grandpa Bill's ashes divided between them in paper bags and periodically one of them would take out a handful and sprinkle it around. Laurie went off by herself to the Japanese Gardens and scattered the last of her share among the exotic plants by the koi pond. Then she sat and watched the turtles swim in the murky green water. It seemed a better existence than her own, or Ron Tuggle's: Both air and water were equally breathable. And if things got tough you could pull in your arms and legs, like the little sculpture that Gabe carried on tour, and sink into the soft, warm mud at the bottom of the pond.

Corky found her there. "You okay, sis?"

She looked up at him.

"Okay," he said. "Bad question."

Corky sat on the bench next to her and they watched the turtles together. After the agony of the memorial service it was a relief for her to be with somebody who understood what she was feeling without her having to talk about it.

Eventually he said, "Did Mom tell you I'm thinking about joining the Navy?"

"She told me. I hate the idea of it. How could you stand to have somebody tell you what to do every minute of the day?"

Corky laughed. "Like I've done such a great job running my own life the last four years? Flunked out of school, quit or got fired from every job I've had? Maybe . . ." His voice changed, developed a sudden artificial nonchalance. "Maybe I should go on the road with you instead. I could sleep on the bus, eat the leftovers from those party trays backstage, meet girls, get high every night. What do you say, could you use an extra roadie?"

She saw he'd been thinking about it for months, pinning his hopes on it. Panic chased all her words away.

"Corky, I . . ."

"Yeah, I know, it was a dumb idea. What do you need a loser like me for?"

"Corky, there's no bus. There's no party trays. Somebody might hand us a joint once in a while, but other than that we're lucky not to have to pay for our own beer. I'm sorry."

"Yeah, it's okay. Don't worry about it."

"Corky, *I can't save you.* I'm not sure I can even save myself."

Corky's expression changed from self-pity to wonder. "It's that bad?"

"It's getting that way."

"Whoa," Corky said. Then, softly, "Whoa."

That night she called Sid the Shark and told him to find somewhere for the band to play.

I N T O   T H E   B R E A C H

Eight days later, on February 19th, she flew to Dallas to meet the rest of the band for a gig in the Deep Ellum arts district. No banners or signs this time, just tired smiles; still, she felt a tension go out of her that she'd been carrying since the Minneapolis airport.

During the long week in San Antonio Melinda had FedExed her a dub of the "Carry On" video. Laurie watched it for the first time while her mother was at work and quickly found out why the director hadn't cared about traditional coverage. He had processed and manipulated the footage until there was some question about whether he'd needed the band as a starting point at all.

A recurring shot of Laurie anchors the video, most of her face in darkness, the rest in washed-out black and white, a grainy sunburst behind her, a ball of light erupting from her mouth as she sings in ultra-slow motion. During the verses a hugely magnified drop of sweat runs down Gabe's face. Mitch's guitar neck bends under the weight of pounding chords. Dennis seems to be screaming in pain as he flails in single frames with his drumsticks, thick tendrils of oily smoke winding around him. Shots of the crowd show roiling bodies and an occasional demented face swimming into focus and then slipping away.

It was a hellish nightmare of a video and Laurie loved it without reservation. Gabe, whom she'd been calling at least every other night, assured her the rest of the band loved it too. VH-1 had passed on it—"too murky, not their sort of thing" according to Melinda—but MTV had scheduled it for *120 Minutes* the following Sunday night.

That Sunday they were in Boulder with the night off, crowded around the TV in Laurie's room, snow falling outside, Laurie and Gabe lowballing again. "They're not going to play it," Laurie said.

"They'll play it," Gabe said, "only Rachman will come on first and make snide remarks about 'Don't Make Promises,' which he was of course much too cool to ever play."

"No," Laurie said, "they'll start it and then Beavis and Butthead will come on and stop the video and talk about how much it sucks."

"Will you guys shut up?" Dennis said. "I'm trying to watch the show."

In fact "Carry On" appeared just before the end, sandwiched between two other videos, aired, as it were, without comment. When the show was over Laurie turned off the TV and Dennis said, "That was cool."

"It was brilliant," Gabe said.

"It was," Laurie said, "a black rose among broken beer bottles."

After a brief silence Chuck nodded. "That about says it all."

The next Friday they were in Flagstaff for their first-ever return engagement, where Melinda faxed them to say that "Carry On" had not made it into MTV's Buzz Bin, where it would have gotten maximum exposure, "for reasons not clear to me or anyone else involved." It was "in the rotation" but not "in the power rotation." Ardrey had suggested they shoot "Neither Are We" with a "VH-1–friendly" director. "Better VH-1," Melinda quoted him as saying, "than no TV at all."

NEITHER ARE WE

A week later—on Monday, March 4th—they were in Provo, Utah, which had been transformed by an influx of software companies into a shiny miniature Silicon Valley. They came back to the motel from a nearly all-male audience to find a fax from Ardrey. It read, in hand-printed block capitals:

I KNOW YOU GUYS DO NOT HAVE MUCH FAITH IN ME AND I CANNOT SAY AS I BLAME YOU. BUT WE HAVE ONE MORE SHOT AT A VIDEO, SO WE ARE GOING TO GO OUT IN STYLE. NEXT FRIDAY, THE 15TH, GENERAL RECORDS WILL FLY YOU TO LA FIRST CLASS. A LIMOUSINE WILL PICK YOU UP AT LAX AND TAKE YOU TO A MEETING WITH DONALD BAILEY, WHO HAS DONE VIDEOS FOR SARAH MCLACHLAN AND MELISSA ETHERIDGE. YOU WILL STAY AT THE CHATEAU MARMONT, WHERE JOHN BELUSHI DIED. THIS SOUNDS LIKE THE SECOND PLACE PRIZE ON JEOPARDY! BUT I THINK IT WILL BE PRETTY SWANK. THANK YOU JOHNNY GILBERT. SEE YOU IN LA LA LAND.
 SINCERELY, MARK J. ARDREY

"Cool," Dennis said, after he'd read it. "A limo."

"They're just going to recoup it out of our royalties," Laurie said.

"Not to be heartless, here," Gabe said, "but I don't think royalties are an issue at this point."

"You're right," Laurie said. "Let's take it while we can get it."

Though she realized she was supposed to be jaded, the idea of being in another video kept her up that night and got her out of bed fully charged the next morning. She'd been ready for it since the first time she saw MTV, back in 1982, before Warner Cable carried it in San Antonio, watching it at her cousin's house in Houston. They'd made their own video late that night, self-consciously lip-synching to Hall and Oates, leaving behind a devastating piece of blackmail if anyone ever discovered it.

The band was getting the rhythm of the road again, playing well, drawing good crowds, especially when they went anywhere near a city they'd visited the previous fall.

Laurie finished "Letting Go" and when she brought it in to the band she felt more awkward than she had since their first days together. "This is okay, isn't it?" she kept asking.

"It's fine," Gabe said. "It's just the first song you've ever brought us that wasn't written from somebody else's point of view. This is actually you talking, for once."

"Yow," she said, reaching for the lyric sheet. "Let me have it back. I'll fix it."

Gabe snatched it away from her. "Don't even think about it."

On Friday, March 8th, they checked into a Motel 6 in Albuquerque. It would have felt like spring, if there had been any trees or flowers to bloom. Mitch was nursing a cold and it had left the whole group sluggish, as if their collective battery had run down. Laurie went to register while the others sat in the van, out of sight of the desk clerk, a habit that saved time, questions, and the occasional request for a security deposit.

After she'd filled out the card, the clerk handed her two keys and a fax from Melinda.

"Can't believe the news from General," it began. "I have calls in to everybody. Don't panic, don't believe anything you hear. I'll be in touch soon."

In fact they'd heard nothing, and panic seemed the only option. The desk clerk pointed her to a pay phone at the gas station next door. Laurie walked, then ran toward it, forgetting to say anything to the others. As she dialed, it occurred to her how much she'd come to hate pay phones: It was impossible to have a human, private conversation there, and yet the alternative, using a room phone in front of the rest of the band, was even worse. It was such a part of the road experience, where everything was rented and disposable, no home-cooked food, no animals to pet, no trace left behind, not even the scent of her perfume on a pillow.

She got Melinda's machine at the office and no answer at home or on her cell phone. The receptionist at the Warner office in Burbank hadn't seen Melinda and told Laurie that Mark Ardrey was "unavailable."

Laurie got in the van and handed the fax to Gabe, who read it once in silence and once out loud. "No Melinda," Laurie said, "no Ardrey."

It was sound check time. They drove downtown to Gold Street, where Sid had booked them a return engagement at the Fabulous Dingo Bar. They set up the equipment, then Laurie called Melinda and Ardrey again and left the number of the club. After sound check they sent Chuck out for breakfast burritos from the Frontier and they all sat at the club and waited for a call that didn't come. Every hour Laurie called both Melinda and Ardrey again, until Warner's switchboard closed, and then she just called Melinda.

Laurie felt like she had a sunset inside her as she got up on stage. Her stomach burned from eating too fast with too much on her mind, from total somatic tension, from a formless sense of doom. All of them except Dennis played distractedly, with too many mistakes. The crowd forgave, but did not surrender their hearts.

At two o'clock California time, as Laurie was turning in, there was still no answer on Melinda's cell phone, still the same message on her machine.

Laurie finally fell asleep before dawn and woke up stunned and disoriented at ten o'clock. The phone was ringing. She fumbled the receiver off the cradle and then couldn't remember what to say.

"What?" she said. No, she thought, that's not right. Was it "hello" you were supposed to say?

"Laurie, it's Mark."

"Who?"

"Mark Ardrey. Did I wake you up?"

"No, I had to get up to answer the phone." She lay down, on the verge of sleep again. "Where am I?"

"You? You're in Albuquerque, at least that's what Melinda told me. So what have you heard?"

The previous night came back to her. "Heard? Other than an ominous and incomprehensible fax from Melinda, we haven't heard anything." She sat up, finally awake. "So what's all this mystery about?"

"Much as I hate to be the bearer of bad news . . ."

"Out with it, Mark."

"General fired me."

"Oh God. What happens to us?"

"Don't I even get a 'Sorry, Mark, hope you're okay'?"

"Maybe another day. What happens to the band?"

"I'm sure nothing's going to happen to you. You've sold thirty thousand units, which is respectable considering how little money and effort they put behind you. You've got great reviews and great word of mouth on the live shows. They'll assign you to somebody else at the label until it's time for the next record, at which point you can look around the company and figure out who you want to work with."

"So what happens to you? Are you set up with another label yet?"

"Me?" Ardrey said. "I'm gone. I'm out of this business. I'm going to find someplace where you're not washed up at thirty-four. Maybe I'll go to some podunk town and write record reviews in the Sunday paper. Maybe I'll buy a horse and wagon and go live with the Friends."

"Sorry, Mark," she said. "Hope you're okay."

Melinda was still not answering. Laurie went to the front desk, borrowed a magic marker, and wrote, "ARDREY CALLED, CANNED. WHITHER MOSS & BAND?" and talked the desk clerk into faxing it to LA.

Melinda finally called as Laurie was closing up her suitcase. Gabe was already on his way down to the van.

"I can't find anything out," Melinda said. "It's the weekend, everybody's gone. Yes, Ardrey's out, but that's not necessarily bad for you. Maybe he's taking the fall for you."

"What fall would that be?"

"It's a figure of speech. Everything's going to be fine."

"I assume this means no video shoot next week."

"Don't assume anything. Just play hard, drive safe, and I'll call you on Monday."

The video shoot indeed turned out to be canceled. It wasn't until April 1st, however, that Ross Claybeck actually called Melinda and told her that he was dropping Laurie from the General roster.

The band was in Atlanta trying to catch up on a week's worth of too little sleep. Laurie took the call at two in the afternoon. Gabe was reading with a book light in the heavily draped room and Chuck was snoring in a sleeping bag near the door.

"It's not just you," Melinda said. "They're letting all of Ardrey's artists go. I mean, Claybeck has a point. The record's had six months and three videos, and nobody else is going to have the motivation to work it. They're all looking ahead to the fall releases."

Laurie didn't say anything. Against her silence, Melinda's words began to spin like tires in loose sand. "All is not lost," Melinda said somewhat desperately. "You've made a good start, you've got name recognition, all we have to do is find a friendly ear at another label. I was talking to David Anderle at A&M the other day and he said something nice about you, I've got a call in to him, I—"

"I have to go," Laurie said.

"Laurie, sweetie, are you okay?"

"It's not like we didn't see this coming," Laurie said, amazed at how normal her voice sounded. She knew that sounding reasonable would get her off the phone faster than anything else, and getting off the phone was what she wanted most at that moment.

"That's true, isn't it?" Melinda said, and Laurie could hear how badly Melinda wanted off the phone herself. "Now we have to make some decisions about—"

"I'll call you later," Laurie said, unable to hear the rest from Melinda's end because of the rushing sound in her ears. She put the phone down and took her journal off the nightstand and did some figuring, carefully checking her work. Then she went outside to stand in the gray daylight and hold on to the railing with white knuckles.

The temperature was in the sixties and clouds were moving fast overhead, too many of them for the sun to break through. The air smelled of rain and gasoline and fresh-cut weeds by the roadside.

All she could think about was the previous night's gig, their most pathetic in weeks, playing to two dozen people across the street from a cemetery in what had obviously once been a pair of double-wide trailers. They'd gotten forty dollars and a free meal, something with canned corn and tomato skins and big chunks of nearly raw onion in it. The owners were two old Southern hippies with shoulder-length white hair and Lau-

rie had felt so sorry for them that she'd eaten what she could and suffered
with heartburn most of the night as a result.

Chuck was awake now, in jeans with no shoes or shirt. "Band meeting?" he asked gently.

Laurie nodded. From the corner of her eye she saw Chuck pad
downstairs and some time later—a minute? fifteen minutes?—the others
had all gathered back in the motel room.

She walked in, leaving the door open, and saw them sitting on the
unmade beds or on the floor. She loved them fiercely. They didn't want
to look at her because, clearly, they knew what was coming. She said,
"We've been cut." She went over the conversation with Melinda, twice.
Gabe, quietly, said, "Fuck."

Mitch opened his mouth to say something inspirational, but Chuck
saw it coming and put a hand on his arm. "Another time, Mitch."

"Okay."

"So," Dennis said. "I take it this is not April Fool's?"

"Indeed," she said, "it is not. So here's the deal. We've got a solid
month of gigs booked, but no more tour support from General. In fact
they still owe us for the receipts we sent in for the last couple of months
and I wouldn't count on us ever seeing that, either. The gigs won't actually bring in enough to keep us on the road, but we've probably got
enough in the bank to make up the difference, barring further disasters.
We can cancel everything and split the money that's left, or we can go
ahead and take this thing as far as it will go."

Now they were all looking at her.

"Drive it into the ground," Dennis said.

"All the way," Mitch said.

"Do it," Gabe said.

"I'm in," Chuck said.

"Okay," she said. A gust of wind lifted her hair and dried the perspi-
ration on the nape of her neck. "Thank you," she said.

"I don't know why you're thanking us," Chuck said.

Dennis said, "But you're welcome."

Later, as they were alone in the room, packing, Gabe said, "Tell me
you're not kidding yourself that some miracle is going to happen in the
next month."

"No," Laurie said. "But I grew up believing that if you worked hard and did everything you were supposed to do, then eventually justice would prevail."

"If you were black that thought would never have crossed your mind."

"I know. But the point is, if I quit now somebody could say I didn't try hard enough, that I could have gone on one more month and maybe that would have made the difference, that I gave up."

"That's it? That's your motivation?"

Laurie nodded. "What about you?"

Gabe shrugged. "I guess I'm just not ready for it to be over yet."

Www.lauriemoss.com

I got the news first on Laurie's Web site. Jim had put the site together shortly after he left the tour, perhaps as an obscure act of penance, and I'd offered him, via e-mail, the raw transcript of my interview with Laurie.

When I saw that General had cut the band I knew, with complete fatality, that I was going to write a book about Laurie. In less than a second she walked into my book proposal for *Struggling* and threw everyone else out.

I also knew, with a sort of high-wire terror, that I might never sell the book, that it was going to take many hours on the phone, many days on the road, and many, many hours of transcription to do it right. And that both the writing of it and the not selling of it would make Barb unhappy, each in its own way. In short, that it could be the most expensive book I'd ever written, in every possible sense of the word.

THE LAST TIME

They did their last show on Tuesday, May 7th, in Missoula, Montana. If Laurie had hoped for epiphany, what she got was anticlimax. They were second on the bill, with only forty-five minutes on stage. The substandard PA was in the hands of a grizzled and apparently deaf sound man. Only thirty people showed up, already drunk when they arrived midway through the set.

The band did what they could. When Laurie looked around during "Don't Make Promises" Mitch and Gabe were wearing huge green foam-rubber cowboy hats. Before "Carry On," their traditional last song, Gabe got on his mike and said, "We've been on the road since September, and this is our last show for a while. We wanted to show Laurie how much we've appreciated crowding into a broken-down van and sleeping three to a room and hauling our own equipment in and out of gigs we barely got paid for. Since we've been living our lives in public we thought we'd share it with you folks here tonight." Then they sprayed her with Silly String, and then they sprayed the audience, and then Dennis counted down the last song and before she knew it they were in the middle of it.

Remember this, she told herself, and tried to fix the feeling in the cells of her body: Know that there was a time when you were not alone, but were part of something bigger than yourself. Know that you made music that was both solid and full of beautiful detail, that you moved people physically and emotionally, that you lived this and it will always be inside you.

L O O S E   E N D S

Though the band money was gone, she still had a little money of her own when she arrived in LA on May 9th. Between the advance, publishing royalties and her savings, she had close to five thousand dollars, enough to buy a car to replace the LBD. She would need it if she stayed in LA and went back to work for Sav-N-Comp and tried to start again.

And she would need it even more if she packed up everything that was still at Jim's and drove to Texas.

Jim insisted that she stay at his place while she made up her mind, and he took her car-shopping on Saturday the 11th. She found another Datsun, this one blue, only a year older than the one she'd originally driven to LA. She paid forty-five hundred in cash, which left her without enough to make a deposit on an apartment. It was only then that she realized her subconscious had already made the decision for her. She would not be staying.

She was tapped out.

The next day, as she sat in the bathroom with the door open, putting on makeup, Molly knocked at the doorjamb. "Going to see Skip, are you?" she asked.

Laurie blushed. "I don't know. Maybe."

"What do you want to do that for?"

"I hate not knowing. Does he blame me for what happened? Is he okay?"

"Girl, look at yourself. *Smell* yourself. You're wearing all that perfume and makeup and that slinky dress to make sure he's got groceries?"

"Maybe I want him to know what he's missing."

"He *knows* what he's missing. From the looks of you, he might not be missing it much longer."

Laurie put her mascara down and looked at Molly in the mirror. "You don't think I should go."

"No, I don't. But you're going, that much is obvious. I'm just saying, Jim has tried to call him three or four times since they both, you know, came home and everything. Skip never called back. People have seen him out at that jingle factory, but he's keeping to himself. I don't think he wants to see any of us."

"Is he still strung out?"

"Who knows? Who cares? He's an asshole."

"I know," Laurie said. "I know. But I feel responsible."

When she pulled up in front of his apartment she saw his Mustang and it made her legs unsteady as she got out of the car. As she walked up to the porch she could see his open window and smell the cigarette smoke that drifted out, as if the eight months she'd been on the road had never happened.

She went into the front hall and hesitated, knowing that she could still turn around and walk away. While still considering the option she saw her own right hand make itself into a fist and knock on Skip's door. "Who is it?" Skip's voice said, and she found that the air in her throat had coagulated and she couldn't speak. A minute later the door opened. He wore old, faded jeans, an untucked white T-shirt, a lit cigarette in the corner of his mouth. Bare feet, bloodshot eyes, rumpled hair. Her eyes strayed involuntarily to the crooks of his elbows. No visible needle tracks.

"So," he said. "It's you." He very slowly shifted his weight, opened the door the rest of the way, and stood to one side. "Come on in."

She closed the door and leaned against it as he crossed the room and flopped on the couch, legs stretched straight out. "How's the tour?" he said.

"It's over. Ardrey got fired, we got dropped."

Skip shrugged. "A blessing in disguise. You'll get on a better label and they'll break you properly. It's only a matter of time."

"I don't think so," Laurie said, "but that's not why I came here."

"Okay. Why did you come here?"

Now it was her turn to shrug, and to look at her feet. "I guess I wanted to know you were okay."

"I'm here. I'm alive. Due in part to the publishing royalties I've gotten for songwriting credits I didn't deserve. You shouldn't have done that."

"Is that Skip Shaw for 'thank you'?"

"No, it's me saying you really shouldn't have. I'm a waste of perfectly good money."

She looked around the room, at his paintings of suicide and betrayal and despair, at the ashes and the peeling paint and threadbare furniture, and realized what it was she'd come to see. The Skip Shaw that had twisted her up inside was there in front of her, but overlaid on that image like a double exposure was an old, bitter man who had nothing left to do but feel sorry for himself.

"You should call Jim sometime," she said, straightening up, ready to leave. "He's not going to yell at you. He misses you."

Skip nodded, a nonbinding promise to think it over. Then he said, "Are you guys going to be playing in town for a while?"

Her hand was still on the knob. She turned it and let the door come ajar behind her. "No, we're done. I'm going back to San Antonio, the other guys will go back to whatever they were doing before."

Skip tilted his head, as if she'd spoken in a foreign language.

"Don't look so shocked," she said. "It's the way things are. You believe in justice because you happened to get what you deserved. You had talent, you got rich and famous. You screwed up, you lost it. It doesn't work that way for everybody."

"It should have worked for you."

"I thought so too. I was wrong. But I can't really complain." She could, but she was damned if she would do it in front of Skip Shaw. "I got enough breaks that I actually got to make a run at it. How many people can say that?"

"Don't go," Skip said. "Come on inside and sit down for a while."

"I don't think so," Laurie said. "You take care of yourself, you hear?"

Traffic was already bad by the time she got on the 10 for Whittier. She remembered the night the sky had rained fireworks on her and thought how much she was going to miss LA, traffic and cost of living and disposable culture notwithstanding.

I will not cry, she thought. She had her guitar and her beautiful amp, now with added character from its hard-earned scratches and dents. She had her Little Blue Datsun and the last hundred copies of the homemade edition of *Of the Same Name*. She had five hundred dollars, a place to stay once she got to San Antonio, and the skills she'd learned at Sav-N-Comp.

She rolled down her window and smelled, faint but undeniable, the perfume of orange blossoms.

F R E E

That night she packed everything in the LBD for an early start in the morning: the amp in the bottom of the trunk, the guitar next to it, her clothes and CDs and books packed all around. Whatever didn't fit in the trunk went into the back seat.

She went to bed early, feeling nothing beyond her own fatigue, slept nine hours, and got up at seven ready to drive.

The car was gone, stolen in the night.

THE REST

MITCH GAINES

Mitch, through Melinda, landed a deal with the specialty label Mayhem to do an album of heavy-metal instrumentals.

"I loved playing with Laurie," he says, when I finally catch up to him at a signing party for the record in June of 1997. His hair is loose and long, and he's wearing a mesh T-shirt and leather pants. "I learned a lot about restraint and taste from her. I'm definitely a better musician for the weeks I spent in her band. But this music, the music on my album, that's where my real roots are.

"If she ever does another record, though, and wants some guitar on it? I'm there."

MARK ARDREY

Mark Ardrey continues to politely refuse all interviews. Dominick Fetrillo in New York, who has never been particularly shy about talking to the press, told me Ardrey is now with an ad agency in Philadelphia, not far from Amish country. According to Fetrillo, "He says it's a clean, honest day's work compared to the record business."

JIM PEARSON

Though Jim is still working half-time at circuit design, the increased visibility he got from *Of the Same Name* has brought him enough paying production work that Molly was able to quit her Parks and Recreation job. When I stop by to see him he's at work on a new Estrogen album, which the band will again release themselves.

I'm startled to find how comforting it is to be in his kitchen again, having written so much about it over the long winter and spring. I can feel Laurie's presence there.

"Listen," Jim tells me, "the most amazing thing happened yesterday." He takes me to the garage, where the members of Estrogen are tuning up, and shows me a guitar case. "Open it," he says.

I do. Inside is a mid-sixties Strat, very clean, maple fingerboard and cream-colored body. "It's Laurie's guitar," I say. "I thought . . ."

"It was," Jim says. "After her car got stolen I put Laurie on a plane for Texas and I talked to the cops myself. Laurie had given me the serial number of the guitar and I passed it on to the cops and all the guitar stores that were interested. And sure enough, some guy showed up last week trying to sell it. The cops hauled him in but they couldn't find any way to tie him to the robbery. The guy says some stranger sold it to him for fifty bucks, and stupid as that sounds, it could be true. Anyway, the cops called me yesterday and I went out to Pomona and got it."

I touch the neck as gently as if it were flesh. "Does Laurie know?"

"Not yet. We're trying to decide whether we want to call her and tell her or just ship it to her and let it be a surprise."

"Let me take it to her." The words are out before I know I've had the idea. "It makes sense," I say, my rational brain trying desperately to cover the tracks of my subconscious. "I can stop off at some of the clubs where you guys played and get local color for the book."

And the darkest part of my brain believes that if I show up with her guitar she'll have to be grateful to me.

C A T H E R I N E   C O N N O R

I drive by Laurie's old place on my way to my motel on the far side of the San Fernando Valley. I knock on Catherine's door and a young man answers: rimless glasses, a day's growth of beard, khaki shorts, and a long-sleeved white shirt. I introduce myself and explain that I'm looking for the woman who used to live there.

"Catherine?" he says. "She was the one that got me into this place. I used to work at the same temp agency she did, and she turned me on to the apartment when she got married."

"Married?" I say. "When?"

"I don't know. I moved in at the beginning of June."

"Do you know who she got married to?"

He looks wary. "I can give you the number of the agency. They might be able to get a message to her."

"It's okay," I tell him. "It doesn't matter." I give him one of my cards. "Give her my best if you run into her."

SUMMER WALSH

Following the lead of Ani DiFranco and others, Summer has started her own record label, Sly Duck Records, with financial backing from Brad Mueck. She's released one album of her own and has a second one on the way; she's also produced two other records by musicians from the Duck.

"The time is right," Summer tells me over the phone. I'm in my motel room, trying to figure out how to tell Barb that I'm going to Texas. "The Lilith Fair is the hottest tour of the summer, and there's a window now for women like us to get themselves heard."

"If General hadn't done Laurie's album, would you?" I ask.

"Laurie doesn't need Sly Duck Records. She's a major-label talent. She's down now, but sooner or later she'll be back up and she'll go all the way."

After I hang up I wonder where people get the peculiar confidence they have in others. Barb insists that one day I'll make a fortune from my writing, maybe because it would reflect badly on her if I didn't. Summer is sure that Laurie will be rich and famous, and that confidence lets her avert her eyes.

Laurie is seeing somebody, Jim told me. He doesn't know any details, but he thought he should warn me.

GABRIEL WONG

Gabe is on tour with Dick O'Brien, playing a chain of clubs called Dick's Last Resort. With Melinda's help I track him down in Dallas and call him from the same Motel 6 in Tempe where he had stayed when he was on tour with Laurie.

"I saw her just last night," Gabe tells me. "She came out to our show on the Riverwalk in San Antonio. She looks good, she's put on a little weight. I tried to get her up on stage, just to do one song, but she refused in a pretty final way and I didn't push. She was glad to see me, though you could tell it was making her really sad at the same time.

"I thought about telling her that you were bringing her guitar, except she was so definite about not wanting to play that I got to thinking, maybe just as well to let you surprise her."

Was she with anybody when she came to see you? I wanted to ask. There was no way to do it without giving away entirely too much, without admitting things to myself that I wasn't ready to say.

"She ruined me," Gabe tells me toward the end of the conversation. "I miss her and I miss being in a band. I never thought I'd say that."

C O R K Y   M O S S

Laurie's brother Corky did in fact join the Navy, and is stationed in San Diego, where he's working on submarine engines. When he gets a weekend pass he hitchhikes from the National City shipyards to wherever Dennis's new band is playing, and hangs out with them afterward.

In his letters home Corky raves about the weather, the ocean, and the women. "Laurie," he says, "was crazy to ever leave California."

L A U R I E   M O S S

For three months Laurie stayed with her mother, working temporary jobs and setting money aside until she could get an apartment and make a down payment on another Datsun, this one red.

The same week that she moved out of her mother's she landed a job with a computer company as an entry-level technical writer. She'd never been on salary before, and she was as amazed and puzzled by the permanence of it as she was by the size of the check.

I call her on Monday afternoon at three o'clock, from a pay phone in a Taco Cabana. I'm sweating, not just from nerves, but from the Texas heat that the restaurant's air-conditioning can barely keep at bay.

We agree to meet that night at her apartment and order pizza. Then she says, "My boyfriend may be there. Is that okay?"

"Of course," I say, as if it really is. "No problem."

She's living in an anonymous complex of dark-gray brick apartments, mirror images receding to infinity. I ring her bell at seven o'clock exactly. The guitar is sitting on the landing, invisible from inside the apartment. All the moisture in my body is rushing to my palms. I wipe them furtively on my jeans.

Laurie opens the door. She is shorter than I had imagined her, only about five-foot-six. She's heavier than in her photos and there's a blemish on her right cheek. Her hair has reverted to its natural brown and is cut just below her ears. Still I sense what Fernando saw when she first came to Los Angeles: the strength in her hands, the life in her eyes. And I am captivated by her mouth, which smiles at the sight of me.

She holds out her hand and I take it. "You look exactly like I pictured you," she says. "Down to the sport coat and the pink T-shirt. Except completely different. Come on in."

I reach for the guitar and look up to see the emotions suddenly streak across her face: curiosity, wariness, hope, doubt, pain. "They found it last week," I say tentatively, afraid now that I've done this the wrong way.

"Oh my God," she says. She backs up, her eyes never leaving the guitar case. I can't tell if there's any joy at all in her reaction. I step into the apartment. It is small and sparsely furnished—a couch, a card table, some folding chairs. A man gets up from the couch and looks at us. He has short dark hair and a mustache; he's wearing a green polo shirt and khaki pants, and there is a thick tangle of hair on his chest. He looks to be no more than thirty. For some reason I think to myself, a little sadly, that he is nothing at all like me.

I set the guitar case down and close the front door and move a few steps away, into the living room. Laurie kneels in front of it, slowly lays it flat, opens the latches, then looks up at me, as if for reassurance that this is not another of life's cruel jokes. I nod and smile and she opens it up.

We stay that way for a long time. I see at last that Laurie is simply overwhelmed. Eventually she closes the case and latches it again. "I'm

sorry," she says. "I know this is terribly rude, but . . . excuse me." She
picks up the case, takes it into the bedroom, and shuts the door.

"Is that really her father's guitar?" the man says.

I nod and introduce myself.

"Oh, I know who you are," he says. "I've been hearing about you for
weeks now. I'm David Rabkin." We shake hands, he brings me a beer,
and we sit on the couch. He asks about the book, and about my trip, and
then, while we wait for Laurie, he tells me how they met.

It turns out that he's a music writer, so we do have something in
common after all. He does a weekly column for the San Antonio *Express-
News* and works one afternoon a week on the Third Coast Network, a
local radio show that features Texas and Louisiana music.

"I've been playing Laurie's record since that first homemade release,"
he tells me. "That album absolutely bowled me over."

"I know the feeling."

He nods. "Of course you do. So when I looked up one night at this
barbecue place and saw her, I had to go over and ask if she was Laurie
Moss. She was with a bunch of her girlfriends from work and I got this
completely icy reception. She told me she wasn't playing much these
days, which was an understatement, and so I shrugged and gave her my
card and went back to my table.

"Fifteen minutes later she came over and apologized for being stand-
offish and said—I'll never forget this—that it was like I had mistaken her
for her twin sister, whom she had loved very, very much, but who'd been
run over by a cement truck. Then she told me what had happened—getting dropped, folding the band, coming back to Texas and living with her
Mom. I think I fell in love with her on the spot."

"How is she doing? I mean, day to day."

"Not so good. I've been around creative people all my life, and she's
got as much creative juice as anybody I've ever seen. She's so smart it
scares me. And every once in a while she'll forget herself and sing along
with the radio and there's that incredible voice. She's got all this talent
and no place to put it, and it's flat out got to be killing her."

Laurie reemerges a half hour later and all three of us pretend she
hasn't been crying. During the two hours in which we finally order pizza,
and eat, and talk about inconsequential things—movies, politics, other
people's music—and then long into the night when I'm alone in my

motel room, I try to reconcile this real, physical Laurie—sturdier, and yet more easily hurt than I expected, possessed of a startlingly coarse laugh, devoid of the languid sensuality that I'd imagined—with the fantasy creature I've been carrying around in my head for two years, a creature patched together from photographs, a disembodied voice, and words on a computer screen, like a digital voodoo doll.

Sometime after midnight I put *Of the Same Name* on my Discman and the Laurie of my imagination is there, unchanged, waiting only for me.

Tuesday Laurie leaves work at noon and we drive to Brackenridge Park. She takes me to the Sunken Gardens, where we sit looking down at the bamboo and flowering trees and koi. Out of nowhere she says, "Did you come to Texas to seduce me?"

I'm too flustered to answer. She says, "It's my fault. It was very sexy to open up to you that way, and have my little fantasies, and not have to think seriously about consequences. When I first started writing you I had this tiny, hermetically sealed existence. You were the one good thing I had left from my life as a rock star. And I didn't want to let go of that. Though I should have told you about David."

I shrug. "He seems pretty crazy about you."

"He's wonderful and sweet and supportive of all the crazy moods I go through these days. He's undoubtedly better than I deserve. But it's early yet. Maybe I'll grow into him."

"Jim warned me you were seeing somebody."

"And you came anyway?"

"I had to bring you your guitar."

She smiles. "You're very sweet. And very unhappy, I think."

Of course our six-month-plus correspondence has not been one-sided. My interviewing style—even when an interview is all it is—has to do with conversation, and quid pro quo.

"Let's not talk about me," I say.

"Oh, let's do. Could it be that you came all the way to Texas to seduce me so that you'd have an excuse to leave your wife?"

I feel dizzy. The heat and the humidity are making it hard for me to breathe.

"You can just leave her, you know," Laurie says. "You don't need me for that. You can do it all by yourself."

She stands, giving me a moment to collect myself, and looks out across the water, very still, as if she'd slipped loose from her body for a moment. A hot breeze gently touches her hair. Then her eyes snap into focus and she says, "Look! The turtles I wrote you about."

I stand next to her and follow her pointing finger. There are two of them, the larger gliding rapidly underwater, the other paddling quietly on the surface. They remain close together without obvious intent, as if connected in ways that I can't see. The sight of them is somehow enormously comforting, and gets me through the moment and on to the next.

"I never thanked you for bringing my guitar," she says as we walk downhill toward the carousel and the zoo. "Thank you." A minute or so later she says, "I wrote a song last night, after you left. I haven't touched a guitar or let myself think in anything but the past tense for over a year, you know, trying to convince myself that everything was over for good, and then, wham." She stops and faces me with a coy smile. "You want to hear it?"

It is a stupid question. She sings the first lines for me:

> God blew into town last week
> In his fat white Cadillac
> Bought the house next door to me
> And commenced to dealing crack
> Put a truck on blocks in the front yard
> And a pack of wild dogs in the back.

"It goes on in a similarly bitter and self-pitying way for seven more verses. I doubt it'll be on the next album."

Before I can recover from that particular bombshell she runs up to a concession stand and buys cotton candy. "Do you want anything?" she calls to me. I shake my head.

"So," I ask when I catch up to her, "were you toying with me, or are you really going to do another album?"

She sighs. "I'm going to have to, aren't I?" The pain and reluctance in her voice seem completely genuine. "I didn't sleep last night, thinking about it. I've got all those new songs that I wrote on tour, and the song I wrote for Grandpa Bill. I can do the guitars and lead vocals here on my four-track and send them to Jim. He can add himself and Dennis and Gabe."

"And then . . . ?"

"That's the hard part, isn't it? We'll have to scare up the money to put it out ourselves. I couldn't face another record company, not now, probably not ever. Jim can sell it on our Web site, I'll sell some if I play out anywhere, which I suppose I'll have to do now, at least in town." An ironic smile flickers across her mouth and disappears. "Now that I have a guitar again."

"Is that going to be enough for you?"

"I guess it's going to have to be. Because I can't go through another year like the one I just had. When I picked up the guitar last night I remembered all the times that the music was enough, and it seemed possible. It seemed like I could settle for just a part of what I used to have, if it was the right part." She stops and makes a face and throws the cotton candy in a trash can.

"People *can* change, can't they?" she asks, looking straight into me. "If they have to, if their lives depend on it?"

"I don't know," I say, speaking for myself at last, wondering if there is in me any part of the courage I see in her.

She drops me at my car, which we've left in the parking lot of her office. Without her needing to say it, I know that this day has been my reward for bringing her guitar from California, and it seems generous indeed. I doubt I will have another day like it.

I walk around to the driver's side and Laurie rolls down her window. "Thank you," I say.

"Are you—"

"I've got what I came for. I'll head back first thing tomorrow morning."

She nods. The air is hot and still, and the sun glares from the mirrored glass of the building in front of me. I lean forward slightly and she tilts her face toward me and I kiss her. It lasts little more than a single warm, soft, heart-stopping second. Then I step away and raise my hand and watch her until her Little Red Datsun crests the entrance ramp to the freeway and disappears.

T H I S   R E P O R T E R

I took the long way home, via Durango, Colorado, and Flagstaff, Arizona, thinking all the way. When I got home I asked Barb for a divorce. I won custody of Tom on Mondays through Fridays, and came away with child support and the house. I work mornings at a frame shop while Tom's in school, and we get by. As Jerry Lee Lewis used to sing, I can make it through the week, but oh, those lonely weekends.

" F E R N A N D O "

I see Fernando one last time, in March of 1998. I am in Los Angeles with Tom to celebrate finishing the second draft of this book, and to listen to Laurie's new album on the cassette player in Jim's kitchen. The record is called *Based on a True Story* and in contrast to the detached character studies of the earlier songs, these are all in first person immediate. Laurie has asked me to write the liner notes, and I know from the first sound of her voice on the tape that it will be a labor of love.

An urge to tie a few last loose ends makes me stop by Fernando's guitar store afterward. He is glad to see me and invites Tom and me out to dinner.

We drive to a beachfront restaurant in Venice where I learn that Fernando too is recently divorced. I'm even more surprised to find out that he's about to be married again—and not to Summer.

His fiancée is in fact the young, tanned, blonde waitress who is bringing us our blackened chicken sandwiches, and who leans over to kiss Fernando on top of his newly shaven head.

"In a weird way," Fernando says, "Summer was actually a part of my first marriage. I know that sounds weird, man, but when the marriage finally fell apart, so did Summer and me."

From where we sit we can see a neon-pink sun sink slowly into the haze over the Pacific. It is the kind of view that makes Corky wonder why Laurie went back to Texas. I look at my hands, as they rest on the edge of the table, and then look at Tom, whose neck is craned to watch the TV set over the bar. I have the sudden and comforting knowledge that there is nowhere else I have to be.

"I know I've let people down in my time," Fernando says. "And I've had some days that I didn't think I was going to make it through. But dude, what can I tell you?" He too looks out at the picture-postcard sunset, and then he shrugs and smiles. "Life goes on."

ABOUT THE AUTHOR

LEWIS SHINER has written
about music for *Crawdaddy!*, the
Village Voice, Reflex, Pulse, and others.
His novels include *Slam, Deserted
Cities of the Heart, Frontera,* and the
award-winning *Glimpses.* He lives in
North Carolina with his wife,
Mary Alberts.